Straight Talk

Judith Keim

BOOKS BY JUDITH KEIM

THE HARTWELL WOMEN SERIES:
The Talking Tree – 1
Sweet Talk – 2
Straight Talk – 3
Baby Talk – 4
The Hartwell Women – Boxed Set

THE BEACH HOUSE HOTEL SERIES:
Breakfast at The Beach House Hotel – 1
Lunch at The Beach House Hotel – 2
Dinner at The Beach House Hotel – 3
Christmas at The Beach House Hotel – 4
Margaritas at The Beach House Hotel – 5 (2021)
Dessert at The Beach House Hotel – 6 (2022)

THE FAT FRIDAYS GROUP:
Fat Fridays – 1
Sassy Saturdays – 2
Secret Sundays – 3

SALTY KEY INN BOOKS:
Finding Me – 1
Finding My Way – 2
Finding Love – 3
Finding Family – 4

CHANDLER HILL INN BOOKS:
Going Home – 1
Coming Home – 2
Home at Last – 3

SEASHELL COTTAGE BOOKS:
A Christmas Star
Change of Heart
A Summer of Surprises
A Road Trip to Remember
The Beach Babes – (2022)

DESERT SAGE INN BOOKS:
The Desert Flowers – Rose – 1
The Desert Flowers – Lily – 2 (Fall 2021)
The Desert Flowers – Willow – 3 (2022)
The Desert Flowers – Mistletoe & Holly – 4 (2022)

Winning BIG – a little love story for all ages

For more information: **http://amzn.to/2jamIaF**

PRAISE FOR JUDITH KEIM'S NOVELS

THE BEACH HOUSE HOTEL SERIES

"Love the characters in this series. This series was my first introduction to Judith Keim. She is now one of my favorites. Looking forward to reading more of her books."

BREAKFAST AT THE BEACH HOUSE HOTEL is an easy, delightful read that offers romance, family relationships, and strong women learning to be stronger. Real life situations filter through the pages. Enjoy!"

LUNCH AT THE BEACH HOUSE HOTEL – "This series is such a joy to read. You feel you are actually living with them. Can't wait to read the latest one."

DINNER AT THE BEACH HOUSE HOTEL – "A Terrific Read! As usual, Judith Keim did it again. Enjoyed immensely. Continue writing such pleasantly reading books for all of us readers."

CHRISTMAS AT THE BEACH HOUSE HOTEL – "Not Just Another Christmas Novel. This is book number four in the series and my introduction to Judith Keim's writing. I wasn't disappointed. The characters are dimensional and engaging. The plot is well crafted and advances at a pleasing pace. The Florida location is interesting and warming. It was a delight to read a romance novel with mature female protagonists. Ann and Rhoda have life experiences that enrich the story. It's a clever book about friends and extended family. Buy copies for your book group pals and enjoy this seasonal read."

THE HARTWELL WOMEN SERIES – Books 1 – 4

"This was an EXCELLENT series. When I discovered Judith Keim, I read all of her books back to back. I thoroughly enjoyed the women Keim has written about. They are believable and you want to just jump into their lives and be their friends! I can't wait for any upcoming books!"

"I fell into Judith Keim's Hartwell Women series and have read & enjoyed all of her books in every series. Each centers around a strong & interesting woman character and their family interaction. Good reads that leave you wanting more."

THE FAT FRIDAYS GROUP – Books 1 – 3

"Excellent story line for each character, and an insightful representation of situations which deal with some of the contemporary issues women are faced with today."

"I love this author's books. Her characters and their lives are realistic. The power of women's friendships is a common and beautiful theme that is threaded throughout this story."

THE SALTY KEY INN SERIES

FINDING ME – *"I thoroughly enjoyed the first book in this series and cannot wait for the others! The characters are endearing with the same struggles we all encounter. The setting makes me feel like I am a guest at The Salty Key Inn...relaxed, happy & light-hearted! The men are yummy and the women strong. You can't get better than that! Happy Reading!"*

FINDING MY WAY- *"Loved the family dynamics as well as uncertain emotions of dating and falling in love.*

Appreciated the morals and strength of parenting throughout. Just couldn't put this book down."

FINDING LOVE – "I waited for this book because the first two was such good reads. This one didn't disappoint.... Judith Keim always puts substance into her books. This book was no different, I learned about PTSD, accepting oneself, there is always going to be problems but stick it out and make it work. Just the way life is. In some ways a lot like my life. Judith is right, it needs another book and I will definitely be reading it. Hope you choose to read this series, you will get so much out of it."

FINDING FAMILY – "Completing this series is like eating the last chip. Love Judith's writing, and her female characters are always smart, strong, vulnerable to life and love experiences."

"This was a refreshing book. Bringing the heart and soul of the family to us."

CHANDLER HILL INN SERIES

GOING HOME – "I absolutely could not put this book down. Started at night and read late into the middle of the night. As a child of the '60s, the Vietnam war was front and center so this resonated with me. All the characters in the book were so well developed that the reader felt like they were friends of the family."

"I was completely immersed in this book, with the beautiful descriptive writing, and the authors' way of bringing her characters to life. I felt like I was right inside her story."

<u>COMING HOME</u> – *"Coming Home is a winner. The characters are well-developed, nuanced and likable. Enjoyed the vineyard setting, learning about wine growing and seeing the challenges Cami faces in running and growing a business. I look forward to the next book in this series!"*

"Coming Home was such a wonderful story. The author has a gift for getting the reader right to the heart of things."

<u>HOME AT LAST</u> – *"In this wonderful conclusion, to a heartfelt and emotional trilogy set in Oregon's stunning wine country, Judith Keim has tied up the Chandler Hill series with the perfect bow."*

"Overall, this is truly a wonderful addition to the Chandler Hill Inn series. Judith Keim definitely knows how to perfectly weave together a beautiful and heartfelt story."

"The storyline has some beautiful scenes along with family drama. Judith Keim has created characters with interactions that are believable and some of the subjects the story deals with are poignant."

SEASHELL COTTAGE BOOKS

<u>A CHRISTMAS STAR</u> – *"Love, laughter, sadness, great food, and hope for the future, all in one book. It doesn't get any better than this stunning read."*

"A Christmas Star is a heartwarming Christmas story featuring endearing characters. So many Christmas books are set in snowbound places...it was a nice change to read a Christmas story that takes place on a warm sandy beach!" Susan Peterson

CHANGE OF HEART – *"CHANGE OF HEART is the summer read we've all been waiting for. Judith Keim is a master at creating fascinating characters that are simply irresistible. Her stories leave you with a big smile on your face and a heart bursting with love."*

~Kellie Coates Gilbert, author of the popular Sun Valley Series

A SUMMER OF SURPRISES – *"The story is filled with a roller coaster of emotions and self-discovery. Finding love again and rebuilding family relationships."*

"Ms. Keim uses this book as an amazing platform to show that with hard emotional work, belief in yourself and love, the scars of abuse can be conquered. It in no way preaches, it's a lovely story with a happy ending."

"The character development was excellent. I felt I knew these people my whole life. The story development was very well thought out I was drawn [in] from the beginning."

DESERT SAGE INN BOOKS

THE DESERT FLOWERS – *ROSE* – *"The Desert Flowers - Rose, is the first book in the new series by Judith Keim. I always look forward to new books by Judith Keim, and this one is definitely a wonderful way to begin The Desert Sage Inn Series!"*

"In this first of a series, we see each woman come into her own and view new beginnings even as they must take this tearful journey as they slowly lose a dear friend. This is a very well written book with well-developed and likable main characters. It was interesting and enlightening as the first

portion of this saga unfolded. I very much enjoyed this book and I do recommend it"

"Judith Keim is one of those authors that you can always depend on to give you a great story with fantastic characters. I'm excited to know that she is writing a new series and after reading book 1 in the series, I can't wait to read the rest of the books."!

Straight Talk

The Hartwell Women Series – Book 3

Judith Keim

Wild Quail Publishing

Straight Talk is a work of fiction. Names, characters, places, public or private institutions, corporations, towns, and incidents are the product of the author's imagination or are fictitious. Any resemblance to actual events, locales, or persons, living or dead, is coincidental.

No part of this book may be reproduced or transmitted in any form or by any electronic or mechanical means including information storage and retrieval systems without permission in writing from the author, except by a reviewer who may quote brief passages in a review. This book may not be resold or uploaded for distribution to others. For permissions contact the author directly via electronic mail:

wildquail.pub@gmail.com

www.judithkeim.com,

Published in the United States of America by:

Wild Quail Publishing
PO Box 171332
Boise, ID 83717-1332

ISBN# 978-0-9909329-5-6
Copyright ©2015 Judith Keim

Dedication

For Peter,
With love always

CHAPTER ONE

A bruising hand gripped my upper arm and jerked me around. Startled, I dropped my purse. A tough guy glared at me with glassy eyes. His thin lips curled into a sly sneer that turned my mouth dry.

A young drug addict. My stomach fisted. Damn! I should have been paying more attention to my surroundings. The chill of the rainy Tuesday evening in Boston crept into my body stiffened with fear.

"You're Samantha Hartwell, ain'tcha?" the druggie demanded. His eyebrows angled into a fierce scowl that sent fear skittering down my spine.

I nodded, surprised he knew my name. Not a good sign.

He moved his face close to mine. His warm breath reeked of garlic and alcohol. I swallowed hard and yanked against his painful grasp.

"You stay the hell away from Caitlin, you hear?" he snarled. He jerked me closer, making me stumble. "Stop fillin' her head with all that art stuff. She's not doing that no more."

My mind took a moment to grasp what he'd said. *This was about Caitlin? The guy was shouting and practically wrenching my arm off because of Caitlin Rafferty?*

"I don't know who in hell you are, but Caitlin has real talent." My voice shook, but I forced myself to stand my ground. Nobody was going to tell me what I could or could not do.

He jabbed a finger at me. "Stay away from Caitlin, bitch. She ain't no artist. She's my woman and she does what I tell 'er. If I hafta come back and find you, you're gonna be sorry."

He shoved me against my car and marched away as if he owned the sidewalk beneath his feet.

Adrenaline left me in a torrent of tumbling waves, turning my bones to jelly. I collapsed against the car and glanced all around, but the leather-jacketed goon who'd threatened me was nowhere in sight.

Gathering strength, I picked up my purse and made my way up the stairs to my fourth-floor office in the Back Bay. I'd need to calm down before I could drive home. Caitlin had told me about her boyfriend, Anthony Carbone, but I had no idea he was such a controlling jerk.

Inside my office, I paced restlessly trying to shake off the fear that clung to me like a tiger's claws. I'd founded Straight Talk, my non-profit consulting business, to help other young women grab a foothold in business and get a grip on their unsteady lives. For some, the task was easy, but for others, like Caitlin Rafferty, the challenge was overwhelming.

Taking a deep breath, I told myself to be strong. But Anthony's sharp-edged words, the way he'd so easily bruised my arm, and the sickening odor of his breath made my stomach churn. I eased myself into a chair. It would take more time to gather my wits before I attempted to return to my car.

I wouldn't call the police. That would cause problems for Caitlin and might hinder what I was doing for the other women who'd asked for my help. I'd come too far to let anyone ruin my plans. Running Straight Talk was what kept me focused...and sober. Without it, I didn't know what I'd do. It wasn't until I'd stated my name before a circle of people in AA that I'd begun to understand what I'd been given—another chance at life, an opportunity to help others, a reason for living.

Friday afternoon, I replaced the phone receiver and sighed.

I'd told no one Caitlin's boyfriend had threatened me. Too many people would tell me to forget her; it was too dangerous. But I couldn't do that. As I saw it, her entire future rested in my hands.

Advising troubled women in start-up businesses was no easy task. I rose to stare out the window of my office and watched college crews in their shells row steadily along the Charles River, dipping their oars in the water in a regular rhythm that soothed me.

Zach Adams stuck his head into the office. "Tough day?"

I turned and smiled at my best friend. "Tough week. Glad it's Friday."

"Me too. Let's get out of here and party."

I laughed. Zach was a recovering alcoholic like me and our idea of partying was to have an extra Diet Coke.

"Derek Roberts' photographs are showing at the Winthrop Gallery on Boylston Street. I said I'd drop by. Want to come?"

"Sure. He's famous and I'd like to see his work. Anything to shake off this bad feeling I've got about Caitlin."

He raised his eyebrows.

I was still at a loss at how best to handle the situation. She hadn't shown up for our meeting yesterday. Her absence could be due to any number of reasons. I hoped Anthony Carbone wasn't one of them.

"Between her family problems, her boyfriend, and her drinking, she's like a freight train running out of control. There's no stopping her."

"Some people just don't know when they're on the right track," Zach grinned at me.

I groaned at his usual wacky sense of humor and picked up my purse. "You're incorrigible. Let's go have some fun and meet this Derek guy. Could be interesting."

"You sure you won't marry me?" Zach's voice was teasing, but his expression told me he might be serious.

"You know how I feel about you." I gave him a little punch on the arm. He was my best friend and I adored him.

"Yeah, you think of me as some kind of brother."

We looked at one another and smiled. I would never have made it through recovery without him, nor he without me. I could give him friendship, loyalty, and a kindness he didn't receive at home, but I couldn't give him the type of love he desired. There was no mystery, no magic, no moving of mountains between us. I couldn't imagine sex with him.

"You deserve the works, Zach Adams, not my kind of love. You'll see. Some woman is going to knock you off your feet, and I won't even be able to get you to say hello to me."

The corner of his lip lifted in a lop-sided, mock grimace. He didn't believe me.

"Zach, I've seen the way girls look at you. You just don't notice."

"Not with you around, I don't. Not with those smoky gray eyes of yours."

I shook my head, wishing I could give him what he desired. "You're hopeless. C'mon, let's go."

As we walked along Boylston Street to Winthrop Gallery, I noticed our images reflected in the glass windows of the storefronts. Zach's outline was tall and muscular, his strong facial features definitely a plus. Any girl would be lucky to have him. Next to him, I seemed short and slim, though no one would call me fragile. My dark, straight hair, I noticed, swung back and forth in rhythm to our brisk stride.

"So tell me about Derek Roberts. How do you know him?"

"We went to prep school together. He wasn't one of the jocks but used to spend his time taking photographs of various sports. In college, he won a Pulitzer for a shot he took of the Bruins' goalie catching the puck in overtime play, taking the win away from Montreal."

"It's supposed to be a great show." I'd read about it in the *Globe*. "I'm pleased for the gallery. I know the owner. He's been struggling to attract a younger crowd, and this may be one way to do it."

"Is he still helping you with your art project?"

"We're putting together an art show of paintings done by women in recovery. It should help fund the new, proposed shelter in Southie."

Zach pulled me to a stop. "See why everybody loves you, Sam?"

My thoughts flew to George Hartwell, my elderly father. "Not everyone."

"Well, most people do." Zach took hold of my shoulders and gave me a long look. "I know all about your father, but, Sam, you can't let one person destroy how everyone else feels about you."

He was right. My relationship with my father was an old story. Most likely it was why I worked hard to excel at everything I did and might even have been the reason I'd turned to alcohol at an early age. No matter what I accomplished, I'd never be what my father really wanted. Thank God my mother, Adrienne, was as sweet and as strong as they come. She'd counterbalanced my father's unreasonable attitude as best she could, but she couldn't prevent the damage done to me.

Determined to have some fun, I looped my arm through his and skipped along the sidewalk with exaggerated steps.

Zach grinned and hurried to keep up with me.

The Winthrop Gallery was deceptively large, extending deep into the storefront from the street. Inside, I took a moment to get my bearings. The high-ceilinged rooms were discreetly lit and the walls, of varying shades of neutral colors, were the perfect backdrops for the colorful photographs mounted on them.

The gallery owner waved his hand in recognition and broke away from a group of people to greet us.

"Samantha! Glad you could make it."

I smiled and accepted his hand. "Me, too."

As I was introducing Zach, someone called out, "Hey, Zach!"

Zach grinned. "Hi, Derek."

I turned to find a tall, dark-haired man striding toward us. He smiled at Zach then turned his gaze on me. Our eyes met and shivers traveled down my spine. Derek Roberts was one of the most attractive men I'd ever seen. The contrast of dark hair with light-brown, almost gold eyes was intriguing. They lit with pleasure as his crooked smile settled on me before turning back to Zach.

"Zach! I swear you look just the same, you old jock." Derek winked at me. "Bet you didn't know that St. John's Prep has a football trophy named after him." He grinned and gave Zach a bear hug.

I blinked in surprise. *Football trophy?*

Zach shook his head. "If you stop telling stories about me, I'll introduce you to Samantha Hartwell."

Derek's eyes widened. "The same Samantha Hartwell who sits on the board of Rivers Papers?"

"Yes, but..."

He cut me off, taking hold of my hand. "Great to meet you! Rivers Papers is talking to me about shooting a series of photos on the paper mill industry. And I understand you're someone I need to talk to about it."

His smile settled on me, and it all came back. In order to promote goodwill and a better understanding of the industry, Rivers Papers was considering publishing a book on the history of Maine and its paper mills. The Hartwells were one of the founding families of the industry, going back to my great-grandfather. My cousin, Marissa Cole, and I hadn't been won over on the proposal, but we were trying to be open-minded about it. One of the board members was exploring the idea.

"I thought you limited your photography to sports," Zach said to Derek. "You're doing industrial work, too?"

Derek grinned. "If the money is right, I'm flexible. Besides, I haven't changed. I still like to go where the action is. Travel is like an aphrodisiac for me."

"No family yet?"

Derek shook his head. "C'mon. Let me give you a personal tour."

Zach and I followed him to a room in the back of the building where a number of black and white photographs were displayed against a black backdrop.

Derek turned to me. "As a kid, I suffered from asthma. It really bothered me to be stuck on the sidelines while most of my friends played sports. One of my fifth-grade teachers suggested I take pictures of them and handed me a little camera. I was hooked from then on. Big time."

A group gathered around us.

"What kind of camera was it?" a woman asked.

"An Instamatic." Derek good-naturedly spoke louder so everyone could hear.

While he answered questions, I stepped away from the crowd and wandered over to the display on the far wall.

In one black and white photograph, a toddler had swung a leg onto a bottom step and was glancing up a long stairway as if it were a mountain to climb. The picture captured both the eager look of anticipation on the child's face and the sense of determination in the set of his little jaw.

Impressed, I moved on to the next photograph. In it, a man had just kicked a soccer ball. His arms were out, balancing his body. One foot was high in the air, the other remained connected to the ground by just the tip of his shoe. The ball was a blur. As masculine as the scene was, the way Derek had captured the action made it appear as if it was a movement in a lovely ballet.

Moving from one photograph to another, I found myself attracted to the man behind the pictures. Behind a handsome exterior, there lurked a man who appreciated the beauty around him.

"Cool, huh?" Zach's eyes lit with approval.

"Touching. He's captured the freedom, the joy, the beauty of being a participant in life."

"That's exactly it. Well put." He left to greet a friend while I continued my private inspection, drawn to the spirit of the photographs.

"What do you think? Am I good enough for Rivers Papers?"

My pulse sprinted. I turned and smiled at Derek. "Maybe."

His lips curved as he settled his golden gaze on me. "If it means I could get to know you, I'd sign on tomorrow."

My smile faltered. *Did he think I'd fall for a line like that?*

Before I could respond, Zach approached us. "Guess who's here? Ted Beers."

My hands turned cold. Ted remained the Chairman of the Rivers Papers board. Efforts to throw him off the board had failed by one traitorous vote. He was carefully monitored, but he remained a thorn in my side.

Someone called to Derek. He bid us good-bye and left the room, and I planned my escape.

"Well, well, Samantha Hartwell." Ted's bass voice echoed across the room, drawing attention as he approached me.

I stood there, trapped. My blood bubbled at the insolent tone of his voice.

Zach, bless his heart, moved closer to me.

Ted held out his hand. I took it and pasted a smile on my face, which I hoped would temper the deep animosity I felt. "Good evening, Ted. You remember Zach Adams?"

A frown creased Ted's face. "Yes. We've met before. Everybody in Boston knows who he is. He refused a lucrative position in one of the top New York law firms to go into family law here. It made all kinds of news in certain social circles."

Ignoring the angry scowl that crossed Zach's face, he turned to me with a sly smile. "Checking out Derek's work for us?"

"No, as a matter of fact, I didn't make the connection between him and Rivers Papers until Zach introduced me to his friend."

Ted's eyebrows shot up. He faced Zach. "You know Derek?"

"He and I went to prep school together," Zach answered shortly, and I knew he was still upset over Ted's earlier remark. Ted wasn't the only one who thought Zach was a fool for giving up a lucrative career and status. His parents had all but disowned him over the decision. In a competitive family like his, it was unacceptable to disregard his rightful place among the socially elite.

I gave Zach an overly bright smile. "Time we were on our way." His temper was sometimes hard to control, and Ted's mere presence was enough to make anyone edgy.

Outside, we both drew a deep breath and sighed.

"What is it about that guy that makes me want to smash in his mouth?" Zach grumbled.

"I know exactly how you feel. It's good we both left the gallery before we ruined things for Derek."

"Yeah. By the way, I told Derek we'd meet him for a late supper after the show."

"Sorry. I'm going home. It's been a rough week and I just want to curl up with a book. I'm meeting my parents for dinner tomorrow. You know how difficult that can be."

"Your father's a moron."

Zach and my father had never gotten along. Observing Zach's hair curling over the collar of his shirt, and his worn Docksiders, I almost laughed out loud. Zach's casual appearance would irritate the hell out of my father.

Zach accompanied me back to the office to get my car. I was glad he did. Since the terrifying incident with Caitlin's boyfriend, I was jumpy about being on the streets after dark. I didn't want anyone to know that every time I saw a dark-haired man in a black-leather jacket, my heart pounded in panic.

At home inside my apartment, I couldn't stop thinking about Derek. His good looks had been a pleasant surprise, his pictures even better. But I wondered at his self-assurance. No doubt, he was accustomed to having women throw themselves at him. Still, his talent was evident, a good reason to talk to my cousin about the book project.

The jarring sound of the phone brought my musing to a standstill. "Hello?"

"Sham? It'sh me. Caitlin. I blew it tonight. I'm drunk as a schkunk ..."

My heart sank. "Where are you?"

"With Anthony. My shponsor is meeting me. Just wanted to let you know I can't meet with you tomorrow. Good-bye."

"Wait!" But she'd already hung up. I let out a worried sigh. Caitlin liked living dangerously. I didn't know where it would lead either of us.

CHAPTER TWO

I pulled open the front door and entered Lia's, one of several new restaurants in downtown Boston near Faneuil Hall. Though I'd never been there before, I knew their menu was a fusion of Asian and classic European cuisine that had become very popular. And pricey. Done in black and silver with just a touch of red accents, the interior décor was contemporary, almost too stark for my taste.

The maitre d' hurried over. At the mention of my name, he said, "Yes, of course. This way, please."

The rooms were softly lit, casting intriguing shadows among the diners. Though it was eight o'clock, a prime time for diners, I wasn't at all surprised to be led to a coveted corner table. My father wouldn't have settled for anything less than the best. Always the gentleman, he rose to his feet as I approached. My mother waved gaily and beamed at me.

I smiled a greeting to my father and gave my mother a quick hug. "You look fabulous."

She smiled and patted her hair. "I decided it was time for a new, shorter do."

"Your mother was fine, just the way she was," snapped my father in his usual gruff way.

Mom's shoulders drooped ever so slightly.

My stomach twisted. Intentional or not, he had a way of demeaning things. Frustration burned a trail through me. "Father, every woman needs changes from time to time."

"Adrienne didn't need to make any changes. She's beautiful, all the same." My parents smiled affectionately at one another. As difficult as my father sometimes was, he loved my mother.

In her sixties, my mother had classical features, dark hair streaked with a natural gray that others paid for, and hazel eyes that gleamed with natural warmth. It still astonished me that she had married my father, twenty-some years older than she. She surely could have had a life far different from the staid one she shared with my father.

I studied him surreptitiously. White-haired, he looked much younger than his years. Mentally, he was as sharp as he'd always been, still practicing law in Maine, albeit on a scaled-down schedule. As they talked about wines, they seemed total opposites. That might be why it worked. Her enthusiasm for life kept my father young.

After making a point of ordering *imported* bottled water for me, Father ordered wine for dinner. Once the wine steward had opened the bottle and poured wine for my parents, we lifted our glasses in a silent toast, and then Father cleared his throat. "Ted Beers called me this morning. He told me he'd seen you and that friend of yours at the Derek Roberts exhibition at the Winthrop Gallery last night. So, is Rivers Papers going ahead with the book project?"

My nostrils flared. "That friend of mine? Do you mean Zach Adams?" Father had taken a deep dislike to Zach, probably because he didn't fit any usual mold.

Sensing my mother's tenseness and her silent plea to avoid any arguments, I drew a deep breath and controlled my irritation. It was more than Zach. Ted continued to garner my father's support for board decisions even though the family's interest was well represented on the board by me and Marissa.

"The board hasn't taken a final vote on the project. I'm sure Ted must have explained that to you."

"He did, but we thought you…"

"Please, Father, don't even go there. Marissa and I will handle things our way."

To cool my outrage, I took a sip of water. Ted Beers was someone I'd come to despise. He and I had dated briefly, but I'd found him to be interested only in money and power. It still infuriated my father that I, instead of my brother Hunter, sat on the Board of Directors. Where his children were concerned, only his son mattered. The bitterness of that truth lingered in my mouth.

"Ted says Derek Roberts is a find," my father persisted. "It'd be best to bring him in to help promote the company. Goodwill and all that."

A worrisome thought came to me. *Had Ted worked a side deal with Derek?* He seldom promoted anything that didn't benefit himself in some way.

My mother fluttered her hands as if to shoo away the tension that throbbed in the air. "I talked to your sister today. Allison told me her friend, Dawson Smith, might be coming to Boston to see you. Is he someone we should meet?"

I smiled and shook my head. "Mom, you're hopeless! We're just friends." My mother was in despair that, at age thirty-four, I was still unwed. I'd had marriage offers and had one serious romance go sour. Since then, I'd decided I could only accept a man who'd be able to stand up to my father and allow me to continue working. After seeing what some of my friends had gone through and my sister suffer through a marriage that had turned bad, I didn't regret my decision to remain single. Never one to give up, my mother smiled brightly. "Well, bring him to Maine if you'd like."

"Thanks, but we probably won't have the time. He's coming to interview one of my clients for a scholarship to the Art Institute."

"That's wonderful, dear," she commented.

Father's expression turned sour. "Still don't know why you're wasting your time doing all this free work when you could be making money at one of the big law firms," he grumped.

In the past, I'd sought his approval by earning first an MBA and then getting a law degree from Harvard. "It's about making choices, Father. I got help when I needed it; now, I want to help others. That's why I founded Straight Talk."

He remained stonily quiet.

"Besides, I applied to a big law firm, and you're the one who prevented me from being accepted into Hartwell, Smith, and Lowell."

He frowned. "That place is reserved for your brother. I expect Hunter to eventually come into the firm."

Jealousy's sharp edges twisted my insides. Like me, my brother was a late bloomer. He'd played around for years and was finally engaged to Bettina Browning, the daughter of one of Father's friends. Personally, I wasn't sure if they'd make it to the altar. Hunter was growing restless with the life my father had more or less chosen for him. I didn't think he even wanted the position the firm kept open.

"Let's talk about something pleasant." My mother reached over and clasped my hand. "Your sister said her business is going very well, and I wanted to thank you. Allison told me that if it hadn't been for your help working on the figures to get it started, she isn't sure how she could have done it."

"Sweet Talk is a great concept, and Treasures is a growing art gallery. She's got a great sense of business." I was proud of my sister for all she'd accomplished in a short period of time, including marrying one of the nicest guys I knew.

Before we could continue, the waiter brought our first course. I dug into the bay scallops marinated in lemon, ginger, and sesame oil. No matter how tension might grow between us, we'd always enjoyed good food in our family.

The rest of the evening was spent in safe conversation away from any talk of law, Ted Beers, or the paper business. My mother kept us amused with the details of her latest trip to California to visit my sister.

"Someday, I'd like to be there for the pressing of grapes at the winery," she said. "Allison said I could even stomp on a few with my bare feet."

Father and I laughed.

When it came time to say good-bye, I kissed my mother and gave my father a quick hug. He wasn't much for displays of affection, but I'd learned it was important for me to be more open. He responded, which made me happy. Beneath the protective wall I'd built around myself with him, I still felt like a little girl who wanted her father to love her.

I waited until they were settled in a cab to the Four Seasons hotel and headed for the Green Line of the MBTA, determined to keep an eye on Ted Beers. Sitting on the board of Rivers Papers with him wasn't the easy job I'd once thought it'd be.

My back would need protection.

The ringing of the office phone greeted us as Zach and I returned from lunch one August day. My heart thumped with anticipation. It might mean another project. I lifted the receiver.

"Samantha Hartwell."

" Hi, Sam, it's Dawson Smith."

At the sound of his voice, I grinned. Dawson was a wealthy former executive in the computer industry who'd retired from the rat race and now spent a lot of his time creating stunning raku pottery pieces. We'd met in California through my sister. He had promised to help fund any projects of mine that revolved around art. Heading a non-profit, I'd enthusiastically responded to his offer. Now, his generosity was being put to the test.

"You got my message?"

"Yes," he said. "I'm curious about Caitlin, the young woman you told me about. You say she's quite an artist?"

"I've seen some of her work and it's very intriguing. She does three-dimensional collages of found pieces, mostly things she picks up along the beaches on the South Shore and Cape Cod. Friends of mine have evaluated her work and think she's got real potential."

"I'd like to meet her. Perhaps at the end of the week. Is that possible?"

"That would be wonderful!" Pleasure hummed through me. We'd clicked from the beginning.

"Coming to Boston will give me a chance to meet her on a more informal basis. I could stick around for the weekend. Would that be okay?"

"Perfect." Spending time with him would be a pleasant diversion after a few rough weeks. "I'll think of things to do and we can talk later. Can't wait to see you, Dawson!"

I hung up and found Zach staring at me from the doorway of my office. "This guy special or something?"

I smiled. "Dawson is a very likable guy. You'll see."

Dawson had requested we meet at the Four Seasons hotel, situated opposite the Public Garden on Boylston Street. The Five-Star hotel was an elegant reminder that his appearance as merely a creator of fine raku pottery was deceptive. Though he normally lived a simple life, he was used to very nice things, which he eagerly shared with others. I admired him tremendously. If things went well, he'd assist Straight Talk in helping Caitlin. Then I could go onto other projects.

As I walked through the entrance into the lobby, Dawson quickly rose from an overstuffed chair, grinned, and strode across the lobby to greet me. His thick gray hair curled softly around his strong-featured face, and his dark eyes glistened with warmth. Of average height, he appeared casually elegant, trim, and muscular, wearing faded blue jeans, Italian loafers, a blue-striped shirt, and a navy blazer. I held out my hand and then gave him a quick peck on the cheek. "It's been a while, Samantha." He gave me an admiring look. "Your sister told me good things about what you're doing."

"It's so nice to see you again, Dawson. I can't wait for you to meet Caitlin. And I want to tell you about some of the other women who've come to me for help."

He motioned me to a chair and settled down on a couch opposite it. "I read the business plan you put together for Straight Talk. I'm impressed."

My heart warmed at his words. As determined as I was to do things my way, it felt good to receive reassurances from others. We talked about his trip and more about my business, becoming comfortable with one another.

I checked my watch and stood. "We can walk to my office from here. Do you mind? It's just a couple of blocks away and it's such a beautiful day."

"Sounds great. I'm used to a lot of exercise."

We walked along Arlington Street, past the Public Garden and the Taj Hotel, crossed Commonwealth Avenue and entered a narrow brick building on Marlborough Street. I led him inside, up flights of stairs to the small office I rented from Zach. Without his consideration and the generosity of Zach's grandmother, who owned the building, I could never have afforded this location. Their low rental rate, a contribution to the business, was a tremendous help.

Inside my office, Dawson and I looked out the window at the Charles River. Triangular white sails on a number of small sailboats dipped and soared above the water, like seagulls playing in the wind.

"Beautiful view," Dawson commented. "But then, Boston, itself, is charming."

"Especially in the summer. On cold, windy days in winter, I envy my sister living in sunny California."

He gave me a warm smile. "Perhaps we can persuade you to move to the west coast."

I laughed. "It won't work. She's already tried. I've got too much to do here."

A knock on the door made me turn. Caitlin, her bright-red hair curling without restraint, gazed uncertainly at me with light-blue eyes. Not beautiful, she was attractive in her own way. I sighed with relief at her put-together appearance. Her sponsor and I had worked with her all week on the importance of staying away from Anthony Carbone. She stood before me now, well-groomed and bright-eyed.

"Caitlin, come meet Dawson Smith." I took her hand.

Her fingers were icy cold. From an underprivileged background, her family did not consider art a worthwhile pursuit. It had taken Caitlin by surprise that so many other people loved her creativity.

Dawson greeted her with a smile. "Glad to meet you. I've looked at photos of your collages. They're really quite wonderful."

Caitlin gave him a disbelieving look and accepted his extended hand. "You liked 'em, huh? Anthony doesn't know what everyone sees in them. I like to put things together and add color. It's just something I enjoy doing."

I bit my lip, pushing back my resentment of Anthony's ability to undermine all my attempts to build Caitlin's confidence. He was Caitlin's downfall. Aside from encouraging her to continue drinking, he was hooked on gambling. Betting on sports teams or any other form of vice had, apparently, always been a big part of Anthony's wayward life. At times, Caitlin understood this was dangerous for her. At others, well...

"Okay, Samantha?"

Dawson's question snapped me out of my musing. "I'm sorry. What did you say?"

"I'm suggesting we go somewhere for a nice lunch and talk about the Art Institute there, rather than staying in the office."

. "Good idea. It won't seem so formal."

Caitlin shot me a grateful look. "How about something in the North End," she said shyly. "I know lots of good places there."

I turned to Dawson. "Do you mind another walk? A longer one? There are several excellent Italian restaurants there, though it's several blocks away."

"A long walk? On a day like today? Not at all."

White puffy clouds danced in the bright, blue skies above us, like dollops of meringue. The temperature held a hint of the future fall weather but still clung to the warmth of summer. A pleasant on-shore breeze cooled us as we strolled along.

It being a Friday, I remembered that the Haymarket was open. "Wait until you see all the fruit and vegetable stands set up near the Bostonian Hotel," I told Dawson. "I usually come late Saturday afternoon, if I'm in town. That's when I can find some great buys."

We walked past the gold-domed State House on Beacon Hill and crossed Government Center Plaza to Faneuil Hall Marketplace and beside it, Haymarket Square. There, a number of vendors selling fresh fruits, vegetables, and cheeses had set up their booths. Brick buildings faced the booths, which extended into the street. Inside the buildings, a number of shops sold everything from meats, sausages, and other staples to hot, homemade pizza, and assorted sandwiches.

"We can grab lunch here if you want. Keep it real simple."

"Let's sample some things and then decide," Dawson said agreeably. "This is a real slice of Americana."

Caitlin pointed out one of the pizza vendors. "A neighbor owns that one. Let's go there."

We stood amid a small gathering of people waiting for the man behind the counter to slice up a fresh pizza.

A burly young man pushed between me and Caitlin, forcing me off-balance. "Where's Anthony?" he snarled at Caitlin.

I felt the blood leave my face and quickly glanced around.

Dawson caught my elbow to steady me. "My God! Are you all right?"

My mouth was so dry, I could only nod. I glowered at the scruffy, young man who'd shoved me aside.

He ignored me and shook a finger at Caitlin. "You tell Anthony that Johnny P is looking for him. If he fuckin' knows what's good for him, he'll fuckin' take care of business. Got it?"

I placed a protective hand on Caitlin's shoulder. "Look ...," I began ...

He turned and barreled his way through the crowd, and was soon out of sight.

Still shaking from the scare, I said to Caitlin, "What's that all about?"

The corners of her lips turned down. "I don't know. I never saw him before."

I let the matter drop, but worry edged through me. Anthony could ruin everything for Caitlin.

The three of us nibbled pizza as we continued our stroll

through the market. Even as we admired the produce and other wares, I kept a careful watch on the people around us, looking for a dark-haired man in a dark jacket, a man who wouldn't hesitate to hurt me.

Dawson wiped his mouth with a napkin. "That pizza is not going to do it for me. I want a bigger lunch than that. What do you suggest?"

"The Union Oyster House is right around the corner. We can get chowder or something more substantial there."

Dawson's face lit up. "Perfect. Lead the way."

The brick building housing the restaurant had been a local landmark for more than 250 years. After being seated inside, I picked up the information card on the table and read aloud. "The Union Oyster House is the oldest restaurant in continuous service in the United States and has been open to diners since 1826."

Dawson grinned. "In business since 1826? If the food tastes as delicious as it smells, I believe it."

A waitress took our order. After she left, Dawson cleared his throat. "So, Caitlin, tell me about your artwork. What prompted you to become involved in your projects?"

Caitlin glanced nervously at me and blurted out, "I don't know why I like it so much, maybe because it's my own thing. I don't have to ask anyone how to do it. I just know how I want to place things on a canvas and what colors should go where." A shy smile brought color to her cheeks. "Anthony doesn't see why everyone likes it. He says they're just a couple pieces of wood, and shells, and other pieces stuck on colored paper."

"Do you think he's right, that that's all they are?" Dawson asked quietly.

I held my breath, knowing how important her answer was,.

"No," she said. "Each piece tells a hidden story. Like one time, I found a small piece of a bird's eggshell. I wanted to show how that mother had taken care of her baby and how the little bird had flown away. I put some straw in the picture and some seeds and all kinds of stuff against a light-blue background, like the sky, and swirled it with black. Everyone likes that one."

Dawson smiled. "It's great that you like to tell stories in your special way."

Listening to the exchange, pride filled me. My work with her was paying off.

"Samantha thinks it's a good idea for you to go to the Art Institute," Dawson told Caitlin. "What do *you* think?"

Caitlin's blue eyes grew brighter. "I don't care what anyone says, I want to learn about different ways of doing things. It would be like a dream come true, you know?"

"Okay, I've done some investigation on this and if you commit to working hard, you won't need to worry about tuition. Knowing how Anthony and your family feel about your artwork, can you make that kind of commitment?"

"This is important, Caitlin," I interjected, unable to contain myself. "You have real talent. Other people are prepared to help you, but they need to have a sense of commitment from you. Are you able to go against Anthony's will on this?"

Caitlin drew herself straighter in her chair. A look of determination settled on her face. "It's *my* life. He won't like it, but I want to do this."

Dawson shook hands with her. "Well, then, Samantha tells me you can start right away. She's taken care of all the details. You and she can work it out."

Tears came to Caitlin's eyes. She clasped her hands together. "Thank you! Thank you! Both of you!"

I smiled at her and turned to Dawson. "Thank you, Dawson. It's such a wonderful thing to do."

"I know how much my pottery-making means to me. I'm

glad Caitlin is sincerely interested in pursuing her art."

Our food came, and I ate my oyster stew in a party-like mood, wanting to shout for joy. Bringing two people together to create a wonderful opportunity for them both was exactly what I'd dreamed of doing after I got my own life in order.

Caitlin finished the last of her fries and fidgeted in her chair. "Mind if I leave? I promised my mother I'd babysit my younger brothers, and I can't wait to tell her I'm going to art school. She told me it would never happen, that things like this didn't happen to our family. Now I can prove to her she was wrong."

Dawson got to his feet.

Caitlin threw her arms around him. "Thank you. Thank you so much."

A look of tenderness crossed his face, making my heart swell for all he'd given her.

Caitlin gave me a big hug and moved through the crowd, looking back at me with a triumphant grin.

Dawson turned to me. "She seems like a nice girl, but what's with the boyfriend? I don't like the sound of him at all."

"Neither do I." A shudder crossed my shoulders. Two nights ago, I'd dreamed of Anthony attacking me. I'd awakened in a panic, my heart beating so fast I thought I'd faint.

CHAPTER THREE

Saturday morning, Dawson and I headed to Maine. Marissa had invited us for dinner and to stay overnight. She'd met him in California and liked him.

Though there were plenty of cars heading north from Boston, the summer weekend traffic jams were disappearing as families prepared for schools, making the trip to Maine more pleasant. Bright sunshine matched our spirits as Dawson and I chatted comfortably about details of our lives. He was a remarkable man; a nice man. I found myself warming to his shy demeanor.

"Harrison Edwards of the Winthrop Gallery in Boston would like to meet you sometime and possibly set up a show of your work," I said.

"Sounds good." Dawson gave me a wink. "Gives me more excuses to come to Boston."

I returned his smile and studied him from the corner of my eye as he gazed out the window. He was attractive, successful, and generous. Though he was much older than I, my parents would think he was perfect for me. The age difference had worked for them, but is that what I wanted for myself?

As if he knew my uncertainty, Dawson reached over and patted my shoulder, his expression serious. "I'd like to get to know you better, Samantha. I've been intrigued with you from the start. But then, I guess you knew that."

"Yes. I felt the same way." But inside my emotions were whirling. Relationships in the past had been easy for me. Way too easy. I'd had fun, shared love, and moved on. In this new life of mine, I was much more serious, more vulnerable, and more determined to avoid sticky situations.

We drove into New Hope past the picturesque marina. Small, quaint shops lined the main street, clustered together like gossipy women whispering enticements to the stream of tourists who crowded the walkways.

"Nice," murmured Dawson.

"Wait until you see Briar Cliff and the beaches. It's even more beautiful."

We continued through town and beyond and reached the entrance to Briar Cliff. I drove between the stone pillars marking the driveway, past the open, wrought-iron gate. The house, like a well-endowed dowager from another era, sat beside the beach at the end of the drive. The three-story, brown-shingled structure seemed immense compared to my small condo. I pulled up to the back of it and turned off the motor.

"Here it is." I stepped out of the car and inhaled the tangy, salty scent from the ocean mere steps away on the other side of the house. "There's a wonderful story behind Marissa inheriting it. She's brought a breath of fresh air to the family. To everyone, that is, except my father."

Marissa burst out of the house and hurried toward the car, a huge smile on her face. "Sam! I'm so glad you're here."

She embraced me and turned to Dawson, who had quietly observed us.

"Glad to see you again, Dawson." She hesitated and gave him a quick hug. "Come inside. Brad is on the phone. Legal business, of course."

"I'll get the bags," Dawson offered.

"Thanks." Marissa pulled me toward the house. Out of earshot of Dawson, she whispered, "He's so-o-o-o nice. Is there something you want to tell me?"

I shoved her playfully. "We're just friends. I'm not sure I'm ready for a relationship."

"You?" Marissa laughed. "Honey, it's been what, a couple of years?"

"Yeah, and you know what? I'm scared. Besides, I've sworn off men. Remember?"

"Oh, hon..."

Lady, Marissa's golden retriever, bounded toward us and barked. Happy for the interruption, I rubbed her soft ears. My last bout of dating had left me convinced to concentrate on my work and forget thinking about a suitable husband. The men I'd met seemed so one-dimensional.

Brad opened the screen door and walked over to us with a welcoming smile.

"Hey, there!" He gave me a bear hug. "Glad you're here." He looked up as Dawson approached us. "You must be Dawson. Here, let me give you a hand."

Each carrying a suitcase, they headed inside the house.

"He's so-o-o-o nice," I teased in a whisper, mimicking Marissa.

She grinned. Her gray eyes, like mine, shone. "Plans for our wedding next year are coming along. Marissa Crawford has a nice sound to it, don't you think?"

I laughed and followed her into the house. Brad and Marissa were a perfect couple. They'd grown up together in Barnham, New York, never dreaming they'd be engaged one day.

We left our suitcases in the front hall and went into the kitchen. A simple lunch of assorted sandwiches was laid out.

The four of us attacked them and then relaxed on the porch like two old married couples—leaning back in rocking chairs, our feet on the porch rail. The men snoozed while Marissa and I caught up on all the family gossip.

"Guess we ought to think about dinner," said Marissa, getting to her feet, stretching and yawning.

"Tonight's easy." Brad came to Marissa's side and wrapped his arms around her. Growling with mock ferociousness, he gave her a lingering kiss.

When they broke apart, she laughed and pushed him away. "Down, boy." But I knew from the flush on her cheeks and the sexy look she gave him that if Dawson and I weren't there they might have bolted for their bedroom.

Observing their interplay, a stab of jealousy surprised me.

Marissa smiled at me. "Becky made one of her famous fancy chicken casseroles. It's in the refrigerator. All we have to do is heat it up."

I grinned and turned to Dawson. "Becky Cantwell's cooking is great."

"I don't know what we'd do without Becky and Henry," said Marissa. "This place couldn't run without them. As a matter of fact, she's the one who prepared the guest rooms for you. Come on, I'll show you to them."

Marissa led us up to the second floor where there were six bedrooms.

"This is the room I thought Dawson would enjoy, looking out over the beach." She gave me a questioning look.

"And my room?" I said quickly. I had no intention of sharing quarters with Dawson at this stage.

"I've redone Arinthia's corner room."

I gave her a grateful smile. She knew that, of the three kids in my family, I was the one who'd most admired my aunt. It made me happy to be placed there.

The room, done in soft, gold tones, was warm and welcoming. I was drawn to the two large windows, one overlooking the side garden, the other, the beach. The play of sun on the water was captivating. Waves rushed onto the shore and hurried away again like a teasing child giving a quick peck on the cheek and then racing away.

Later, as we sat in the sunroom before dinner, I surreptitiously observed Dawson. Though he was several years older than Brad, they were in a deep, animated conversation about a variety of subjects. I knew Dawson was interested in me and wasn't sure how I felt about it. Shifting in my chair, I wondered where it all might lead.

Dinner continued in the same, easy-going atmosphere. In the presence of good company and stimulating conversation, the tensions of my work week melted away. Anthony, I told myself, was nothing but a creep who enjoyed bossing people around.

After the meal, the men retired to the den to watch the Red Sox game. Chatting comfortably, Marissa and I cleaned up.

When Marissa had put the last of the dishes in the dishwasher, she said, "How about a walk on the beach? It's a beautiful night."

"Perfect."

I stepped onto the porch and breathed in the salty tang of the night air with a happy sigh. Boston was a convenient, attractive place to live, but the scenery there couldn't compare to the natural beauty along the coast of Maine.

The others joined me.

"Beautiful, isn't it?" said Dawson. "I've forgotten how different the coasts are." He took my hand, and we headed out onto the wide expanse of sand, stopping to watch the movement of the waves, silver-tipped in the moonlight. They rolled in to greet us then rushed back out to sea in a night-time game of chase.

Marissa and Brad came up behind us, Lady at their heels. "It's a gorgeous night," said Marissa.

Brad led off down the beach ahead of us. Dawson and I held

hands and hurried to match their brisk pace.

"I've been thinking about a show at Winthrop Gallery," said Dawson. "It might work."

We became engrossed in conversation about his art world, and our steps slowed until we lagged far behind. I figured we'd gone about a mile when Brad and Marissa walked toward us.

Brad gave us a knowing smile. "Take your time. We'll meet up with you at the house."

They set off again at the same fast pace, leaving us on our own.

Dawson drew me into his arms. "I've wanted to do this all day."

He tilted my chin and gazed into my eyes. A surge of warmth swept through me as his lips met mine. I relaxed under his gentle, but firm kiss. It had been a while since I'd dated anyone and the contact felt good.

We pulled apart and Dawson gently traced my lips with a fingertip. "You're beautiful, you know." He grabbed my hand. "C'mon, hon. Let's head back. I'm too old to grapple on the beach."

My emotions whirled as we walked hand in hand. Dawson attracted me, but I wasn't sure my feelings went beyond that. Did he think I'd just go to bed with him?

It seemed to take no time to reach Briar Cliff.

A large, white note was taped to the porch door. Puzzled, I picked it up and read it aloud. "We've gone to bed. Make yourselves comfortable. See you in the morning. Hugs, Marissa."

I swallowed hard. No doubt Marissa thought she was doing me and Dawson a favor by giving us all the privacy she thought I desired.

Dawson took me in his arms and kissed me, pressing his body close to mine. When he pulled away, he wore a tender expression. "I think you know what I want to do, but I'm not sure this is the proper time and place. Perhaps you'll come to California ..." His eyes lit up. "Better yet, I have a trip to London coming up...You could come with me."

I gazed uncertainly at him. He was asking much more of me than I was ready to give.

"Samantha, my dear, there are so many things I want to show you. London is just the beginning."

I stared at him, speechless. His words made me realize what it would feel like to be treasured and pampered, to not have to worry about paying rent on office space or taking on everyone else's problems. I sometimes felt as if my whole life was a constant struggle; my facing the world alone; seeking approval from someone who was not about to give it; trying to find myself, accept myself, and be successful, whatever that was.

He brushed a strand of hair away from my face with a gentle hand. "Just think about it." He gazed lovingly at me and reached for me. Disappointment glimmered in his eyes when I involuntarily took a tiny step backward.

My stomach clenched at the thought I'd hurt him. The moment grew awkward as I wondered how to tell him what was on my mind.

Dawson solved my dilemma by leaning over and giving me a chaste kiss on the cheek. "We'll talk later. See you in the morning."

Entering my bedroom, I was drawn once more to the silvery scene outside. I told myself to be practical for once, that my parents would be so pleased if I settled down with someone as reliable as Dawson.

I turned away from the window, shaken by my thoughts.

Is that what *I* wanted?

###

The next morning I rose early. Nagging thoughts of Dawson's proposal of a trip to London had kept me tossing and turning all night, making it impossible to sleep.

Dawson Smith was a wealthy man who was used to doing exactly what he wanted when he wanted. He wouldn't have been able to succeed in both the business and art worlds without a drive that matched my own. If I entered into a relationship with him, would he, like my father, toss my pride and my wishes aside to maintain control over our lives together?

I quietly dressed and tiptoed down the stairs, needing some time alone to sort things out.

At the entrance to the kitchen, I stopped short. Marissa sat at the table in her robe, sipping coffee. She looked up and greeted me with a Cheshire cat smile.

"Well? How did it go last night? Anything you want to share with me?"

I laughed. "You're bad. A hopeless romantic."

She cocked an eyebrow. "Is there anything serious going on between you and Dawson? I saw the way he looked at you."

I poured myself a cup of coffee and sat down at the kitchen table opposite her. "He wants to take me to London and have me come out to California and stay with him. I don't know what to think. I'm attracted to him because he makes me feel so safe and comfortable, but ..."

"Safe? Comfortable?" Marissa's eyes widened. "Is that what you truly want, Samantha?"

My insides squeezed. "I don't know. It's been so long since I've had any interest in anyone." An unbidden image of Derek Roberts flashed in my mind. Comfortable wasn't a word I'd ever use to describe him. He'd drawn me in with those golden eyes of his, reminding me of a lion surveying the jungle. Just thinking of him set my heart to pounding.

"Dawson is very nice. He has such an air of ...I don't know...authority." Marissa studied me. "He reminds me a little bit of your father."

Dismay swept through me. "Omigod! Do you think that's why I'm attracted to him? Some father figure thing?"

"I hope not." She placed a hand on my arm. "Forget it. I don't know where that thought came from."

Inside my room once more, I gazed out at the water below. Its continuous movement soothed me. I let my thoughts drift as free as the waves. The sound of my cell phone startled me out of my reverie. Frowning, I checked the number. Nobody I knew. I hesitated and took the call.

"Samantha? Where are you? This is Caitlin."

"What's wrong?" I could hear tears in her voice.

"It's Anthony. He's all mad 'cause I'm going to the Art Institute. He says I'm getting too good for my own britches. He thinks I owe him for all the things he's done for me."

Though hot anger boiled beneath the surface of my mind, my entire body turned cold. "And just exactly what has he done for you?" I couldn't hide my sarcasm.

"You know. He buys me things and takes me out and all."

"It doesn't mean he owns you, Caitlin. Nobody should have that much control over anyone else." I lowered myself onto the edge of the bed.

"I know ... but he's the only good thing I've got going right now. I've had another fight with my mother. She says I'm costing her too much money, and, unless I get a full-time job, I can't stay there."

She paused, and I could hear sniffling. "Anthony thinks we ought to get married. I don't know what to do, but art school is out. My work stinks. Everyone thinks so."

Darn it! I'd worked so hard to help Caitlin see the value in herself and her work. Anthony managed to drain all of Caitlin's self-confidence each time she attempted to do something positive for herself. Her mother was no better. Saddled with too many children at too young an age, Caitlin's mother saw her as a built-in babysitter and housekeeper so she could go out drinking.

I fought to speak calmly. "Caitlin, don't make any rash decisions. Give me time to work something out. And, remember, people like Harrison Edwards and Dawson Smith, real people in the art world, think your work is wonderful. Don't let anyone tell you differently."

"Here comes Anthony now," Caitlin whispered and hung up.

I clutched the buzzing phone in my trembling hand, wishing I could shake some sense into her. Yet, I understood how trapped she felt, torn between family, finding love, and helping herself. I was dealing with all of it myself.

Against my father's wishes, Straight Talk had become my life, filling me with the need to be productive. But love, the real kind—hot and exciting, sweet, and gentle—would make my life complete. Having observed Marissa with Brad, I knew without a doubt that I didn't want to settle for just a 'comfortable' relationship. I wanted more. Much more.

A knock sounded at my door. I opened it slowly.

Dawson stood there, fully dressed. "There's been an emergency at my studio on the ranch in California. I need to go back there today. Can you drive me down to Logan Airport? I've arranged for a morning flight."

My heart pounded. "Oh, no! What happened?"

"A fire started in one of the sheds and spread to the barn. I've lost a horse and lots of equipment." He swiped a hand through his hairs and blinked rapidly.

"Oh, Dawson, that's horrible. I'm so sorry. I'll be ready to leave in a few minutes." I quickly changed clothes and packed.

Downstairs we said a hasty good-bye to Marissa and Brad and hurried out to my car.

My mind raced as Dawson and I traveled through the small town of New Hope and out to the Maine Turnpike. I gripped the wheel tightly, so unsure what to say to him, so afraid of hurting such a sweet man.

He turned to me. "It was nice to be back in Maine again. It's beautiful. Charming, really."

I wondered how I could begin to tell him what I was feeling inside.

"Samantha, there's something I want you to know." Dawson gave me a long look. "You're a lovely, beautiful young woman. I admire you and your work very much, but as far as a romantic relationship between us is concerned, I understand it's not right for you. That shouldn't stop us from working together. I want to be a part of your success by helping you. Will you allow me to do that?"

Relief did the tango with embarrassment. My emotions dipped and swirled in a dance of their own.

As if he could read the feelings I couldn't get out, he gave me a gentle smile. "I'd like to set up a scholarship program for anyone who would like to go to school to learn something new—any school, not just for art."

My heart filled with gratitude. He was such a dear, sweet man. I pulled over to the side of the road, stopped the car and threw my arms around him.

"You're wonderful! I'm so sorry about...about...us."

He patted my back. "Don't worry about it. Sometimes, it just doesn't work out. It's not your fault."

I hugged him harder. "You're the best, Dawson. I really

mean it."

He smiled and caressed my cheek. "I'm proud of you, Samantha. You're doing a remarkable job, not only for Caitlin but for other women as well. Not everyone your age would be so self-sacrificing."

My throat grew thick. Dawson's approval meant so much. I thought of my father who could never easily say words like that to me and blinked hard, struggling for self-control.

"Hey," said Dawson gently. "I didn't mean to upset you."

There was so much I wanted to say. "Can we *always* be friends?"

"Of course. You, Allison, and Marissa—the Hartwell women as you call yourselves—are remarkable people. I value your friendship."

I gave him another squeeze, thinking I'd never met a man as wonderful as Dawson.

I returned to my apartment looking forward to curling up on my couch. Exhausted, I quickly fell asleep, even though it was just after midday.

A phone call from Marissa woke me from my nap. "How are you? I'm dying to know what happened between you and Dawson."

I told her the whole story and how sweet Dawson had been to me. "I realize when the time comes, I want what you and Brad have—not something simply nice, something more wonderful than that, a relationship that would last a lifetime."

"You're right," she quickly agreed. "You shouldn't settle for second best. I can't imagine settling down with someone who didn't turn me on by simply walking into the room. It's like that for me with Brad. Know what I mean?"

My thoughts flew to Derek Roberts. A shiver danced across

my shoulders. *That's the effect he'd had on me, and I'd only seen him once in my life!*

Marissa continued, "Another reason I called was to let you know that your father cornered me last night to talk about Derek Roberts. He thinks it's a good idea for Rivers Papers to go ahead with the promo book Ted Beers is championing."

My senses were on high alert. "What's the connection between Ted and Derek? Did he say? You know Ted doesn't promote anything that doesn't benefit himself. If Derek Roberts is associated with Ted, it can only mean trouble."

"I agree. That's why I wanted to warn you. Too bad Ted is still on the board. He doesn't give a damn about Rivers Papers. Not really."

"I don't understand why my father has anything to do with him."

"Brad told me that Ted is one of your father's best clients."

A nagging thought entered my mind. "Has my father approached Brad about joining his law firm?"

Marissa hesitated and then spoke. "Actually, he did, but Brad told him no. He's going to help me with the charitable trust I'm setting up with Arinthia's money. He'll also continue to work with his father in Barnham."

My father had gone ahead and asked Brad, not me, to join the firm? Pain like sharp-edged knives pierced my body. I'd graduated from Harvard Law with high honors and had been sought after by the most prestigious firms on the east coast. But my own father had refused to give me a position, telling me he was waiting for my brother to assume it. My heart ached. It had always been like this in my household.

Marissa sensed my hurt. "Are you all right?"

I pressed my lips together, determined I'd show my father how wrong he was about me. "I'm fine," I answered, though my words didn't ring with confidence. How could they?

CHAPTER FOUR

At the close of one of my evening support meetings, a striking, nicely dressed woman approached me. Her honey-brown hair was styled in a sleek, shoulder-length cut that nicely set off her features. She appeared to be in her middle forties. I tried not to stare at the jagged scar that ran the length of her left cheek, marring what would otherwise be a stunning face.

"Hello, I'm Liz Sanderson." She held out a hand. "I heard what you said about Straight Talk. Can we speak privately about it?"

"Sure." I shook hands with her. "Do you want to go somewhere for a fresh cup of coffee?"

Her dark eyes brightened. "That sounds good. The coffee at the meeting was awful."

"There's a Dunkin' Donuts on School Street. We can go there." I kept wondering if I'd met her before. Something about her seemed so familiar.

We walked down the street together, and, after buying our coffee at the counter, we sat down at a table in the corner of the room for privacy.

I took a sip of the hot liquid, noting the lack of a wedding ring on her left hand. "Are you contemplating going to school or setting up a business of some kind?"

"I'm a travel writer. Or *was*. With all the changes in my life, it's time to settle down and do something more practical. I'm thinking of taking a few computer classes to learn Excel and PowerPoint so I can get a job as an administrative person."

"Is that what you really want to do, Liz?" Dressed impeccably and wearing sizeable diamond earrings, she didn't fit the image of an office worker.

She shrugged. "At this point, it might be the best thing. At least it's a steady salary. My son, who's away at school, is about to turn eighteen when child support payments will stop. I've got to do something, or I'll be out on the street." She pointed to the scar on her face. "My husband did this to me. In the past, he's faithfully made his payments to me. Guilt, I suppose. Now, it's about to stop. He's met a young girl who wants to marry him. All at once he's backing out of all the unwritten agreements we had in place about continued support." Her voice turned bitter. "It seems no matter how much money he spends on her, it's not enough."

"When did the...accident... happen?" I asked, caught up in her story.

Liz fingered her scar. "Five years ago this Christmas. We were in the islands for the holiday so I could write a story on Barbados. My husband and I had way too much to drink and got into a fight. Funny thing is, later, neither one of us could remember what the argument was about. At any rate, I made him mad enough to pick up a knife in the condo where we were staying. Who knows if he ever intended to maim me? I'm not sure. But it woke me up to our bad marriage and to our drinking problems. I opted out of the marriage and into sobriety."

We sat quietly for a moment, sipping coffee, letting her story settle between us. Finally, I could resist no longer.

"Liz, with all the plastic surgery that can be done today, why haven't you had your scar altered?"

She gave me a sheepish look. "I was so mad for so long that I left it there as a symbol of what can happen if you drink. I think I'm finally convinced it's time to take care of it."

I laughed. I liked this woman with a glimmer of humor in her eyes. She'd be pleasant to work with and would, I was sure, be a success at whatever she did. She'd already proved herself as an independent writer.

We talked about her writing for a while.

"*National Geographic* assignments were my favorite. My mother stayed with my son, Rick, and my husband would meet up with me when he wasn't working on something for the governor."

It hit me then. I felt my eyes widen. "Is your husband's name Howard?"

Yes. That's another reason I kept the scar—to embarrass Howard, one of the top advisors to the governor of Maine." She laughed. "It still makes him crazy."

I chuckled. Liz Sanderson was nobody's fool.

"I'm putting that all behind me," she went on to explain. "That's why I want to have a fresh start, try something new and be there for my son."

I studied her. At some point, Liz might make a nice addition to the staff of Straight Talk. "Come into the office tomorrow and fill out some paperwork. I believe we can help you sign up for a few courses."

Liz's eyes watered. "You realize I'll pay you back as soon as I can. I'm in a financial bind at the moment, but I fully intend to make my own way. I refuse to let Howard have the satisfaction of knowing how devastating his behavior is to me. All the planning I'd done for the future means little now."

I gave her hand an encouraging squeeze. "Yours is a perfect example of why I started Straight Talk."

I checked my watch, and we rose to leave. Outside, I glanced around warily. Confronting Anthony had made me realize I needed to be more careful. In the growing darkness, I hurried the few blocks to my car. A black cat jumped out from an alley and I stifled a scream. He slid back into the shadows and I let out a shaky laugh.

Seated inside the SUV with the doors locked, I drew a deep breath, and silently railed against Anthony. He'd turned the city I'd always loved into a frightening place.

I decided to call Caitlin before going to work. After all of Dawson's effort to make things happen for her, I couldn't just let her situation go.

"Hello?" she said in a sleepy voice.

"How are you doing today?" I listened for signs of slurring.

"Uh...better. I'm staying with my sponsor."

"Good. I'm calling to see if you've decided to go to art school after all."

"My sponsor thinks I should."

"It's your choice, Caitlin, but I don't think either one of us should let someone else, including Anthony, make those kinds of decisions for us." There was no point in pursuing this dream if she wasn't willing to fight for it. "Do *you* want this, Caitlin?"

I held my breath.

A long pause played with my emotions.

"Yes, I really, really do, Samantha. Tell me what I have to do."

We made the arrangements and I hung up feeling giddy with joy. I could already envision her works hanging in the Winthrop Gallery.

The day took off in a flurry of activity. Liz Sanderson came in to fill out paperwork, and several new women came in for interviews and to apply for help. Rosie's Place, a well-known women's shelter in Boston, called and asked if I would do a presentation through their adult learning program on filling out job applications and developing resumes. I quickly accepted. Many women didn't appreciate how much knowledge they had, and that some simple homemaking skills were applicable to the job market. Granted, some of them would perform menial tasks at first, but those situations would, I hoped, lead to better-paying jobs.

By Friday, I was in my usual, exhausted state.

"Are you going out tonight?" Zach asked me at lunch, munching an egg roll from our favorite Chinese restaurant.

I shook my head. "I think I'll crawl home, watch a sappy movie and call it a day."

"Guess who I've got a date with?" He wiggled his eyebrows.

I studied the glow on his face. "Don't tell me Edwina Nichols finally agreed to go out with you."

Zach's smile was infectious. "We're going to the movies. How's that for dull and safe?"

I rolled my eyes. "I thought if it wasn't worthy of the society pages, Edwina wouldn't participate."

He patted my hand, and gave me a wicked grin. "Jealous, are we?"

"You know that's not it. I just want to be sure that whoever you date realizes what a great guy you are. I've heard Edwina thinks everyone is beneath her."

His expression grew serious. "I've known her all my life. She's not that way. Her mother is the one who is constantly pushing her into society. She even named her only daughter Edwina after a rich uncle. How fair is that to good ole Eddie?"

I laughed. Perhaps I was being overly protective of Zach, but I knew how sensitive he was beneath his jovial manner. Then again, maybe Zach would be the best thing that ever happened to her. Either way, I'd keep a watchful eye on good ole Eddie.

#

I dragged myself through the door of my condo to find the message light blinking on my phone. Marissa. "Sorry I missed you. Give me a ring when you can."

I smiled and punched in her number. She picked up immediately.

"You phoned?"

"Yes, I've got some v-e-e-r-r-y interesting news. I ran into Ted Beers in Portland. He was with a drop-dead gorgeous guy. Guess who? Seems Ted and Derek Roberts were in town to talk with a publisher about the book for the company. Ted's sister is going to write all the descriptive material for Derek's photographs. He went ahead and made all the arrangements. How's that for brass balls?"

My body tightened. Ted was already working behind the scenes to set things up his way? He was up to something. And, it would appear, Derek Roberts was in on it too.

"Know any writers?" Marissa gave a wicked chuckle. "Maybe we could beat him at his own game."

A smile played on my lips. "As a matter of fact, I do. Earlier this week I met someone who has the qualifications for this kind of writing. She's even done work for *National Geographic*."

"Good. Give her a call and see if she'd be interested in writing about the history of Rivers Papers and the paper mill industry as a whole, along with creating interesting captions for the photos."

I hung up with Marissa and called Liz to tell her about the possibility of becoming part of the book project.

"I'd love it! I've done a lot of research on the rain forests of Brazil, and the paper business would be another fascinating assignment. Yes, Samantha, I'd definitely be interested."

Pleased, I said, "Submit a bio to me, along with a list of

projects you've worked on and samples of your writing. I'll see that each board member receives a copy."

"Samantha? Please don't give the board members my name. Not right away. Some of them may know Howard. He may try to interfere if he hears about the project. He still likes to retaliate when he can."

"Okay, I'll give them the paperwork without any name." Howard was a powerful figure in the state of Maine, where Rivers Papers operated. He had, no doubt, many connections, even some on the Rivers Papers board.

The tensions of the busy week seeped out of my body as I relaxed, reading on the couch. I thought about Derek. Though he was a bit full of himself, he'd seemed pretty straightforward when I'd met him at his art show. I wondered again about the connection between him and Ted Beers. Theirs was such a contrast of personalities.

The phone rang, jarring me out of my contemplation. Startled, I reached for it. "H-hello?"

"Samantha? This is Derek Roberts. I'm still kicking around in the area and wondered if you're free tomorrow? We could maybe take in dinner or something."

My pulse raced. Speak of the devil!

"You're here in Boston? But I thought you were in Maine."

"Ah, your cousin Marissa must have told you we met in Portland. But I'm in Boston for the weekend. So, are you free for dinner?"

Every instinct told me to say no. He was dangerously attractive and if he was in cahoots with Ted Beers, he was not someone I wanted to be with.

"Yes, that would be nice." The words defiantly slid out of my mouth. Flustered, I listened as Derek told me he'd pick me up at seven o'clock. He hung up before I could gather my wits and change my mind.

"Well, that was stupid," I said to the empty room. "Not only is he going to take you to dinner, he's picking you up here, and you didn't even give him your address."

I frowned. Zach must have given him my phone number, my address, everything. The next time I saw him, I'd wring his neck.

CHAPTER FIVE

Getting ready for the date with Derek, I changed my clothes twice before I settled on brown pants, a turquoise silk blouse, and a Gucci scarf my mother had brought back for me from Italy.

The nerve-tingling sound of the doorbell thundered into the apartment. I tensed, then, silently admonished myself for acting like a flighty teen and opened the door.

The smile that crossed Derek's face when he saw me sent my emotions reeling. I'd never had this kind of chemistry with a man before and it caught me off balance.

"Hi, there," I said shakily, caught up in those golden eyes of his.

His gaze took in all of me. "You look great."

Goose pimples marched up and down my spine. I took a deep breath and stepped back.

He glanced around the apartment. "Nice. A real home. Something I'm not used to."

"It works for me." Though my apartment in the Back Bay was small, it was well laid out. A living room with a dining area snuggled up to a sizeable galley-type kitchen. A large bedroom and roomy bath stretched out on the other side of the living room. Outside, a long narrow balcony ran the width of the apartment, adding another dimension to the space.

"I didn't know what kind of food you like, so I played it safe and made reservations at Harris'. I figured that would give us a wide choice." Derek smiled at me.

"Good idea. They have wonderful food, and we can walk

from here."

"You don't mind?"

I shook my head. "Boston is a walking town, and I enjoy the outdoors after being stuck in an office all week."

We stepped out to a pleasant evening. Crisp air and clear skies hinted of another fine day ahead.

"So you really enjoy Boston?" Derek asked as we ambled along.

"Yes. It's a beautiful city, full of history and educational opportunities."

"It seems that way," Derek agreed, "but I think my favorite city is Paris."

He described his favorite off-beat places in the city I, too, had loved on a visit.

As I listened, my gaze wandered over him. Tall and trim, he seemed at ease in his body. After knowing how he'd been unable to play sports as a boy because of his asthma, I realized how frustrating it must have been for a well-built man like him. He carried himself with assurance and an efficiency of movement that indicated frequent exercise.

Derek broke into my thoughts. "How long have you been in Boston? And have you known Zach for a long time?"

"I came from Maine to Boston almost three years ago," I smiled at the memory. "I met Zach the first night I was here. We're best friends."

"Zach was a wild man in high school, but he's one of the most honest people I've ever met."

"Honesty is a top priority for me." Wanting to make my point, I looked Derek square in the eye. "If I can't trust someone, I don't want anything to do with him."

Derek stopped and studied me a moment. "Odd. Ted told me to be careful dealing with you, that you're not the woman you seem. He said you're a shrewd businesswoman determined to have her own way. Is that true?"

My jaw dropped. "Wha-a-a-t?"

Derek studied me. "I enjoy a challenge. That's why I gave you a call—to find out what I could about you."

I silently fumed. Ted, the slime ball, had no right to tarnish my reputation. Furthermore, I wasn't about to become anybody's 'challenge.' My nostrils flared. "So, you think of me as one of your ... your travel adventures?"

His eyes rounded with surprise. "What's wrong with having an adventure with a beautiful lady?"

I felt as if I'd had acid thrown at my face. His words burned, destroying any idea of a pleasant evening. He'd made me feel as if I were some kind of experiment, the results of which would be reported back to Ted. My stomach twisted at the idea. "I'm sorry, Derek, but I can't do this ... this adventure thing with you. You'd better go on to the restaurant alone. I'll find my way back to my apartment."

Mumbling to myself, I marched away from him. I was not about to be taken for a fool. Ted and I had a history. An ugly one.

"Wait!" Derek cried.

I turned around.

Derek stood in the middle of the sidewalk, an incredulous look stamped on his face.

Shaking my head, I kept on walking. I'd be darned if I was going to be treated as part of Derek Roberts' world experiences. I deserved better than that.

He caught up with me and grabbed my arm. "Whoa! Slow down. I'm sorry. I didn't mean to make it sound that way."

I narrowed my eyes. "What's your business with Ted Beers, anyway?"

A sheepish look crossed his face. "I dated his niece for a while. It didn't last. She thought I should marry her."

An idea unexpectedly occurred to me. "This niece of his, is it her mother who Ted's proposing to write the text for your book? Is that the deal?"

Derek's surprise seemed genuine. "How'd you know about that?"

"Marissa told me." My curiosity grew. "Why is that so important to Ted? What else is going on?"

He let out a long breath. "I don't understand all the politics on the board, but I learned that Rivers Papers sells a high gloss paper to Beaver Crossing Press. Ted is part-owner of it. Why? Is that a problem?"

My mind racing, I caught the corner of my lip with my teeth. "I'm not sure. It's just that Ted always puts his own interests above anyone or anything else—including Rivers Papers."

Derek moved aside to let an older couple pass by on the sidewalk and stood to face me. "Samantha? Can't we simply enjoy the evening? What's the harm in having dinner together?"

The sincere appeal caught my attention. As much as I hated the thought that Derek had discussed me with Ted, that he was on a date with me as a lark of some kind, I admitted to myself I'd let my temper get the best of me. Maybe, by going to dinner with Derek, I'd learn what else Ted was doing behind the board's back.

"All right, let's start over. Where are we going for dinner?"

"Come wiz me to zee Casbah," he joked.

I grinned and took his arm, determined to relax and enjoy the evening for what it was. A one-time date.

Harris' was well-known for its club atmosphere and excellent range of food from filet mignon to sole almondine.

The paneled walls and dark green furnishings made me think of stuffy New York scenes, but the mix of people inside, with their young ages and hip manner, defied that image. The martini bar was packed, and the music was definitely upbeat.

We were seated at a table in one of the small dining rooms.

Derek grinned as we settled in our chairs. "I requested a table away from all the hoopla. I figured it was better that way." His golden eyes penetrated mine. "I really do want to get to know you, Samantha."

"And I want to know what you have in mind for the book," I responded, telling myself not to be drawn in by his charm. "If your photographs are going to tell the story of the paper business in Maine, it's important to me that you have a clear understanding of it. My great-grandfather and his brother started the paper business back in the late 1800s."

Derek frowned. "Wasn't there a family feud or something?"

"Yes." I was surprised he already knew so much about the family. "Marissa wanted to put an end to the ongoing arguments. That's why she appointed me to the family seat on the board. She still oversees decisions because she owns so many shares of the business."

"Isn't dioxin a problem for paper mills?" Derek asked.

Our waiter appeared, interrupting us.

We placed our orders, and I explained to Derek that dioxin was a very real concern and that most mills had addressed the issue by using non-chlorine bleaching processes.

"Ted hired a plane to fly us around the state so he could show me the mill and processing plant from the air. We flew over several large tracts of land that supply the timber for your company. It's beautiful country."

My mind spun around the fact that Ted had hired a plane to show Derek around. No doubt he'd charged it to the company.

"What else did Ted show you?" Though my suspicions ran deep, I fought to keep my voice neutral.

Derek shrugged. "Just some land he and your father are going to develop. Big condos, the whole works."

"Coldstream, I bet. It's quite a controversy."

"That's the name." He leaned closer. "Now, tell me, how did such a beautiful woman become all caught up in the paper mill business?"

His smile was lazy, his manner confident.

I tamped down sudden uneasiness at the way my body was reacting and changed the subject. "Tell me about your travels."

During dinner, Derek kept me amused with tales of his various trips throughout the world.

"It's fascinating to see how other people live. In my photographs, I like to capture faces of old and young people who live in out-of-the-way places—people in Burma and some of the desert tribes of Africa, those who are willing to let me photograph them."

"I admire that." Some of his pictures at the exhibition had captured that exact essence. He seemed to be a man of contrasts—bright and bold, quiet, and sensitive to others.

The waiter cleared away our entrée dishes.

"Would you like anything else?" Derek took a last sip of coffee.

I shook my head. "No thanks. My veal was delicious. In fact, everything was wonderful."

"Everything? You mean it wasn't as bad as you thought, spending the evening with me?"

I responded to his grin with a smile of my own. It had, in fact, been a very pleasant time.

We left the restaurant and slowly walked toward my condo, maintaining a comfortable silence. As another couple walked toward us, Derek held onto my elbow to help me navigate by them. I looked up to thank him and was rocked by the tenderness I saw in his eyes.

He gave me a cocky grin, and the gentle look disappeared, making me wonder if I'd only imagined it.

When we reached the outside of my building, I turned and faced Derek.

"Thanks for a wonderful evening. It's late. I think I'll go on up." I read surprise in his expression and realized he'd expected to be asked inside. But in spite of a powerful physical attraction to Derek, I had no intention of becoming involved with a traveling man, especially one associated with Ted Beers. If the time came for a meaningful relationship, it would be with the "marriage, kids, forever" kind of person and I didn't think that fit Derek, not with his yen for travel.

A car screeched to a halt next to the curb beside us. I gripped Derek's arm. The tinted power window on the passenger's side rolled down. Anthony Carbone stuck his head out and shook a fist at me. He wore a mask of fury that turned my legs to jelly.

"Hey, you! Samantha! Didn'tcha get my message the other day? Leave Caitlin the hell alone! If you don't, you're gonna be sorry you ever met her ... or me! Fuck off, lady, or you won't live to regret it!"

Horns blared. The car took off with a roar that went right through me. I wobbled on my feet and clung to Derek's arm to keep from collapsing on the ground.

Derek stared after the black Escalade. "Who in hell was that? What's going on?"

Dizzy, I lowered myself to the curb. I'd thought that Anthony was merely a bully, not a dangerous murderer. Tonight, I realized how wrong I'd been. The man who was driving the car looked like a hit man out of a mob movie, and

Anthony, himself, was just as frightening. What in hell had I gotten myself into?

Concern written all over his face, Derek squatted beside me. "Samantha? Take my hand. You can't sit here. It's dangerous with all the traffic rushing by. C'mon. I'll walk you up to your apartment."

I took a deep breath and rose. In recovery groups, I'd heard a lot of stories about violence and, Heaven knows, I'd seen enough of it on television. But my personal life had been basically free of it. Until now.

Derek followed me inside. I was so grateful for his presence that I clung to the hand he offered me. The elevator in the lobby now seemed like a trap, the other occupants of the building an unknown threat.

At the door to my apartment, I turned and faced Derek. "Thank you so much for staying with me. I'm a little shaken by all this."

"I'm not leaving until I see you inside. Go ahead, open the door. I'll make sure you're all right and then, if you want, I'll take off."

I realized how silly I'd been acting. "Why don't you stay for a while? I'll make some coffee."

"Deal. I'll look through the apartment, make sure nothing is wrong."

My surroundings grew fuzzy as my pulse went into overdrive. "Omigod! You think someone could be inside?"

Derek put his hand on my shoulder. "I'm probably being overly cautious—an old habit of mine from some of my travels."

Thinking of some of the more controversial political photographs Derek had displayed in his show, I understood.

I waited inside my apartment by the door while Derek quickly checked the rooms for any disturbance. He returned, giving me an encouraging smile.

"Everything seems fine. How about that coffee?"

I let out a sigh of relief. "I may even have some cookies in the cupboard. Sound good?"

He grinned. "You're on."

He followed me into the kitchen, plunked down on a bar stool, and watched while I got the coffee going. I pulled the Oreo cookies out from their hiding place, where they couldn't tempt me.

"Nice to watch a woman in a kitchen," he murmured.

At such a sexist comment, I whipped around, ready to do battle.

He chuckled at my expression. "I didn't mean it quite that way." The laughter softened his angular features. I felt a sexual pull like I'd never felt before. Warning myself to remember that he was in Ted's camp and, therefore, the "enemy," I sat down on a bar stool beside Derek and waited for the coffee to finish dripping.

Derek leaned back against the counter and studied me a moment. "Are you going to tell me what's going on? It's not every day a date of mine has her life threatened by a young punk."

I told him about Straight Talk and Caitlin Rafferty. "She has real talent and is thrilled with the school. She wants to have a better life than the one she's destined to have if she goes back to her old lifestyle. No matter how much Anthony threatens me, I feel I've done the right thing by helping her. I just wish he could see it that way."

Derek was silent. Then he tilted my chin and studied my face. "Do you have any idea how beautiful you are? When you were talking about Caitlin, a fire lit your eyes. You have a sense of purpose not many people have. I'd love to be able to photograph you sometime."

I stirred on the bar stool restlessly. I didn't know what to say. Was this one of his standard lines? Sexual tension building, we stared at one another until I finally looked away. Derek was too dangerous for my own good.

Derek sipped his coffee and nibbled on cookies. "Are you going to be at the board

meeting at the paper mill next week?" he asked. "Ted wants me to make a presentation to the members of the board. He's asked me to tell them about my work and describe what I envision for the book. If you're going to be there, I was wondering if I can take you to dinner. Not as an adventure, mind you, just because I'd enjoy it."

I told myself I owed it to him to be nice after all he'd done for me. "I know a great little restaurant right outside Riverton. The couple who owns it is originally from French Canada and the food is to die for."

Derek's lips curved. "I hope that doesn't happen—the 'to die for' bit. I want to get to know you a lot better, Samantha Hartwell."

I ignored the heat that burned my cheeks. No doubt he always made such statements to the legions of women he met around the world. Pointedly, I checked my watch. "It's getting late, Derek. I have to be up early. I promised to meet someone for breakfast."

He rose reluctantly. "Guess I'd better go. It's later than I thought."

At the door, I faced him, trying to find the right words. "Thank you for helping me tonight with Anthony. I felt so much safer with you here."

The corners of his mouth lifted. "Damsels in distress are a specialty of mine."

Before I could object, his lips came down on mine—surely, sweetly.

My eyelids fluttered in surprise and closed as delicious sensations rippled through me.

He stepped away, breaking our embrace.

I raised my fingers to my lips, wondering if they felt as hot as the rest of my body.

His golden gaze filled with humor as if he knew very well how I felt. "See you in Maine."

He walked out the door, leaving me aching for just one more kiss.

CHAPTER SIX

Full of excitement, I hurried into my office. It promised to be another busy, fruitful day. As I was removing my coat, Zach wandered in and gave me a sly smile. "'Heard you had an interesting date with Derek."

I blinked with surprise. "He called you?"

Zach shook his head. "No, I called him to make sure he followed through on his promise to me."

"Promise? What promise?"

Zach's gaze veered away from me. "Sort of a gentleman's agreement—in exchange for your telephone number and address."

Hands on hips, I said, "Zach, don't you trust me to take care of myself?"

He shot me a piercing look that stopped me from going full steam ahead with my independence schtick. "From what Derek told me, you just might need help taking care of yourself, Sam. Do you want to tell me what in hell is going on with Anthony Carbone?"

Though I was still bothered by the episode, I shrugged, striving for nonchalance. I'd had a dream about it that kept me awake most of the night.

"He was high, I'm sure, and angry about Caitlin moving on. Derek called him a punk and I've decided that's what he is. That and a bully full of loud noise and idle threats."

Zach placed a hand on my shoulder. Worry creased his brow. "Why didn't you tell me about it? I can pull some connections at the police department, if necessary, and get this guy off your back."

It felt so good to have a steadfast friend like Zach, but over the past several years, I'd learned to handle most things on my own. "I don't want it to escalate into something beyond what it is. But, thanks." Hiding my unease, I gave him a brilliant smile. "So how was the date with Eddie?"

Zach grinned. "Eddie is definitely the wrong name for her. She's all female."

I burst out laughing. "Why, Zach, I do believe you're blushing."

He laughed with me. "I'm going to see her next weekend."

"Good for you." I was truly happy for him. Next Friday, I'd be having dinner with Derek.

At the door to my office, Zach turned back to me. "Sam, take care. Call me if you need me. Anthony may be a little punk, but he could be dangerous."

He left, and I sat at my desk, intent on putting the whole incident behind me. Otherwise, I wouldn't be able to deal with my work. Focused now, I checked my schedule. I'd have just enough time to put the finishing touches on my presentation for Rosie's Place before my first conference call.

A short while later, a knock at the door interrupted my work. I swiveled in my chair and let out a gasp.

Caitlin hobbled painfully toward me, her face so swollen and bruised her eyes were almost completely shut.

"My word, Caitlin! What happened?" I rushed over to her and grabbed hold of her arms as she weaved back and forth on her feet.

"Anthony," she murmured through swollen lips. "He beat me up. Last night."

"Did you go to the police? Have you been to the hospital?" My stomach whirled in sickening circles. I eased her into a chair.

"The police?" The look of dismay she gave me made her eyes appear twice as big through the swollen folds around them. "You're kidding, right? No way! That would only make things freakin' worse. Pretty sure there are no broken bones. I fought him off good. A friend of mine, someone I really trust, checked me out and gave me some painkillers."

I gingerly placed my arms around her. "Oh, hon, we have to do something. You can't go on like this."

Tears tracked down her bruised cheeks. "I'm not going to give up. Not now. If I do, everything you and Dawson have done for me will mean nothin'."

My throat thickened at her determination. I pulled up a chair beside her and held her hand. An angry red mark crossed her knuckles, signifying a struggle. "I'm proud of you for wanting to stick to the plan, but we've got to come up with a way to protect you."

Guilt lay heavy on me. Was it my fault that she'd been attacked? What next? Anthony had threatened to kill me. With me on alert and unavailable, would he take out all his frustration on her? Even try to kill her?

I fought back panic. "Caitlin, I've got a sister in California. She and her fiancé might be willing to have you stay with them. If not, perhaps Dawson Smith knows of a safe place for you. What do you say? Would you be willing to leave Boston for a while to let Anthony's anger die down?"

She nodded and grimaced with pain. "I know I can't stay here no more. He tried to force drugs on me even though he knows I'm trying to stay clean. I don't want to go back to that druggy scene, but he don't care. And my family don't care about me. My mother kicked me out of the house on Friday. I have nowhere else to go."

"Let me call my sister." Alarmed, I rose to my feet. I didn't know Caitlin's situation had become so intolerable.

She put a hand on my arm. "Do ... do you think I could stay with Dawson? He told us he's got lots of space on that ranch of his and art classes are taught there." Her eyes filled. "He's the kind of man I wish I'd had as a father. You know, real nice and quiet like. I trust him not to hurt me."

I paused, wondering how Dawson would feel about it, then, decided to go ahead and call him. He'd always been straight with me. No reason to think he wouldn't be so now. I'd ask him for an honest answer, and if he didn't want Caitlin staying with him, I was sure I could talk my sister into it.

It was still early in California, but Dawson was an early riser. I walked into my small conference room and punched in his number. He answered on the third ring.

"Dawson? It's Samantha Hartwell. I need your help. Caitlin and I both do."

I described the situation for him. As the facts came out, I could sense Dawson's anger.

"By all means, send her out to me," he said crisply. "I've got plenty of room and my housekeeper lives in, so there won't be any sense of impropriety. In fact, why don't you come with her? That'll get you out of Boston for a while, too. Might be safer for you."

"Thanks, I'll think about it. We don't want to put Caitlin on a plane alone. She's in pretty bad shape. I'll let you know all the travel arrangements."

After hanging up, I returned to Caitlin. "It's all set, hon. Dawson is happy to have you stay with him."

She sagged with relief and I realized how truly frightened she was.

"Are you coming to California with me?"

I shook my head. "I don't think so, but I don't want you traveling alone. A friend of mine may be willing to make the trip with you. You'll like her, and she knows her way around any airport."

I left Caitlin and made another call.

Liz Sanderson sounded out of breath when she answered her phone.

"Liz, it's Samantha Hartwell. I have a huge favor to ask of you."

"Shoot. I'm all ears," she said without hesitation.

I filled her in on the details of Caitlin's situation and the proposed flight to California. "Can you take the time to accompany her? I'd go myself, but I have a board meeting at the paper mill this week and would hate to miss it."

"No problem," she answered promptly. "I'd love to do it—for more reasons than one. It'll do my heart good to help her out of harm's way. But, Samantha, what about you? Are you sure you're safe?"

I swallowed hard. I couldn't deny the uneasy feeling that crept through me every time I heard Anthony's name or looked at Caitlin. "Actually, I was thinking I'd go to Maine for a couple of days. I have business there, and Anthony's going to be furious when he realizes Caitlin isn't around. He's such a jerk. I'm trying to convince Caitlin to file a complaint with the police, but she's afraid to do it. But I'm going to take several photographs of her face as proof of what he did to her. We'll use it against him if we can."

"It's wise for you to leave town, Samantha. I'm glad you'll be gone for a while."

"I'll give him a few days to calm down. Then I'm coming back here. If I allow him to interfere with my work, it wouldn't be a good example to the women I help."

"Be careful. Let me know about flights and all. I'll take care of arrangements at this end."

###

Caitlin lay on the couch in my office, eyes closed. I lowered myself beside her and inspected her face. Looking at her wounds, I was enraged all over again.

"I still think you should file a report with the police."

"No." Caitlin struggled to sit up. "Anthony said he'd kill me if I went to the cops. I know too much about all he's doing."

"You mean he's been dealing?" I wouldn't put it past him.

She shook her head. "He's been running numbers, gambling, and a whole bunch of stuff. Please, don't talk about it anymore. It only makes things worse."

Groaning softly, she lay back down again.

I squeezed her hand. "Get some rest." I left her nodding off and went down to Zach's office.

He waved me into his office, and I sat in a chair, waiting for him to get off the phone.

"What's up?" he asked as he hung up.

As I filled him in and described Caitlin's injuries, my stomach grew queasy. It might have been me.

Zach's expression was grim. "Caitlin has to go to the police with this. She can't let him get away with it."

"What can I do? She's adamant about not reporting it to the police. Legally, I can't make her." Frustration ate at me.

"You're going to take photographs of her face?"

I nodded, and he continued. "Let's have her sign a statement, which I'll have my secretary notarize, stating exactly what happened and why. I'll keep it here along with the photographs, ready to be used if we should need it in the future."

He gave me a worried look. "The notarized statement might help you, too. If Anthony ever threatens you in any way again, we'll use it to go to the police. Going to Maine for a few days is a good idea. I don't like the idea of your facing him alone."

"I left Caitlin sleeping. It might be a good time to take those pictures. Can I borrow your camera?"

"You bet."

We hurried upstairs to my office.

Caitlin was curled up in a ball. Snores rumbled from her open mouth and through her swollen nose.

We approached her on tiptoes.

"The son of a bitch." Zach's soft whisper did nothing to hide his disgust.

Quietly, so as not to disturb her, I snapped several pictures of her, and we stepped out of the office.

"When will she fly out to California with Liz?" Zach asked me.

"I'll try to put them on an early evening flight. The sooner she leaves Boston, the better."

Zach put his hand on my shoulder. "I don't like this whole thing, Samantha. Anthony's a loose cannon. We don't know where he'll aim next."

My body turned cold. Zach was not prone to melodramatic statements.

I dropped Caitlin and Liz off at Logan Airport and headed north on Route One. As I drove through Revere, I thought of Anthony and his gambling habit. The defunct Wonderland Greyhound Park was nearby. I could easily picture him gambling, owing money to others, too cocky to know when he should stop. That's probably why the guy at the pizza place in Haymarket had been searching for him.

After I pulled onto I-95, I called my mother from the car to let her know I was on my way. I hadn't had lunch, so I stopped for a light supper in Portsmouth at a seafood restaurant overlooking the Piscataqua River.

Running home to my parents was something I'd avoided in the past, even during the worst of times. But now the large white colonial home I'd grown up in beckoned to me with its sturdy columns and protective size. I could hardly wait to get there.

Shortly after eight, I pulled into the driveway of my parents' home outside Portland. It sat in a small, upscale neighborhood of what real estate agents liked to label 'estate' homes. Seeing the house ablaze with lights, I was glad I'd made the trip. Their brightness was a welcome beacon in the dark. I already felt safer.

My mother greeted me at the door. "I'm so glad you're here. Come in. I have decaf coffee brewing and a plate of your father's favorite cookies."

I set my suitcase down at the bottom of the stairs with a sigh and stretched. "Where's Father? In bed?"

"He had a busy day. Though his stamina is becoming weaker, he's really quite remarkable for a man his age."

Thinking of the age difference between my parents, I followed my mother into the large kitchen. We settled with our cups of coffee at the cherry gate-leg table in the sunny yellow kitchen.

My mother gave me a worried look. "So, tell me, what is going on with this fellow, this Anthony Carbone you told me about earlier."

I gave her the whole story, downplaying the threats he'd hurled at me.

Her features became coated with concern. She patted my hand. "What you've done with Straight Talk is very admirable, Samantha, but you're dealing with unpredictable people. This instance proves it. Perhaps the time has come to close your doors. You've done enough and I don't want anything bad to happen to you."

"I can't stop now. It's people like Caitlin and Liz who make it all worthwhile. I need to stay focused on something positive. It gives meaning to my new life."

My mother withdrew her hand and studied me. "But it's people like Anthony Carbone who make it dangerous. Promise me you'll put an end to the business when the bad appears to outweigh the good."

That was fair. "Speaking of good things coming out of Straight Talk, one of the reasons I asked Liz Sanderson to accompany Caitlin was so she could meet Dawson. I think she and Dawson might get along very well. She's a terrific woman, and Dawson is such a sweet guy."

My mother took a sip of coffee and spoke. "What happened between you two? Allison said you make such an attractive pair."

Putting my thoughts together, I gazed into the distance. "Dawson's too old and too nice, if that makes any sense. I don't want to settle for 'comfortable,' as Marissa puts it."

My mother's eyebrows shot up. "I understand about wanting magic. But in the end, you need a friend as well as a lover. Don't lose sight of that, darling."

"Are you and Father friends?" I challenged.

Her expression turned troubled. "We are, to a point. Times have changed dramatically in the last forty years since we became an *item*, as the old folks used to say. Your father's thinking and mine would not mesh as well today as it did back then. Women were not as liberated and independent." She laughed, a little sadly I thought. "Heaven knows, I'd probably give you a run for your money if we were the same age, setting up a business, becoming independent. You certainly know how much I admire your spirit. Allison's, too. You girls make me so proud."

My heart warmed at her compliment. She was a good foil for my father's silent and not so silent criticism. She'd always encouraged my sister, me, and my brother. Thinking of him, I said, "How's Hunter doing?"

My mother let out a long sigh. "I've tried talking to him, but lately, he's become so defensive about discussing any plans for the future, I've finally decided to step back. Something is wrong and I'm not sure what it is."

"Do you think he really loves Bettina? I'm not sure he does."

My mother appeared genuinely surprised. "Why wouldn't he love Bettina?"

"You and Father have really pushed the relationship. You did the same thing to Allison and look where it got her. Thank Heavens, she found her soul mate. Now, she's as content as can be."

My mother knotted her hands. "Oh dear, you might be right. Your father and Bettina's father think it would be a wonderful way to blend businesses." She sighed. "No wonder Hunter looks so unhappy. I'll ask him about it. No, *you* talk to him. Find out what's troubling him. He may open up to you."

Though I resented my father's old-fashioned ideas, I said, "Don't blame yourself. We're all adults and, in the end, we make our own choices."

"I do know Hunter hates law school." My mother exhaled again. "I hope the dear boy doesn't disappoint your father. He has such high expectations for him."

Forcing myself to remain silent, I clamped my teeth together. Even so, my stomach clenched. It seemed so unfair. Hunter didn't care one whit about a position at Hartwell, Smith, & Lowell, while I had always desperately wanted it. But it would never be offered to me. Not when Father considered it Hunter's rightful place.

My mother stifled a yawn. "I'm glad you're here, Samantha, where I know you're safe. It's late. Time for me to go up to bed. It's been a long day."

My work week was far from over. I'd closed the office for a few days, but work behind the scenes was ongoing and I still had the board meeting at the paper company on Friday.

I smiled to myself. And a dinner date with Derek Roberts.

CHAPTER SEVEN

I awoke sometime in the night, my pulse racing. Disturbing images of Anthony Carbone attacking me continued to play out in my mind. Breathing deeply, I sat up and forced myself to calm down.

I climbed out of bed and walked over to the bedroom window. Tall pines edged the back lawn, their outlines exposed by the street lights that streamed soft light to them; they stood like sentinels. Oddly, I felt more trapped than safe. Anger filled me. How dare Anthony, that tough punk, make such a mess of my life!

I stumbled back into bed and lay awake, staring at the ceiling. Maybe my mother was right. Perhaps it was time I moved along; tried my hand at corporate law; gave up the dream of going into my father's law firm. At the thought of leaving Straight Talk, the business that gave me such purpose, sadness pierced me. I swallowed hard, feeling adrift already.

Tossing and turning, I counted from one to ten over and over again until the fading numbers lured me to sleep.

My eyes fluttered opened. I blinked at the light that filled my room. The sun shone through the window blinds in bright fingers of light that beckoned. I rose and opened the blinds to greet the new day. My gaze was drawn to the colorful maple tree on the side lawn. Its leaves were already beginning to show signs of turning to the beautiful reds and golden colors of autumn in New England. In another couple of months, the 'leaf peepers' would come in droves to see their brilliant fall display and to enjoy the crisp air. Today, I'd have the chance to relax and enjoy myself without dealing with those tourists.

Looking forward to letting the day slowly unravel, I put on a sweater over my silky pajamas and headed downstairs. My father was leaving for the office as I walked into the kitchen.

"Hello, Father. It's going to be a beautiful day," I said, cheerfully.

"Half over," he grumbled. He pointed to the kitchen clock, which showed nine o'clock fast approaching.

I fought to keep my mood upbeat, and walked over to the coffee pot.

My mother smiled at me. "Your father has just informed me Ted Beers is coming for dinner tonight to discuss their plans for Coldstream. He wants you to join us." She gave me a pleading look, silently asking me to cooperate.

My heart sank. I most assuredly did not want to spend any time with Ted Beers. My mind raced for excuses. Maybe Marissa had no plans. I could ask her to call me...

"I expect you there." Father's words broke into my rebellious thoughts.

He rose and prepared to leave. "See you ladies later."

I sipped my coffee silently. Ted and I were not good together, more like the proverbial oil and water. His self-centered arrogance irritated me, and my dislike of him ate at his ego. Now, I had another bone to pick with him—his unfair words of warning to Derek.

My mother beamed at me as I took a seat opposite her at the table. "It's been forever since we've had a girls' day out. I'd like to treat you to a few things."

My spirits rose. Since opening Straight Talk, my discretionary funds had all but dried up, and I hadn't allowed myself much time to enjoy outings like this. Spending the day with my mother always brought a sense of fun to my hectic life. After listening to stories of women in crisis and coming up with ways to help them, it was a relief to relax with someone so settled, so content.

We headed down to the discount stores in Kittery on Route One. Taking our time wandering through stores, we laughed and chatted like friends. We'd both ordered hot, creamy clam chowder for lunch at the Weather Vane restaurant when I received a phone call from Liz.

"I'm just calling to let you know Caitlin and I arrived safely in California. She was so tense before we left Boston last night I was afraid she'd be too ill to board the plane."

"How is she now?" Poor thing must have been scared Anthony would find her.

"She's so much better, smiling a little. At the moment, she's out at the barn with Dawson, looking at the new horse he bought after the fire."

"And how're things with Dawson?"

"He's happy to have us here. Samantha, you didn't tell me the man was so attractive." She chuckled softly. "I swear I felt like swooning when we shook hands and he grinned at me. I've never felt quite that way before."

I smiled with satisfaction. "He's a wonderful person. Thanks to you both for all you're doing."

"You have no idea how much I appreciate being out of New England and away from Howard for a while. And to be here, helping Caitlin and meeting Dawson, why, it's just wonderful."

Relieved by the news of Caitlin and feeling smug about Liz's reaction to Dawson, I hung up.

We returned home with a load of packages. My mother had insisted on buying me a couple of outfits and I'd replenished my wardrobe with more mundane things.

"Nothing like a little bit of shopping to make a woman feel good." My mother sat and slipped off her shoes. "You'll have something new to wear to dinner tonight."

My spirits flagged.

My mother placed a hand on my shoulder. "I know you don't like Ted, but it's just for one evening. And it would please your father."

I tried to put a good spin on it in my mind. "I'll get through it ... somehow."

I sat in the expansive living room silently observing Ted as he talked about the land he and my father owned in Coldstream, Maine. Coldstream was an isolated area north of Riverton. The underhanded deal to have Rivers Papers use that site for a kaolin processing plant had been uncovered and successfully squashed by Marissa and me and other board members.

Never one to give up, Ted had followed up with a plan for my father and him to develop condos on the site. As he'd explained in the past, the upscale condos would be for people who wanted to escape to the north during hot, summer months and be close to ski areas in the winter. A small pond lay between their two plots of land.

Now, Ted leaned forward. "I figure we could enlarge the pond. It'd have to be done secretly, though, so none of the anti-development environmentalists realize it. They'd claim it would destroy the natural meadowlands around it."

Listening to him, my skin crawled. I couldn't hold back my dismay. "Surely, Father, you wouldn't do something like that. Perhaps, by keeping things as they are and selling the condos as a nature lover's retreat, you'd make more money in the long run."

Ted glared at me and turned back to my father. "With all due respect, it's not anyone else's business what you and I do."

I waited for my father to blast me for speaking out. He surprised me by remaining uncharacteristically quiet and then tactfully changed the subject to Derek Roberts and the newspaper article he'd read about him recently.

"Derek has agreed to do the photography on a book about Rivers Papers and the paper and pulp business in Maine." Ted shot me a challenging look. "My sister, Isabelle, is going to write the text and captions."

"It's not final, not until it has been brought before the board." I was furious that he'd already assumed the matter was settled. "It'll be addressed tomorrow in the meeting."

"You saw his photographs in Boston." Ted's voice had turned chilly. "Envision the high quality Derek will bring to such an undertaking. And my sister has always wanted to be involved in a project like this. Actually, she thought up the idea. It's a family thing. Her daughter, Alexandra, and Derek plan to be married. Isabelle has already booked the club for the wedding."

The sip of Diet Coke I'd just taken slid down my throat the wrong way. I gasped for air.

"Are you all right?" my mother asked.

I nodded and rose. Derek had told me his relationship with Ted's niece was over. Crestfallen, I hurried to the kitchen for water.

The rest of the evening passed in a blur. I focused in and out of the congenial dinner table conversation between my parents and Ted, torn between disappointment with Derek and anger at myself. Against all common sense, I'd found myself wishing the unusual attraction between Derek and me could lead to something more meaningful.

Ted finally left, and, drained by the effort I'd made to be

social, I helped my mother with the dishes, feeling the stirrings of a headache.

The next morning, I packed up my things and kissed my mother good-bye. My father had already left for the office.

"Good luck with your board meeting." She walked me to my car. "And let me know when you get back to Boston. You're going to stay at Marissa's tonight?"

"That's the plan. She called me from New York and asked if I would check on the house. With Henry and Becky away for the weekend, she wants to make sure everything is okay. I'll talk to you later."

On the two-hour drive to Riverton, I relived my evening in Boston with Derek. I'd really liked the sincerity with which he'd spoken about his work and his apparent love of all kinds of people. I'd been touched by his concern for me after I'd been threatened by Anthony. He wasn't the self-centered man I'd first thought. And as for the chemistry between us? It was an A-plus. But he'd lied about his relationship with Alexandra and, as I'd told him, I was all about straight talk.

I gripped the steering wheel and sighed. I'd been foolish to even think about a relationship with him. Derek traveled the world and no doubt had his choice of women everywhere he went. Why not? He was as handsome a man as I'd ever seen and socially graceful enough to be welcomed into most circles. I told myself the only reason I'd been attracted to him was because it'd been a long time since I'd gone on a real date. But I knew deep down it was much more than that.

Riverton was a small town like so many others in New England. Brick storefronts lined the main street, and a church with a towering white steeple sat like an aged dowager on one of the four corners of the main intersection. Across the street from it, an unadorned, yellow, cinder-block building housed the many little burrows of City Hall. The County Courthouse, the most significant building in town, complete with four Doric columns alongside its massive front doors, held the halls of justice and lay diagonally across from City Hall. Yet, for all its simplicity, Riverton was a center of sorts along the Kennebec River.

Just before the approach to the bridge that spanned the river, I turned into Rivers Papers and stopped at the small guard house that sat outside the entrance to the mill.

Barney Sage, the guard on duty, tipped his hat in recognition. "Go on ahead, Ms. Hartwell. A few of the others are here already."

I waved at him and drove through the opening in the chain-link fence surrounding the paper mill's sleek, white metal buildings.

Stepping out of my car, I inhaled the piney smell.

The low steady hum that filled the air signaled to me that the huge fans on the roof were working to direct heat and steam away from the mill. All was going as expected. I gazed at the result of what my great-grandfather and great-uncle had begun in the late 1800s with pride. They'd be surprised and surely pleased by the modern technology used in today's processing of pulp.

Inside, I signed in at the desk and collected the required hard hat and goggles so that I could visit with my good friend, Jonesy, a long-time employee and respected supervisor.

The guard checked my shoes to make sure they fit the safety code and motioned me through. Feeling like a creature from outer space with the goggles on, I walked into a long, air-conditioned room. A huge, self-enclosed machine took up most of the space. Its inside workings were represented on a one-dimensional display, like a television screen, that dominated one wall and allowed the workers to keep tabs on the process. Covering my ears against the noise, I hurried toward the glass-enclosed supervisor's office.

Jonesy waved from inside and stood at the door to welcome me. The sight of his round, jovial face filled me with joy. I stepped inside the office and into his warm embrace.

"How's it going, Sam? Still doing okay?"

"It's goin' great."

"Good girl. One day at a time will do it."

"Any inside news for me?"

He shook his head. "Nothing big. Earlier, some city fella was trailing after Ted—a looker according to the women here. Heard it said he's gonna take some photos of the processing. Don't know more than that."

Derek was already here. My heart defiantly skipped a beat. "Guess I'd better go. Remember, if you have any problems, feel free to call either Marissa or me."

"Will do. Yessir, you two have made a big difference around here."

I left him, nervous at the prospect of seeing Derek and canceling our dinner plans.

The board meeting was to take place in one of the brick outbuildings that had been part of the original mill. I entered the conference room and stopped, surprised to find it empty. Gazing out the large window, the view drew my attention. The river below was more than a picturesque ribbon of blue wending its way through the town; it was the essence of Rivers Papers. Without it, the mill would never have been developed.

Jake Weatherbee, a vice-president and a member of the board, stuck his head into the room. "Want to join us? Ted has been leading us on a quick tour of the property to demonstrate some of the areas Derek Roberts has in mind to photograph for the book."

I fought irritation. Once again, Ted had assumed control of the group and was pushing forward on his idea of what the book should be. Little did he realize I'd done some research on his sister and discovered that Isabelle Beers Dietrich had published nothing in either fiction or non-fiction. If Rivers Papers was going to produce a high-quality discourse on the paper and pulp business, we needed a professional writer to do the work.

Outside, I joined the group standing beside the river. Derek grinned at me and turned back to Ted, who was addressing him.

"Note the inflatable 'flashboards' that can raise or lower the water by a few feet. We use them for flood control in times of high water or low water. Raising the 'boards' allows the generation plant to maintain head pressure, or the surge of the river, to turn the generators. Doesn't sound like much, but it's a significant deal economically when we can increase electrical output. Lot to learn, isn't there?" Ted said to Derek.

Derek dutifully nodded and shot me another smile.

The group turned to re-enter the building. Before I could join them, Derek took my arm and held me back.

His golden eyes searched my face. "I've been thinking about you a lot, Samantha. Let's break away from the meeting as early as we can."

How I wished the situation was different. There was something about him that enchanted me, but I shook off the feeling with steely resolve. "I don't think so, Derek. It's not a good idea. Not when you're committed to Alexandra."

"Alexandra?" Derek's eyes widened. "What are you talking about?"

I pressed my lips together, taking a moment to control my temper. "Ted came to my parent's house for dinner last night. He said you and Alexandra are planning to be married.

Apparently, what you told me last week wasn't exactly true, Derek."

He stared at me speechlessly, and I hurried away from him to catch up to the others.

"Wait," he called out, but I followed the group inside, refusing to be drawn into a situation that would only hurt me.

CHAPTER EIGHT

Inside the board room, I seated myself at the opposite end of the oblong mahogany table from Ted and Derek and kept light conversation going with the men on either side of me. Derek's gaze returned to me time and time again, but I ignored his silent entreaties.

We went through the business reports and other small matters quickly. Then, Ted introduced Derek once more and spoke about what the board hoped to achieve with the book project. "My sister, Isabelle, has graciously agreed to write the script for the book."

Sim Washburn, a long-time board member gazed at each member of the board. "The paper industry has been maligned for so long the public has forgotten some of the good we've done in this state and others. I'd like to see this book focus on that aspect and highlight the beauty of the natural areas we maintain. We're not perfect by any means, but I'd like to think there is some sort of balance."

"By all means. And I believe we all agree that Derek Roberts' work is exceptional," I said. "However, I think it's only fair to ask what qualifications Isabelle has for participating in this project. The information you gave us never mentioned any past experiences like this and I haven't been able to find anything about her work."

"Neither have I." Walt Coddington was CEO of the largest hardware store chain in the northeast.

Ted shot me a defiant look. "Isabelle has recently become interested in writing. She's doing a memoir of her working days in New York City. She's even joined a writing group."

"So she's never actually done anything like this?" Walt asked, and I wanted to kiss him for his persistence.

"Not really," Ted mumbled, "but she's the one who thought it might be a good project for Rivers Papers. This whole idea came up because of my niece and Derek. They're all but engaged."

My gaze swung to Derek. A white ring appeared around his pursed lips. Surprised, I realized how angry he was.

Unaware of Derek's reaction, Ted continued. "It's also feasible to do this project on a reasonable budget because Beaver Crossing Press is willing to deal with us. I doubt a New York publisher would be interested in doing the book or allowing the kind of input we want."

I nodded, along with the others. That part was true. "I'm friendly with a writer who has done many travel pieces and several special articles for *National Geographic*, among others. Her work is well known. I'd like each of you to review the packet I've put together about her and consider using her to do the writing and captions for the book. In light of what we hope to achieve, I believe she or someone else might be a better choice."

His jaw clenching and unclenching, Ted glared at me. Some of the other board members moved restlessly in their seats. Clashes of opinion were nothing new between Ted and me. I was one of the few on the board who dared to speak against his wishes. Walt was another.

"Excellent idea, Samantha." Walt leafed through the sheets of information I'd passed around. "I'd feel a lot more comfortable with a real professional doing the job. How about you, Derek? Would that satisfy you?"

"A far better choice." He glanced at me.

Ted studied the circle of people at the table. "In that case,

I'm not so sure Beaver Crossing Press will take such a high interest in the project."

Walt's eyebrows shot up. "Are you threatening us, Ted? I happen to know you share ownership of the press with a number of other people, including your sister."

Stunned silence filled the room. Even I didn't know his sister was involved in the publishing company.

Ted cleared his throat and glanced around. "All right, I'll speak to the publisher about the terms of the contract. The committee working on this can schedule an interview with the writer. In the meantime, let's take a vote on going forward with the project with Derek as the photographer. The selection of writer will remain open to discussion at a later time. Do I hear such a motion?"

Sim made the motion and Walt seconded it. All voted in favor, and I was left hoping Ted's natural aggressiveness wouldn't somehow hurt Liz. He did not give up easily.

After the meeting ended, I gathered my things, anxious to be on the road. If I didn't dawdle, I could make it to Marissa's house in time to cook dinner.

Derek sidled up to me. "We haven't finished our talk, Samantha." His voice was soft, but there was no mistaking his will.

I sighed. "Want to walk me to my car? We can talk on the way."

"Okay. We need to get a few things straightened out." He followed me out of the room and stayed right on my heels.

"Hey, Derek! Wait!"

At the sound of Ted's voice, Derek and I both stopped.

"Later, Ted." Derek placed a hand on my waist and urged me forward.

Outside the building, he grabbed hold of my briefcase. "I'll carry it. It's heavy."

I handed it over. "Trying to make me feel like a schoolgirl?" I asked, unable to hide the amusement in my voice.

He grinned. "What the hell, anything to clear the air. You've got everything all wrong; I didn't lie to you. I told Alexandra I wasn't interested in marrying her. But you know Ted. He's one never to give up."

I stopped in the parking lot and faced Derek, determined to clear the air. "Are you still seeing her?" I studied him carefully.

He raised his right hand. "I swear I'm not. They invited me to their house for Thanksgiving, but I've already told Isabelle no. Besides, I'll probably be out of the country. My time is not my own. I have to go where my leads take me."

I continued to my car, mulling over his words. He was right. Ted wasn't one to give up on anything, even a dream of marriage for his niece.

"You're awfully quiet," Derek murmured. "Does that mean you'll reconsider going to dinner with me?"

Silent, I unlocked the car and took the briefcase from him. Would one more dinner with him hurt? If I, who treasured honesty, couldn't be honest with myself, I was in trouble. I wanted to spend more time with him. He made me feel young and beautiful ... and hot.

I gazed into Derek's eyes, trying to be fair. "Why don't I meet you at the restaurant? Pierre's is in a small white house tucked back in the woods about a half mile out of town on the right-hand side of the road. You can't miss their sign."

"I know the place." Derek checked his watch. "It's early. We can sit and talk before dinner."

He leaned down and gave me a quick kiss on the cheek. "You won't regret it, Samantha."

"Hey! What's going on?"

I cringed at the sound of Ted calling to us. "You handle him.

I can't." I climbed into my car and waved. "See you there."

When I looked into the rearview mirror, Ted was gesturing wildly in front of Derek. I couldn't see Derek's face, but I could tell from the way his shoulders had stiffened that he didn't like what Ted was saying.

I headed down the road. At the thought of spending another evening with Derek, anticipation wove through me. He challenged me in a way I'd never experienced. Was it the fact that he could have any woman he wanted but chose to spend time with me? I tapped a finger on my lip. Maybe, as I feared, he saw me as just the woman of the moment. At that unsettling idea, I drew my brow into a knot.

At Pierre's I parked the car, climbed out and inhaled. The delightful aroma of butter, garlic, and spices drifted out from the kitchen. My mouth watered.

Marie and Alphonse Metier greeted me at the door. Middle-aged, their round bodies showed the effect of their wonderful cooking. They beamed at me.

Alphonse took my coat and threw his arms around me. "*Bonsoir*! It's been too long."

Marie hugged me next. "You look beautiful. There must be a man in your life."

I laughed. "Not really, though I'm meeting one here tonight."

"*Bon! Bon!* They are necessary, are they not?" Marie's eyes twinkled with amusement. Alphonse gave me an exaggerated shrug of his shoulders as if to say he'd put up with whatever Marie had to say. I laughed at the two of them, and they grinned happily.

"Are the seats by the fire available? We thought we'd sit there before dinner."

"By all means." Alphonse led the way into what once was a living room but now served as a small bar area. "It's early yet.

You have your choice of places."

I walked over to the small settee facing the lit fireplace. "I'll settle here. Derek should be here any moment."

"I have a special wine for you." Alphonse brought his fingertips to his mouth and kissed them with a flourish. "*C'est magnifique!* A light beaujolais."

I shook my head. "How about sparkling water?"

"For you, the best!" Alphonse hurried out of the room to fill my request.

I watched him go, thinking back to my drinking days. It hadn't been easy to stay on track, but no one in my family, not even my parents, knew how close to death I'd come one night. I'd partied into the wee hours of the morning with friends in New York City. It had started with Bloody Marys in the morning and continued with assorted drinks all day and all night. I couldn't seem to stop. I'd had another argument with my father and was emotionally bankrupt. My whole life seemed a mockery of trying and failing to please him. I think behind my party laughter was the thought of ending the constant struggle.

Sometime during the night I blacked out, and when I awoke, I was in the hospital. My friends told me I'd gone berserk, screaming and shouting and threatening to throw myself off the balcony of the apartment where we were staying. It took two of them to hold me back. I'd frightened them and myself even more—enough to finally seek help.

Alphonse returned shortly. "For you. Water with gas."

"Thank you." I accepted the bubbly liquid and checked my watch. Derek had yet to appear.

I waited, growing more and more concerned.

Marie hurried to the door every time she heard a noise out front. But no one appeared.

Embarrassed by his failure to show, I rose and asked for

my coat.

Marie clucked her tongue sadly. "Maybe another time."

I was slipping my arms into my coat when Derek burst into the entry. He gave me an apologetic look. "Sorry I'm so late. Ted kept insisting I go over a few details with him. I got away as soon as I could."

"So this is Samantha's man?" Marie's voice shimmered with admiration. "I'm Marie. My husband Alphonse and I own Pierre's. Go now. Sit by the fire where you will have privacy. I'll send Alphonse in to you."

Derek took my arm. "Jeez, for a while I thought Ted was going to insist he join us for dinner." He still looked upset.

Imagining the scene between Derek and Ted trying to outwit one another, I smiled.

Obviously relieved by my reaction, Derek's lips curved. "Thanks for understanding."

We settled comfortably on the couch.

Derek glanced at my half-filled glass. "What are you drinking?"

I held up my glass. "Sparkling water. Water with gas, as Alphonse says. But he has a nice wine if you want it."

He shook his head. "I try to avoid the stuff. My father was an alcoholic. Growing up with him was enough to make me stay away from it."

After ordering sparkling water for himself, Derek lifted my hand. "I'm glad you decided to have dinner with me. I've waited all week to see you again. No more news of Anthony, I hope?"

I settled back against the cushions, all seriousness now, and filled him in on the details of Caitlin's injury and subsequent flight to California.

Derek's expression became grim. "You'd better keep away from Boston for a while. Why don't you stay at my place in

Riverton? He'd never think of looking for you here."

I raised my eyebrows. "Your place?"

"No strings attached." He gave me a crooked grin that spelled danger.

"Thanks, but I have family here in Maine. My parents live outside Portland and my cousin, Marissa, has a huge house in New Hope. In fact, that's where I'm supposed to stay tonight."

"Too bad. I was hoping you'd help me decide what to do with all the stuff I bought at a flea market this week. For the next few months, I'll use Maine as my base of operation. I need a woman to help me make sense of it. How about you?"

Lost in dreams of what staying with him might be like, I blinked in surprise. What was he asking? He wanted me to be his woman?

"Like I said, I need help organizing the condo I just rented. Give me a few suggestions, will you?"

My heart stopped, then started on a shaky beat. Good Heavens! All he'd asked of me was to help him fix up his place—nothing more. Feeling like a fool, I shifted in my seat and worked to hide my embarrassment.

"When you set up base somewhere, do you need just the basics or do you try to make it a real home?"

A sad look crossed his face. "Even though I travel a lot, I try to make my living quarters nice. I don't have any place to call home except my temporary bases of operation. I'll stay in Maine for a few months and then go on to something else."

"I see," I said and realized how much I hated the idea of him leaving.

We were seated at a table and quickly succumbed to Alphonse's suggestions for our meal.

As before, conversation between us was easy, intriguing. I liked Derek and found myself drawn into his fascinating stories, seeing the world through his eyes. And when he asked me questions about my work, he seemed genuinely interested.

As we talked, Marie and Alphonse came to the table often, making sure we were well satisfied with the braised lamb shanks we'd ordered and had everything we needed.

"Samantha is a good woman, no?" Marie asked as she placed apple tarts in front of us for dessert.

Derek grinned at me. "That she is."

I shook my head. She was a worse matchmaker than my mother.

A smile of satisfaction on her face, Marie bustled away.

Derek smiled with amusement. "These people are friends of yours?"

"I've known them for years. Whenever I come to Rivers Papers for a late meeting I try to eat here."

"It's obvious they think the world of you. Let's go and see how you do as a decorator."

I hesitated. "Is it far? I really should be on my way soon."

He checked his watch. "What time did you tell Marissa you'd be there?"

I swallowed hard, caught in a trap. I couldn't lie. "Actually, she's in New York with Brad. I was just going to use her house to have privacy away from my parents."

Derek's lips curved. "Aha! So, *actually,* as you put it, nobody is expecting you anywhere." He leered at me with humorous exaggeration.

I couldn't hold back a laugh.

We left the table, and while Derek took care of the bill, Marie helped me on with my coat.

"*Bonne chance,*" she whispered to me. "*Il est très beau, n'est-ce pas?*"

I nodded, thinking he was much more. Trouble, that's what he was, and I knew it.

###

In the parking lot, Derek turned to me. "Maybe you'd better follow me. The condo is in a small development called Piney Woods, just south of Riverton."

"I know where it is." It had been a big deal in town when the development was built.

Derek got into a Jeep and I followed him in my SUV, keeping well behind him as we traveled through Riverton. I had no desire to set tongues wagging at the mill about Derek and me.

Piney Woods was a nice neighborhood whose charm lay in the natural woods around the scattered gray clapboard apartment buildings. Cars and trucks lined the parking lot. Lights inside most of the condos made the complex appear friendly. As a temporary home for someone like Derek, it made all the sense in the world.

I met him in front of a building off to one side.

"What do you think?" He indicated the development with a sweep of his arm.

"So far, I like it."

"My apartment's got everything I need—a fireplace, Jacuzzi tub, spare bedroom for my equipment, and a huge deck looking out over the river. Come on inside."

I followed him up the stairs to the top floor of the three-story building. He unlocked the door to an end unit, turned on the lights, and ushered me into a large living space with a stacked-stone fireplace in the middle of one wall. On either side of the fireplace were empty shelves. Opposite the fireplace, a sofa sat against the wall, the largest piece of furniture in a sparsely filled room. A sliding door opened onto the deck. I stepped outside and breathed in the smell of pine.

Derek came up behind me and wrapped his arms around me. "Beautiful, huh?"

I laughed. "Too dark to really see, but I bet it's beautiful in daylight."

He turned me around to face him. "I've wanted to kiss you all evening," he murmured and lowered his face to mine. His lips were soft and firm, demanding and gentle. The man could kiss. My body burned with a heat I'd only read about. By the time we pulled apart, I was breathless.

Derek studied me. "You feel it, too? This thing between us?"

"Why, Derek, I do believe you're a romantic," I responded playfully, trying to temper the intensity of my feelings. The longing he brought out in me was downright scary.

"Romantic? I don't know about that. I like people. That's why I photograph them with all their foibles. But I don't go chasing after women."

"No, they come chasing after you." I became quiet under his intent gaze.

He drew me to him once more. My eyes closed as his lips pressed against the tender spot on my neck then moved up to capture my lips in a sweet kiss that excited me even more as it deepened. Of their own volition, my arms rose to pull him closer. My heart pounded like jungle drumbeats in my ears.

His hands cupped my breasts and moved to unbutton my blouse.

Trembling, I forced myself to step back.

We stood and stared at one another, breathing deeply, all too aware of the depth of desire between us. I took another deep breath and turned away, straightening my blouse.

"I ... I'm not ready for this."

Derek came up behind me. "I didn't mean to rush you ... I ... I ... couldn't help myself."

I drew in a breath at the awe I heard in his voice, but I told myself I'd be a fool to go too fast with him. At dinner we'd talked about a lot of things, but in reality, we hardly knew one another.

"I'd better go," I mumbled, afraid for him to see how torn I was between being practical and throwing myself into his arms again.

"If I promise not to touch you again, will you stay for a while?"

The yearning in his expression hit me in the gut. It had to be lonely for him to travel the world by himself. My heart went out to him.

"All right. Keep your hands to yourself and I'll stay to help you. Then I'm leaving."

He held out his hand. "Deal."

"Derek! You promised!"

The look of surprise on his face when he realized what he'd done had us both laughing.

I walked into the living room. It needed a lot of help. "Show me what you bought and we can decide where to put things."

Derek led me into a small spare bedroom jammed with items.

"I bought most of this stuff at flea markets and garage sales. Not worth much of anything, really. I'll leave it behind when I take off again. But these things help to make the place feel more like home."

I watched him out of the corner of my eye as I pawed through the collection of lamps, books, and off-beat decorative items. He seemed such a contrast of impressions—sensitive and confident, tender and tough, gregarious, and very much alone.

Sympathetic to his plight, I drew myself up. "Do you want to drive down to Marissa's house tomorrow? I'll show you around New Hope. It's a very picturesque little coastal town."

Derek's face brightened. "Really? I'd like that."

We worked together to fill blank spots in the sterile décor the owner had provided with the lease. Soon, the place looked homier than an impersonal hotel room.

I stood back to view our efforts in the living room. "Tomorrow we'll buy some plants."

He grinned at me. "Thanks. I knew you'd fix it up real nice."

Derek wrote down the directions I gave him to New Hope and gave me a steady look that had me wishing I had the nerve to stay. But I knew it would be best if I held back, kept things on an even keel. What we were feeling was way too much, too soon—lust, not love. Besides, he wasn't going to stick around. He'd made that very clear.

Under my protest, Derek walked me to the car. "Just want to make sure you're all right." He held the car door for me while I slid in behind the wheel.

Holding the door open, he leaned in and gave me a quick kiss on the lips.

"Hey! You promised hands off," I announced when I could get my breath.

His eyes twinkled. "Right. I didn't lay one hand on you, did I?"

I laughed. True, but his lips had scorched me.

CHAPTER NINE

The next morning, I lay awake in the guest room of Briar Cliff, excited about the idea of seeing Derek again. During a restless night, my thoughts had returned to him again and again. I leaned back against my pillow, smiling to myself. Who would have thought that I'd finally discover what it felt like to be giddy over a guy? It was so much more than lust. I liked being with Derek. He was interesting. And ... oh, yes ... so, so sexy.

Imagining him lying beside me, I rolled over and hugged the pillow. After that searing kiss of his, I knew he'd be a very good lover. I checked the brightening sky. Clear blue. My spirits rose even higher. Wandering around New Hope would be a perfect way to spend time with him.

My cell phone rang. Alert, I sat up, hoping nothing was amiss with one of the women I'd helped that week.

"Samantha? It's Derek. I'm at the local Starbucks. What can I bring you?"

"You're already here in New Hope? Do you know what time it is?" I pulled the sheet up over my bare breast as if he could see me.

He laughed. "I've been in town for almost two hours. I know it's early, but it's the best time for outdoor photography. That's when the light is fresh and new."

"Give me fifteen minutes to get dressed. And, thanks. I'll take a grande café mocha, half the mocha, no whip."

I scrambled out of bed and headed for the shower. Eager to see him, I hurried through my morning routine and raced down to the kitchen. I'd just searched through the refrigerator for orange juice when Derek pulled up behind the house in his Jeep Cherokee. I peered out the kitchen window. Even at this early hour, dressed in jeans and a black golf shirt, he looked like he'd just stepped out of *GQ* magazine. I looped my damp hair behind my ears and went outside to greet him.

He gave me a smile that warmed my insides. "Nice digs. You told me she had a large house, but I had no idea it was this big."

"Marissa inherited it from her grandmother. She likes me to use it whenever she's out of town, which is quite often. Brad, her fiancé, still practices law part-time in Barnham, New York, with his father. When he has to go there, she travels with him."

"You guys are really close, huh?" He handed me my coffee.

I took a grateful sip of the steaming liquid. "She's like another sister to me. She put me on the board of directors at Rivers Papers. We work closely together, overseeing it."

"Funny, I never thought much about the making of paper before getting this assignment. Now, I suppose I'll never use it without thinking of Maine, Rivers Papers... and you."

We grinned at one another.

"It's a fascinating business and Maine is a beautiful state," I said, trying to maintain some sense of business. "I'm hoping you can capture all of that in the book."

He followed me into the kitchen. "I think I got a few good shots of the coastline this morning."

"It should be a relaxing day. If you'd like, we can walk down the beach and into town for lunch. In the meantime, I thought you might like to read a little history about my family and how they came into the paper and pulp business."

"Sounds good to me." Derek sat at the kitchen table, stretched his long legs, and gave me a lazy smile.

"How about some eggs?" I said.

"Great." His eyes lit with humor. "Like I said before, I like to see a woman work in her kitchen." He laughed when I threw a dish towel at him.

I went to work, fixing breakfast.

"Do you like Maine better than Boston?" Derek asked.

I shrugged. "There are good things about each."

"Yeah, I get it. For me, each part of the world has its own beauty, its own style."

I stopped and studied him a moment, trying to put my feelings into words. "I suppose it doesn't matter where you are as long as you live life well. I don't mean richly, but a life filled with meaning. I've learned that."

The corners of Derek's mouth lifted in an impish grin. "I see you married to some guy with a lot of little kids running around." His eyes bored into mine. "Why hasn't that happened?"

I shrugged. "I guess I'm a late bloomer. It's taken me a while to realize what I gave up to drink—mostly, the nicer parts of me. Now, I'm back on track."

He looked at me with approval, and a warm glow spread throughout my body. Statements like that sounded so easy to others, but I sensed he knew how much work it had taken on my part to learn that.

"Will you come with me when I photograph the area around Riverton? I want your input. From all I've heard, you're the one family member who cares most about the business. People at the mill told me all about your younger days visiting the mill and how you've always loved being there. I'd like to capture that sincere interest. I think it's important to the book."

Pleased, I smiled. "Establish a time frame within my work schedule and I'd be glad to do it. As Sim said during the board meeting yesterday, most of us aim to temper the business aspect with love of the land. It's something I've always felt."

"Deal. I'd like to complete it in the next few weeks when the autumn colors are vibrant and before another assignment comes up for me."

At the thought of Derek leaving so soon, disappointment coursed through me. I warned myself not to let my fascination with him get out of hand. He'd be on his way, and I had a very busy life of my own.

After a pleasant breakfast, I retrieved the family history that Simone, Arinthia Hartwell's companion, had drawn up for Marissa.

"This might give you an idea about how much foresight my great-grandfather and great-uncle had to buy the land and build the first mill." I handed Derek the booklet. "The whole business then was far simpler from what exists today."

Derek took the leather-bound papers into the sunroom while I cleaned up the breakfast dishes. A short time later, I joined him.

"Well? Do you have a better picture of the Hartwells?"

"Like you said, it's very interesting. Tell me about the rift in the family. I heard it mentioned that your brother Hunter was supposed to have the seat on the board, but you and Marissa changed all that. Jonesy told me it's the best thing to happen to Rivers Papers in a long, long time."

I let out a sigh. "You know how it is in some families. One member becomes successful and the others resent it. That's sort of like what happened with my great-grandfather. His brother bought him out and then made the mill into a huge success. When my Uncle Herbert died, my father thought that naturally, the seat on the board would go to him, being the only male family member of age in the family. But my Aunt Arinthia had other ideas. She was saving it for my cousin Tim.

After he died in a freak accident in the Army, she decided to keep the seat, much to my father's distress. It's been a battle ever since."

"What about your brother? Is he upset Marissa gave you the seat on the board and not him? "

"Not at all." My response was tinged with a bitterness I couldn't help. "It's my father who wanted that for my brother, who's the only young male in the family. Hunter isn't all that interested in the business."

"But you are ..." Derek studied me for a moment.

Trying to hide my hurt, I nodded.

Derek jumped to his feet and held out a hand. "To hell with family conflicts. Let's go outside."

Relieved to avoid further discussion of a painful topic, I grabbed my purse and we stepped out onto the wide porch overlooking the beach.

"What a view!" Derek craned his neck. "Beautiful."

The sandy stretch of beach extended as far as the eye could see in either direction, the view broken by the dark shapes of rocks sitting in the water like giant turtles hiding in their shells. On this fall morning, the beach was all but empty. The only sounds were the cries of the seagulls swooping and diving in the sky and the gentle lap of the waves meeting the sand with a moist kiss.

"Wait! I'll get my cameras." Derek strode back inside.

I drew in deep breaths, reveling in the salty tang of the air. Like Derek had said, to hell with old family stories. It was time for fun.

Derek appeared with a couple of cameras and two different lenses slung over his shoulder. "It's too good an opportunity to pass up, with scenery like this."

I took his proffered hand. "The coastline of Maine is beautiful. The north has a craggy feel, while the southern part of the state has a more traditional sandy beach except for the huge granite rocks that poke up in and around the water."

Derek smiled down at me. "I wish I could show you so many different parts of the world. You're one of the few people I know who might really enjoy the way I look at it."

"Did you get your love of travel from your family?"

His expression became guarded. "My parents divorced when I was a freshman in high school. It got very ugly. I don't have any brothers or sisters so it was just me trying to patch things up. You can imagine how that was. I've already told you about my father. He married the girlfriend who helped break up the marriage. Within a year, he had a heart attack and died. To my mother, that was pure justice. She eventually married her lawyer, an uptight asshole who hates the sight of me."

"Whoa! That's gotta hurt."

Derek shook his head. "Not any more. It took me a while to work it out in my head, but I figure it's my mother's one chance at happiness, and if that means staying away from them, that's what I'll do."

I stared at him. He'd said it didn't bother him, but the hurt in his voice told me otherwise. My family was difficult at times but I'd be crushed if they turned me away.

"You're a really nice man, Derek," I said, meaning it.

He kicked at the sand and looked away before turning back to me. "Yeah? Maybe not."

I wasn't fooled by the sudden roughness in his voice. "C'mon, let's head down the beach and into town."

Hand in hand, we walked along the sand. I thought about the sacrifice Derek had made for his mother and was impressed by his generous decision. That same caring is what made his photographs so special, I decided, liking the man even more.

###

The town of New Hope curled around a small harbor. Shingled, two-story buildings added a texture to the shoreline that complemented the patterns of the rippling water lapping the shore. Several fishing boats and a few sailboats bobbed in the harbor. In the next month or two, the owners of the sailboats would be forced to take them out. Harsh falls and winters in Maine were no friends to the luxury boats owned by the wealthier citizens of New Hope. The fishermen would continue their quests as long as they could in the wintry weather.

As we drew closer to the harbor, Derek stopped and took a few pictures of a ketch, its high mainmast making circles in the sky as it moved with the motion of the waves.

"Do you sail?" Derek asked.

"I did a lot of sailing as a kid."

"It's a great feeling to have the wind carry you along. When I was doing a publicity shot for a resort in Tahiti, the owner took the whole crew of us out on his large catamaran. It was unbelievable!"

"You've been to so many exotic places, perhaps Maine won't seem so special to you."

Derek threw an arm around my shoulders and gave me a squeeze. "How can you say that with you at my side?"

I froze. It seemed like such a phony line. To how many other women had he spoken those very same words? I scolded myself for being so insecure but I honestly didn't know what he saw in me. In many ways, I felt a failure.

We strolled past the cluster of shops on Main Street, nestled in small, wooden clapboard buildings that looked like pieces in the miniature Christmas village my mother set up for the holidays. Tourists wandered in and out of the shops, carrying bags full of treasures. Their excited chatter added to the bustling flavor of the streets.

We walked from one end of town to the other, stopping so Derek could snap pictures of the unique old buildings, the water rushing under the bridge as the tide changed, and a number of people in various sizes and shapes.

We stopped for lunch at Toby's Takeout, a typical fishing shack alongside the harbor where people could order fried clams, lobster, and other seafood. It was one my favorite places in New Hope.

I ordered cokes and lobster rolls and sat with Derek at one of the picnic tables on the large patio next to the building. The sun felt wonderful as we waited for our number to be called for pickup. I closed my eyes and lifted my face to it.

"Hold it right there," said Derek softly.

I kept my eyes closed and maintained the pose, waiting to hear the click of the camera.

"Samantha?"

I opened my eyes and turned to Derek, just as he took the picture. He continued staring at me even as he placed the camera down on the table.

"Beautiful. You, that smile, and that sense of goodness. Someday, I'd like to take a whole series of pictures of you."

My heart pounded at the intensity of his gaze. I waved a hand in dismissal. "Oh, you'll be off to some distant destination, doing your thing."

Derek frowned, but remained silent, and I knew I was right. Derek Roberts would not stick around any place for long. The thought made me sad.

I was still troubled by the idea of my increasing attraction to him as we ate our lobster rolls in quiet companionship. I almost wished he would do something terrible—so terrible I'd never want to see him again.

I got up and tossed our empty paper plates and cups into a

waste container. "Had enough?"

"Yeah, let's head back to the house. I've used up all my film and I'm through with the digital camera."

He rose from the table as a young couple approached us. "Hey, Mister, would you mind taking a picture of us. We're on our honeymoon." A young man, who looked about sixteen but had to be older, handed Derek a cardboard camera.

"Sure, I'd be glad to do it." Derek handled the inexpensive camera as if it were a Leica.

I watched, touched, as Derek took several shots of the young couple gazing at one another lovingly.

Derek handed the camera back to the young man and shook his hand. "Good luck."

I smiled at Derek as we walked away. A treat awaited the honeymooners when the film was developed. "That was sweet of you."

"Good subjects." His reply was gruff, but I knew he was pleased.

Beyond the harbor, we took a trail down to the sandy beach. As we followed the high tide mark along the beach, Derek put his arm around me and pulled me close. I inhaled the faint aroma of the spicy aftershave that clung to his skin and sighed. It smelled so manly. Everything about him was, I thought, my body fluid against his solid shape.

Derek stopped and drew me even closer. He leaned down and kissed me with a mixture of tenderness and need. The cool breeze dancing playfully around us couldn't tamp down the heat that rose in waves of longing within me.

His tongue played with my lips then penetrated my mouth. Desire, sharp and painfully sweet, coursed through me. All I could think of was him and how he made me feel. When we finally parted, his strong hands gripped my face gently, forcing me to look into his eyes. I saw such tenderness there that I drew in my breath with a soft gasp. He was such a sensitive man, sexy and real. And he scared me to death.

We walked again, this time with an underlying sense of urgency that neither one of us attempted to hide.

We approached Marissa's house, and a shiver of anticipation ran through me. Derek smiled at me and I knew there would be no holding back. Neither one of us would deny what we'd been wanting for weeks.

I was about to climb the front stairs to the wrap-around porch when a large figure rose from one of the wooden rocking chairs at the far end. My heart pounded in alarm. I shrieked and jumped back.

Derek tensed and gripped my hand, pulling me behind him for protection. "Who's that? Do you know him?"

Feeling foolish, I let out a shaky breath. "It's okay. It's my brother, Hunter."

Hands on hips, I watched Hunter walk down the steps toward me, looking as if he hadn't slept all night. "What are you doing here? I thought you were away in school at Cornell."

There was a stillness to him I found disturbing.

"What's wrong?"

"I quit law school. Father doesn't know it yet. I need you to help me, Sam. He wouldn't listen to me when I tried to tell him how much I hated law. I told him I wanted to transfer into the hotel school, but he ignored me. You know I've always been interested in that sort of stuff. I've been hanging around with a few of the kids there and, Samantha, it's everything I've ever wanted—culinary arts, business, a little bit of everything. I want to have my own restaurant someday."

Shocked by his defiance of my father's wishes, I rocked back on my heels. "What about Bettina? What does she say about all this?"

Hunter kicked at the sand with the toe of his shoe. "That's

another thing. We're through. It was a mutual decision. Besides, I'm with someone else. We went out a couple of times last year and we've made it more permanent. She's a hotelie from New York City. Her father owns a famous restaurant there."

I gaped at the younger brother I thought I knew. Even though my mind was still trying to sort through all he'd told me, I respected this new young man much more than the old one. Maybe, like Allison and me, he was finally coming into his own at an age when most kids had it already figured out.

Hunter narrowed his eyes at Derek. "Who are you?" His voice held an edge of brotherly concern I didn't like.

Derek held out his hand. "Derek Roberts."

"Yeah? What are you doing with Sam? You'd better not hurt her. She's been through a lot."

"Hunter, please ..." I began, mortified by the way he glared at Derek.

Derek held up his hands, all innocence. "Don't worry. Everything between us is mutual."

"That right?" Hunter asked me. "He's not one of the crazies that Mom told me about?"

I placed a hand on Hunter's arm. "I can take care of myself, little brother. We were just going inside. What is it you want me to do? Can it wait?"

Hunter looked from me to Derek. An understanding smile spread across his face. "Oh, I get it. You want me outta here. I'll go if you swear you'll come to the family dinner Mom has set up for tomorrow. That's when I'll drop the bomb! Mom knows I'm up to something, but she doesn't know all the details. Promise me you'll show up. I know you don't like these family fights, but I need you there."

I gave him a quick hug. "I'll be there, but I'm warning you, Hunter, you'll owe me big time for doing this."

He hugged me back. "You're the best, Sam. I mean it. See you tomorrow. I'm meeting Bettina at her parents' house. We're going to break the news to them today. It shouldn't be too bad. Her father didn't like me that much, anyway."

He gave a salute to Derek and walked around the side of the house without a backward glance. I could tell from his slumped shoulders and the way he dragged his feet that, regardless of what he thought, nothing about this weekend would be easy for him.

"Good luck!" I called softly, knowing he couldn't hear me.

"A family crisis, huh?" Derek threw his arm around my shoulder and pulled me close.

I turned to face him. "Yes, but what was it you told me earlier?"

His lips curved into an alluring smile. He tugged me into his arms. I settled into Derek's arms and he kissed me.

We broke apart, and I unlocked the door and walked inside the house, feeling as if I were opening my heart to him.

I couldn't hide my nervousness as I shed my purse. "Would you like coffee or something else to drink?"

Derek grinned. "That's not what I had in mind."

Standing a few feet away, he studied me. Our eyes locked and the walls and furnishings seemed to melt away.

"Come here," he whispered.

Feeling as if a string was attached to me and Derek was pulling on it, I moved forward into his outstretched arms.

He embraced me and I leaned against his hard chest. The racing beats of his heart matched my own.

I led him up the stairway to the room that had more or less become mine throughout my many visits. At the doorway, we halted.

"You sure about this?" Derek's voice was husky, his face flushed.

I silently took his hand, and we went inside. The king-sized bed with its quilted coverlet seemed to grow in size as I stared at it with sudden shyness.

Derek's lips captured mine and desire outweighed all other emotions. Derek's hands caressed my breasts and thumbed their tips. A moan escaped my lips. With an easy swing of his arms, he lifted me and gently placed me on the bed. His gaze never left mine as he stripped down to his boxers, which couldn't contain his arousal.

My pulse quickened at the sight of such manliness.

He helped me pull off my jeans and shirt, and unhooked my bra, letting my breasts tumble free.

"Beautiful," he murmured, lying down beside me and cupping a breast in his broad hand. "I knew you would be."

We explored one another's body, our lips and hands and tongues discovering the curves and hidden places that made each of us so special.

His kisses trailed down my body, growing in intensity until I cried out for release.

"Hold on," Derek whispered, turning aside to take care of protection.

He stroked me until I moaned with neediness. He kissed me deeply and pulled away, gently brushing the hair away from my flushed face. "I've wanted you so much," he murmured.

His fingers sought the core of my heat, and desire flared through me. Urging him on, I lifted my hips, begging for more.

He entered me, and thrilling sensations rolled through my body. He rode the wave of my pleasure until he too cried out.

Afterward, we lay limp, staring into one another's eyes. The tenderness I'd seen earlier in Derek's expression had reappeared, and I felt as if I was gazing into his soul. I knew a moment of pure joy as I realized we had shared so much more than simple lust. For me, it meant giving my heart away in a way I'd never done before.

My mouth grew dry at the thought. When it came time for him to leave, would I be able to survive the pain of losing him?

CHAPTER TEN

W e stayed in bed until it grew dark. Each time we made love, Derek proved his ardor was not a temporary thing, but a continuous pattern of generosity.

I climbed out of bed on rubbery legs. "I don't know about you, but I'm hungry."

Derek grinned. "I've worked up an appetite myself."

I padded down to the kitchen in my old fluffy, pink robe, intent upon finding some food. As I opened the refrigerator, I heard a knock at the kitchen door. Startled, I went to the window and peered out. Hunter stood in the circle of light cast by the electric lantern outside. He looked terrible. I sighed and opened the door.

"Didn't go well, huh?"

Hunter shook his head. "Bettina's father insisted upon calling our parents so the business deal Father had with him would be nullified, as he put it. Father went on a rampage and told Mom to tell me I wasn't welcome at their house. Mom says he'll calm down, but in the meantime, I need a place to stay."

I caught my lip between my teeth, wondering how I could say no.

"I'm sorry. I really am," Hunter said, as Derek strolled into the room wearing jeans and nothing else.

"What's going on?" Derek put his arm around me, looking as if he'd brook no interference from anyone else.

Hunter glanced from him to me. "Look, I'd better go."

"No. It'll be all right. You need a place to stay. I'm sure

Marissa wouldn't mind. In fact, she's been trying to get you and Bettina here for some time." I turned to Derek. "Father has kicked Hunter out of the house. He has nowhere to stay."

"I understand what that's like. Come on in."

Hunter let out a rumbling sigh. "It wasn't as if Bettina was unhappy about the breakup. She was as relieved as I was when we made the decision to go separate ways. It's archaic, you know, to have children marry for business purposes."

"Yes, but Father himself is archaic. Honestly, you'd think he was living in the eighteenth century."

"Yeah, well, he's going to have to give up on the idea of my going into the firm. I'm not doing it. Period." Hunter gave me a speculative look. "Maybe you can take my place."

My laugh was tinged with resentment. "No one can take your place. Not me, not Allison." Hunter had been a cute little boy with lively blue eyes and an eager smile. He'd grown into a handsome man. Everyone loved him, especially my father. It still stung that he never showed the same enthusiasm for either me or my younger sister, Allison.

Hunter let out a sigh and raked a hand through his dark, straight hair, like mine. "After tomorrow, he'll probably never speak to me again."

I placed a hand on his arm. "One day at a time. Now, how about some dinner? I was just going to see about some steaks, maybe put a salad together."

Hunter smiled at me gamely. "'Sounds good."

I got out steaks to defrost and headed upstairs to get dressed. Derek followed me. In the privacy of my room, I turned to him. "I'm sorry, Derek."

He put his arms around me and gave me a hug. "You're just being a good, big sister. I wish I had had a sister like you growing up." He squeezed me affectionately. "But I'm really glad we're not related." The grin he shot me wasn't the least bit brotherly.

I laughed and snuggled against his bare chest, enjoying the moment before pulling back. "You'll stay for dinner, won't you?"

"Sure. Afterward, I'll head back to Piney Woods. I need to answer an email. Another proposal came in and I want to respond to it."

"Oh ..." Distress at the thought of him traveling prevented me from saying anything more.

Derek tilted my chin so he could look me in the eye. "I'm going to tell them 'no' this time, Samantha. I'll see your project through. You promised to help me."

Relief flowed through me. I wasn't ready to give him up just yet. If, ever.

When I returned to the kitchen, Hunter was sitting at the kitchen table looking like a ten-year-old boy who'd lost the most important ball game of his life.

I took a seat opposite him.

"So what is this guy to you, anyway?" he blurted out.

I looked away, trying to find the right words. "Very, very special," I said, knowing it was already much more than that.

"You love him?"

Hunter's bluntness gave me pause. I stared at him and considered the question. "It's too soon to know for sure. Maybe. I don't know." I worried that if I admitted how much I cared, it might come back to bite me. But I couldn't hide my real feelings or the way my body warmed just thinking of what we'd just shared. "Yeah, I think I love him."

"Do you want me to leave?"

I smiled at Hunter's thoughtfulness. "No, it's all right. Derek's going to have dinner with us and then head back to Riverton."

Derek entered the kitchen and grinned at me. I couldn't

help thinking how handsome he was. Now that I knew every inch of his body I was more convinced of it than ever. But more than that, behind his worldly attitude was a compassion he hadn't been able to hide from me.

Hunter chuckled softly, looking from me to Derek and back to me. "Wow! You guys together are hot!"

I recalled Marissa's warning about not settling for less than that. How right she'd been. Dawson and I never had one-third the chemistry that existed between Derek and me. I felt as if we were soul mates who had found one another at last.

Derek took a seat at the table and turned to Hunter. "So tell me about the hotel school you want."

Thinking it would be a good idea to leave the two of them alone, I rose. A whole lot of evaluating was going on beneath the polite words. Let them figure one another out.

Dinner consisted of steak, salad, chocolate ice cream and pleasant conversation. Both Derek and Hunter made an effort to be congenial, though I could tell Hunter was upset about the forthcoming meeting with our father, and Derek seemed reluctant to leave.

Right after our meal, Hunter disappeared into the sunroom. In the kitchen, I clung to Derek, wishing with all my heart he could stay, knowing it would be best for many reasons if he left.

Derek brushed a lock of hair away from my face. "Are you going to stay here in New Hope for a while longer?"

I shook my head. "I need to get back to the office—so many people are depending on me. Anthony shouldn't be a problem now that he's had a few days to settle down. After beating the crap out of her, he can't be too surprised by Caitlin's disappearance."

"Be careful, Samantha." Derek traced the curve of my cheek with his finger. "I wouldn't want anything to happen to you."

"Let me know when you'll be in the city."

"I think I can stall one of my assignments. Next weekend we'll plan to hit the areas around Riverton and Coldstream, okay? I've taken some pictures, but I want you to show me some of your special places."

"Okay." My body tingled in anticipation of spending another weekend with him.

His lingering kiss was tasty, teasing, tempting. We broke apart and simply stared at one another, wowed by the magic between us.

"Well, I guess I'd better go," Derek said with little enthusiasm.

Overcome with misery, I stood at the kitchen door, watching Derek drive away. I stayed there until the last hint of the red tails lights of his Jeep disappeared into the night.

Morning fog hovered above the ground, cold and damp—a dismal harbinger of the family meeting ahead. Hunter hadn't yet told my parents everything. While he continued to sleep, I made coffee, lit the fireplace in the sunroom and, wrapped in my old pink robe, sat in front of the fire, sipping coffee. I couldn't clear thoughts of Derek out of my mind. Our lovemaking had been wonderful, as much a spiritual thing as physical. And oh, the pleasure!

My cell phone rang, and I quickly snatched it up. "Hello?"

"Good morning, Sam," my sister Allison's voice surprised me.

"What are you doing up? It's barely five o'clock in California."

"Ah, but it's harvest time." Amusement rang in her voice. "I've been up for a while. When the grapes, the temperature, and the weather are ready, there's no holding back. Mother phoned last night to tell me that Hunter and Bettina have called off their engagement. She said Father is furious, that he won't even allow Hunter to stay there."

"That's not the end of it, Allie. Hunter is dropping out of law school and transferring into the hotel school. He refuses to even consider being part of Father's law firm."

"Omigod! Father will have a heart attack over that." She drew in a deep breath. "Maybe now you can go into Hartwell, Smith, & Lowell."

"I doubt it."

"Well, that's his loss. So tell me...Mother also mentioned you had a dinner date with Derek Roberts. If the photographs of him in the magazines are any indication, he's a hunk. How did it go?"

I hesitated. I'd kidded Allison a lot in the past and I didn't want her or anyone else teasing me about what had happened between Derek and me.

"Well?"

"If you promise not to say a word to anyone else, I'll tell you."

"Uh, oh. It sounds serious. Are you all right?"

I couldn't help smiling. "I'm fine. Oh, Allie, he's wonderful. I've never felt this way about anybody."

"What about his travels? Is he through with all that?" Allison spoke with sisterly concern.

I smiled at her role of protective sister. "I don't think so. That's his job, after all, traveling to any place in the world to take the pictures he or someone else wants."

"Hm-m-m-m." Her tone sent shivers of self-doubt through me. Maybe, like I'd previously suspected, I was just another source of entertainment and satisfaction for him during his brief stay in Maine. My self-confidence wavered. Chilled by the thought, I pulled my robe closer around me.

"I've met Liz Sanderson and Caitlin Rafferty," Allison continued. "Liz filled me in on the whole story. Sam, promise me that if you're ever threatened by that boyfriend of Caitlin's you'll come stay here with me, far away from him. I would hate for anything bad to happen to you. There were still ugly bruises on Caitlin's face."

"I don't think you have to worry. He's mad at Caitlin, not me."

"Still, you be careful. Look, I've got to go now. Blake is calling me."

We ended the call and I paced the room, trying to sort through my thoughts. Was I being foolish to brush away concerns of Anthony? I couldn't let him dictate how I was going to live my life. I had to be strong enough to carry on with my obligations. And right now, those obligations included helping my brother through what promised to be a horrible family dinner.

CHAPTER ELEVEN

Hunter and I arrived at our parents' house right after lunch. My father stood at the door and glared at Hunter, then turned his frosty stare to me. He'd already heard the news about Hunter giving up law school. Clearly, he was in no mood to put up with one of his children's bad choices, even if that child was in his twenties. I felt sorry for Hunter but was annoyed that our father had included me in his sweeping look of disapproval.

My mother fluttered around us like a mother hen protecting her baby chicks from an ornery rooster. "Come in. Come in."

We settled in the living room. Father cleared his throat and looked askance at Hunter. "What do you have to say for yourself, son? A broken engagement and a career thrown away. Are you trying to destroy your life?"

Hunter pulled himself up from the defiant lounging position he'd assumed on the couch. "I told you how unhappy I was in law school. You wouldn't listen to me. I've always wanted to go to the hotel school, but you wouldn't hear of it. I decided to follow my instincts and do what was right for me. I don't give a damn what anyone else thinks about it. You can cut me off if you want. I don't care. I'll work my way through hotel school, do anything I can to make it happen."

I knew by the way my father's eyebrows shot up that he was just as surprised as I by Hunter's outburst. I silently cheered my brother.

My father spoke into the humming silence in the room.

"I've held a spot for you at my law firm so you'd have the opportunity few graduates have; that of joining one of the most prestigious law offices in the northeast. I've paid for the best schools for you, contemplating that day. It would behoove you to follow the example of your sister, here, and do the right thing by me."

At the unexpected compliment, backhanded as it was, my jaw dropped.

Hunter's chin lifted. "Samantha's the one who should be in the firm. Not me. She's the one who's perfect for the field of law. She loves it and the paper business, too. Why don't you recognize that?"

Father turned to me. "Is that what you want? To take Hunter's place?"

My body turned cold. My father would never understand me; never really see me as the person I was. "It's much more than that. I don't want to take anyone's place. I want to earn it on my own and have you grateful for who and what I am."

My father turned to my mother. "Adrienne, I'm too old to deal with all of this. Defiance and disrespect are things I'd never have dreamed of showing to my own parents. What have we done with these children?"

I rolled my eyes at my brother.

My mother put a hand on his arm and murmured, "Now, George, these are good children—intelligent and strong. You would never have let your father dictate your choices for your life. Why would you expect anything different from your children?"

My father shook his head in defeat. "Hunter, you're on your own. It's time to prove to me you'll do well under your own steam. If, after a year at the hotel school, your grades are satisfactory, I'll take care of your tuition, nothing else."

Hunter's face lit with satisfaction. "Thank you, Father.

That means a lot to me."

I waited for Father to say something to me about the law firm, but he rose and announced he was going to lie down before dinner. Watching him leave the room, I realized how old he was. He looked and acted his age today. It couldn't have been easy, I thought, for a man to start a family when he was middle-aged, especially for a man as rigid as my father.

My mother spoke to Hunter. "I've known for some time you were unhappy. I wish you could have confided in me."

"I couldn't talk to anyone about it until Bettina and I had decided our futures." The corners of his lips turned down.

"Your father is set in his ways, but he'll come around." She gave him a hug and came over to me, embracing me warmly. "I'm proud of both of you for being strong and thoughtful. Now, let me go see to your father."

Hunter and I were left alone in the emptiness of the room.

"He took it comparatively well." Hunter's face brightened. "I'll prove to him I'm right."

"Maybe, like Mom says, he just needs a little time to get used to the idea."

"How about you, Samantha? Is he ever going to give you a chance?" Hunter's gaze bored into me.

My heart ached. I shook my head. "I don't think so. If it were a real offer, he'd have followed up. He just doesn't get it. Or me."

Hunter gave me a look of sympathy and changed the subject. "Hey? What's the story with that guy who was threatening you? Are you going to continue your work in Boston?"

I gazed at my brother with surprise, wondering why he would think I wouldn't stay the course. Had my mother been telling him I wouldn't? That wasn't the arrangement I had with her.

"I can't let someone like that dictate my life, Hunter. I'm doing good work. Caitlin's whole life is about to change because she has the courage to stand up for what she believes in. I need to show her that same kind of courage."

"Yes, but she'd never be that strong if you weren't there to help her. Who's helping you?"

"I don't need help like she does. I've already decided to stick it out. Anthony Carbone cannot be allowed to scare me off. That job is helping me realize so many personal goals, including staying sober."

"Yeah? Well, just be careful."

Though I nodded, a shiver crawled through me. Recently I'd received warnings from everyone close to me. Was I being too stubborn for my own good?

The rest of the afternoon turned out to be much more pleasant than I'd anticipated. Now that decisions had been made, Hunter was more like his old self, teasing me and my mother in the boyish way he showed his love.

During an early dinner, my father remained subdued. In an effort to keep things light, my mother kept up a steady stream of anecdotes concerning her latest visit to Allison, amusing us with her hilarious experiences picking grapes at the winery in a crazy race to see who could pick the most, the fastest.

"Allie and I were like Lucy and Ethel in an old episode of *I Love Lucy*," ended my mother, dabbing at tears of laughter.

Following dessert, I helped my mother with the dinner dishes, then put on my coat and gave her a big hug, eager to get back to Boston at a decent hour. "Thanks, Mom. I'm glad you'll help Hunter with Father."

I left her and went to my father's den to bid him good-bye.

He rose from his favorite, brown-leather chair. "Be careful,

Samantha. I don't like the idea of you living alone in Boston with some moron trying to take out his frustrations on you."

Aware he was uncomfortable with any lingering shows of affection, I gave him a peck on the cheek. He caught me off guard by hugging me to him and patting me on the back.

"Good girl," he murmured, then abruptly dropped his arms.

My heart warmed. Coming from him, his words were like a benediction.

Hunter insisted on walking me out to the car. Outside, he gave me a hug. "Thanks for being there for me, Sam. It means a lot to me."

"I'm happy for you. You've grown up a lot. It took guts to make those decisions. Good luck at school."

He grimaced. "The work isn't easy, but I'll get by. Maybe next time I'll tell our parents about Kyoko."

"Kyoko's the new girlfriend?" I couldn't help laughing. Yes, my brother had changed a lot in the last few months. Good for him.

I drove into Boston with a new sense of commitment. Nobody, but nobody, was going to stop me from doing my work. Anthony Carbone be damned!

Thinking of the past few days, I hummed a Norah Jones tune. Derek was someone with whom I could envision spending my entire life. The trouble was, he wasn't exactly the marrying kind. He'd once said that travel was like an aphrodisiac to him. How could I compete with that? Yet, he'd hinted at traveling together. Was that his idea of commitment? I stopped humming.

Darkness settled in as I entered the outskirts of Boston. My thoughts strayed to Liz and Caitlin. Liz had sounded so happy on the phone. It would be wonderful if she were given the job of working with Derek on the book. The pay and independence would allow her to carry on with her life.

Pulling up to the curb in front of my condo, I turned off the engine and reached into the backseat for my suitcase. I'd come back for my packages after I opened up the apartment, I decided, and hurried toward the building's front door.

"I've been waiting for you," said a deep voice.

The blood drained from my face.

Anthony Carbone stepped out of the bushes on the far side of the building.

I backed away. Shock froze my body into slow motion.

"What? You're afraid? It's just a gun," he sneered. He waved a handgun at me as if it were a harmless toy. "Where's Caitlin?"

Constricted by the cold fear that stiffened my body, words clogged in my throat.

He drew closer. "I said, where is she, Bitch?" His eyes were glassy. Heaven knew what he was on, but I was in more trouble than I'd ever imagined.

My pulse sprinted in nervous beats. No one was in sight, the street strangely quiet. Fighting hysteria, I took a step back, frantically glancing around for someone, anyone, to see us.

The hand that held Anthony's gun shook. He waved it at me again. "Come on, Bitch! Tell me," he spat out. Spittle formed at the corners of his mouth.

"I saw what you did to her, Anthony. You beat her up. Why?"

"Why not?" He laughed nastily. "The bitch wouldn't listen to me."

"Well, she's far away from you now, Anthony. You can't hurt her anymore."

Anthony's eyebrows shot up. "Where do you get off, playing

God? You think you got the answers for everyone else but, Lady, you fucked up with me." An evil smile spread across his loathsome face. "You wanna play the game of God? Well, now, it's my turn."

The few cars on the street whizzed by in their usual detached fashion. I knew if I screamed, Anthony wouldn't hesitate to shoot me.

Anthony laughed. "Nobody's gonna help you and nobody's gonna stop me." He lifted the gun and aimed it at my chest.

I held up my hands.

His smile was evil. "Any last messages for Caitlin? I'll find her, you know."

I leaped sideways as he pressed down on the trigger.

A shot rang out, echoing in my ears like the scream I couldn't hold back. My left leg felt as if it were coming apart. Trying to stay upright, I shrieked with pain. Blood oozed through my pants.

Anthony grabbed hold of my arm and shoved the gun against my head as somewhere in the distance I heard a dog barking.

Adrenaline pumped through me. *Survive! I had to survive!* I grabbed hold of the gun and twisted it aside.

"What are you doing?" he screamed, struggling to aim the gun at me again.

I fought him with a strength I didn't know I had. We rolled around on the ground grappling and grunting, each of us intent on winning the battle for life. The pain in my leg was like a thousand knives sawing at me as I fought against Anthony's weight. I screamed as Anthony's foot connected with my leg. Then with a grunt of sheer determination, I grabbed his foot, tripping him.

The gun skittered away from his hand.

I grabbed it at the same time he did and fought to keep it

aimed away from me. He let out a growl as I got a better hold on the gun. He threw himself at me, and as we struggled, the sound of another shot registered in my brain.

I lay on the cold ground aware of little else but fiery pain. My vision wavered in and out of darkness. I gazed up at the stars above me—now larger, then brighter, as if I were traveling closer to them. *Am I dying?* I wondered. *Is this it?*

The sound of footsteps and the hum of voices broke through the red-tinged daze that clung to me. I fought to remain alert, to remember. Bits and pieces came back to me— Anthony Carbone, a gunshot, his face full of fury, the fight. He wanted me dead.

And then my world turned black ...

CHAPTER TWELVE

"Where am I?" I muttered, feeling as if my tongue were a dried-up stick in a mound of cotton.

"She's awake," I heard a voice say. A face appeared before my blurry eyes.

"Do you know where you are?" the voice asked.

My mind struggled to make sense of things. I blinked rapidly trying to clear my vision. "Water ... I need water," I croaked.

"Here," came the voice. "I'll moisten your lips. That might help. Do you know what happened?"

The few drops of water that dribbled into my mouth allowed me to move my tongue more freely. I frowned as memory returned. "Anthony Carbone tried to kill me. We fought ..."

"Do you know where you are?" the voice persisted.

I scanned the room, feeling tired, so tired. "Hospital," I murmured and allowed drugs to carry me away into the pain-free nothingness from which I'd emerged.

The next thing I knew, another voice pulled me from my sleep. A familiar voice.

"Hi, darling."

My eyelids fluttered. "Mom, it hurts," I moaned. I struggled to sit up but immediately fell back against the pillow. "What happened? My leg?"

My mother held my hand in hers, and I knew from the way she gripped it how upset she was. "You're going to be fine. The bullet hit a bit of bone and they had to do some surgery. The tibia, I believe the doctor called it, had to be plated."

"Plated? What does that mean?" In my fogginess, I tried to understand.

"They inserted a metal plate to hold the shattered pieces of bone together." Her voice caught. "Don't think about it. Just relax as best you can so you can heal."

My vision remained foggy but it didn't prevent me from seeing the tears that streamed down her cheeks. A movement behind her caught my attention. My father stepped forward and placed a hand on my mother's shoulder.

I stared at him, still trying to grasp all that had gone on. "Hi, Father. What are you doing here?"

His eyes moist, he cleared his throat. "Just making sure you have the proper care you deserve."

"I'm sorry ..."

"Don't concern yourself with that now." His voice broke and I realized he, too, was crying.

There were so many things I wanted to say. Instead, I closed my eyes and let the medicines carry me away.

Some time later, I awoke to discover my sister sitting by my bed. "You're here, too? Everybody's coming to see me. Am I about to die?"

Allison jumped at the sound of my voice, rose and took hold of my hand. "Die? Don't be foolish! It would take more than one gunshot to kill you!" Her smile disappeared into a torrent of tears. "Samantha, you scared me so bad! What would I do without you?"

"I'm going to make it," I responded gamely. "But I never want to see Anthony Carbone again."

Allison's eyes widened. "Didn't they tell you?"

"Tell me what?" At the stricken expression on Allison's face, a horrible suspicion grew.

She waved a hand in dismissal. "Never mind. I shouldn't

have said anything."

"Allison, you'd better tell me now or I'll be even more upset."

"Hold on. I'm going to find the nurse."

After she left, my mind replayed the struggle with Anthony. A second gunshot had shattered the air. Was it possible...? My mind refused to consider anything further.

Allison returned with a nurse. "Samantha? Sherry will give you more medicine if you need it. I know you want to be careful about drugs, but we don't want you too upset."

"It's Anthony, isn't it?" I felt as if I were in the middle of a nightmare that wouldn't go away. "Is he... is he?" I couldn't say the rest. Something like that was against everything I believed in.

Allison rushed over to my bedside and held my hand once more as if to give me strength. "Everyone who came to your aid said it was clearly a matter of self-defense. Remember what he was trying to do. You had to protect yourself."

"Omigod! I killed him? Oh, no! Please, just leave me alone." I turned my face to the wall, filled with such horror I couldn't think.

"Mother is going to be furious with me for telling you. I'm sorry, Sam, I really am."

I ignored her and closed my eyes. I needed time to myself. I'd actually killed someone. How could I live with the knowledge that anyone was dead because of me?

I'm not sure how much time passed when I heard a voice say, "Hello, there."

I swiveled my head around, still stricken by the knowledge that I'd ended a life.

A tall, rangy, middle-aged man walked into my room, wearing a white coat. "I heard you've come around nicely, and I'm sure you're wondering just what we've done to you."

He stood at the side of my bed and held out a hand. "I'm Doctor Swenson, the guy who put that leg of yours together again."

"Like Humpty Dumpty?" I asked, vainly attempting to shake off the depression that had wrapped around me like a damp cloak.

"Much better than that, we hope." He smiled. "We've plated the tibia in your left leg. That's the bone between your knee and ankle. We're going to watch you closely for infection because the fracture caused by the gunshot was a compound one. You'll be off your feet, on crutches for a few weeks, then a walking cast. After that, you should be fine, though you'll probably know when rainy days are in the forecast. Any questions for me?"

Tears filled my eyes. "Dr. Swenson, I have to know. Was Anthony Carbone, the man who shot me, treated here?"

He shook his head. "I'm sorry, I can't answer that. I do know the police want to speak to you. I've held them off for a while, but now that you're awake I won't be able to keep them away. They can give you all the details, I'm sure."

I swallowed hard at the thought of any interrogation. "One more thing. I'm a recovering alcoholic so I don't want to get hooked on any pain medications. Can you help me?"

"Absolutely. We'll keep an eye on them and you." He gave my hand an encouraging squeeze. "If a nurse wants to give you pain medication and you think you can get by with ibuprofen instead, speak up to let her know. I'll make a notation on your chart."

He started to walk away and turned back. "I know you're upset about what happened, Samantha. Anyone would be. But consider yourself lucky. You're healthy and should heal well. Be thankful it was just your leg, young lady. I'll check on you later." He gave me a smile meant to comfort me, but it didn't help. More than my leg had been shattered.

Hunter arrived with a very pretty, tiny Japanese girl who I assumed was Kyoko. He wore a gentle expression as he introduced her to me.

"We're so sorry this happened." Her voice held a lilting note. "Hunter and I drove all night to get here."

My gaze turned to Hunter. "You haven't been home yet?"

He shook his head. "We came directly here." His voice turned gruff. "Had to make sure my big sister was all right."

"Thanks. Do me a favor, will you? Please call Zach. I think I'm going to need his help."

At that moment, Zach rushed into the room, looking as if he'd just come from the court. He stopped and stared at Hunter and Kyoko. "Am I interrupting anything? I couldn't believe it when I heard about it at the police station. Are you okay? Really?"

I burst into tears and shook my head. "No," I managed to say between sobs.

"Look," said Hunter, glancing from me to Zach. "Why don't we leave you two alone? We're going to the Copley Plaza Hotel. Father has secured a number of rooms there for the family." His voice lowered. "Wish us luck."

I sniffled and murmured . "Go for it."

Alone with Zach, I could unburden myself. There was very little we didn't know about one another—good and bad.

"Zach, I killed someone." My lips quivered uncontrollably. "A person is dead because of me." I waited for him to say something.

"Christ, Sam, what are you getting all blubbery about?" he spouted. "The man tried to kill you, not once, but twice, from what I heard. Yes, it's a shame it happened, but you were defending yourself. That's a right of yours. Too bad the asshole was even walking the streets after what he did to Caitlin."

I let out the breath I'd held. Zach was angry as hell, but not at me for being stupid enough to come back to Boston after making Anthony so angry, or for killing someone.

Zach leaned over and gave me a quick kiss on the cheek. "You floating on that pain medication?"

"I'm scared to death I'll go back to where I was."

He took my hand in his. "I'm not going to let that happen. We'll work on it together, just like we did before."

Tears filled my eyes once more. "You're the best friend I could ever have."

"Yeah? Same here." He squeezed my hand. "I know it's a weird idea, but I want you to be my best man at my wedding."

My eyes widened. "Wedding? What wedding?"

Zach's lips spread into a happy smile. "Last night I asked Eddie to marry me. It's going to take her mother a while to accept the fact that my blood is only slightly purple, not blue, but Eddie and I are real happy."

"This is awfully sudden, isn't it?" He'd just started dating her a few weeks ago.

He shrugged. "It isn't like we haven't known one another for a long time. We just hadn't ever hooked up before. She's the one, all right. Talk about hot. I can't imagine not being with her, and she says the same thing about me." His eyes glowed with a joy I'd never seen.

"Oh, Zach, I'm so happy for the two of you. Of course, I'll stand up with you." I glanced down at my injured leg and gave him a weak smile. "Just give me a couple of weeks to get on my feet, will you?"

Zach chuckled at my attempt at humor. "It's going to take Eddie and her mother far longer than that to fight it out over the wedding plans. I've done my part by asking her. Now, I'll sit back and watch the show."

My parents arrived, interrupting our conversation. Zach drew a deep breath.

"See you later." He gave me a kiss on the cheek. "I'll leave my cell phone on. Call me night or day."

I touched his arm, grateful for his support, and watched him leave.

"How are you feeling today?" My mother placed a hand on my brow. "My, you've had a lot of company. Your brother called and told us he'd seen you."

"Zach is going to help me get off the pain killers. It won't be easy. And guess what? I'm going to be in his wedding."

"Zachary is getting married?"

I smiled. "To Edwina Nichols."

"Oh, my!" My mother knew all about the Nichols family. "I wonder what her mother thinks of that."

I laughed, so happy for Zach that I wanted to cry.

CHAPTER THIRTEEN

The next couple of days were as difficult as any I'd ever experienced. Filled with antibiotics against any possible infection, my body ached with pain as I resisted begging for strong pain medications. I often thought amputation might be easier to bear than the constant throbbing in my leg. Support friends of mine kept me focused on how lucky I'd been to escape more dangerous wounds.

Zach came to see me morning and night. I clung to his hand and listened to his pep talks, knowing how lucky Edwina was to have him in her life. Paradoxically, I wished I'd been able to love him in the same way. He was such a good friend, such a good man.

Thoughts like this inevitably led me to dwell on Derek Roberts. I hadn't heard a word from him since the wonderful day we'd shared in Maine. It hurt.

When Zach came to see me my last night in the hospital, I asked him to check my voice mail at home, wondering if Derek had phoned there. "'Call me as soon as you check on all my messages, okay?"

He gave me a worried look. "This is about Derek, isn't it?"

I fought for a noncommittal tone in my voice. "He and I were supposed to go to Riverton this weekend to capture photographs for the book. I need to tell him I can't do it."

Zach studied me a moment and frowned. "You're not falling for him, are you?"

I looked away. I couldn't lie to Zach.

"Be careful, Sam. As great as he is, with the job he has, he's not a stay-at-home kind of guy. Photography is his life's work."

"I know." But secretly I believed with all my heart that what Derek and I had shared might change that. Loving Derek was dangerous, but I wanted to take the chance with him. I'd never felt about any man the way I did about him.

Zach arrived in my hospital room the next morning and handed me a sheet of paper. He ignored my questioning look and walked over to the window and gazed out, his back to me.

I glanced at the list he'd handed me. The normal things were there. Calls from Rosie's Place, the library, Liz and the usual sales calls. At the bottom was a message from Derek, written with quotes around it by Zach.

"Hey! Sorry to have to cancel our weekend together. Something's come up in the Mideast. A promise I'd made earlier. I'll see you when I get back. Ted told me not to worry. The book is a long-term project and the board hasn't even settled on a writer yet. Take very good care of yourself. I don't have your cell number, so give me a call."

My heart pounded with dismay. Everyone had warned me that a relationship with Derek had no real promise of a future. The reality of it hurt. He would drop anything, even plans with me, to go on his merry way. I was so stupid.

Zach gave me a pitying look. "I'm sorry, Sam."

I let out a long sigh. "I shouldn't have let him get to me. I thought we had something special. 'Guess I know better now."

A nurse knocked on the door, interrupting us. "A policeman is here to see you."

I let out a trembling breath. Earlier, I'd given an account of my struggle with Anthony to the police, telling them everything I could remember. They'd left with a promise to get back to me. Now, I'd hear whether they were going to turn the incident over to a prosecutor or not.

"Want me to stay?" Zach asked.

"Would you mind?" My body had grown so cold I had to pull up the blanket on my bed. I still found it difficult to believe I'd actually killed a man. Every time I thought of it, my stomach pitched and dipped like a rudderless sailboat on stormy waters.

With his trim body, dark hair edged in gray and steely blue eyes that missed nothing, Lieutenant Cleary looked like he should be on television.

"'This your boyfriend?" he asked, after greeting me. His gaze raked over Zach.

"A good friend," I answered, faintly amused at Zach's new uneasiness at the suggestion of him being my boyfriend. "I've asked him to stay with me. The medicine tends to make me forgetful."

"Okay. I'm here with good news. Your neighbor, Martha Greene, has come forth as a witness to the fight you had with Mr. Carbone. She's sworn that you were fighting for your life, that in the midst of the struggle the gun went off. Considering forensic evidence and the fact that Carbone was well known to us, we will not be turning this case over to the prosecutor. 'Thought you ought to know."

He patted me on the shoulder. "Shame it had to happen to you at all. But the doc said you'd heal."

I gave him a shaky smile. Yes, my leg would heal. But would my heart?

Zach gave me a peck on the cheek and left for his office. Overwhelmed by emotion, I lay back against my pillow. The good news of being free from prosecution did nothing to erase the disappointment I felt over Derek's message. I blamed myself. I'd known the moment I met him that he was too handsome, too wonderful, too dedicated to his work for my own good. I told myself to learn from this painful lesson and forget him. But I knew it would be a long time before the memories of our lovemaking left me.

My parents arrived. They'd insisted they pick me up at the hospital and take me to their house for the early part of my recovery. Too listless to fight the idea, I gave in. My mother's care and home cooking would do my soul good.

I allowed my mother to fuss over me while we waited for the nurse to bring a wheelchair into the room as part of the discharge procedure.

My mother took hold of my hand and gave it an encouraging squeeze. "We've set up the den for you until you're ready to climb the stairs to your room."

I smiled, wishing now I hadn't agreed to go back home with them. To her, I was already her little girl again. But the thought of returning to my condo and the scene with Anthony was terrifying.

In the quiet of my parents' home, I spent the next few days doing a lot of reading. Hoping to absorb words of wisdom in an attempt to make sense of the killing, I leafed through spiritual books. But images of my struggle, the guilt of killing someone kept me from finding peace.

Marissa came to see me every day and worked hard to distract me from my gloomy thoughts. I tried to respond to her cheerful chatter and to focus on more serious matters concerning Rivers Papers.

"We need to push the board to give Liz the job of writing

for the book," said Marissa. "We want her to be ready to start the minute Derek comes back."

I nodded, but my heart wasn't in the project anymore.

Liz called one afternoon from California. "Caitlin is heading back east. With Anthony out of the picture, she's no longer in danger. She's decided she wants to be back in Boston. Dawson and I tried to talk her out of it, but she's determined."

"How about you, Liz? When are you coming back?"

"I'm not sure. I've made an appointment with a plastic surgeon to have my scar worked on out here. Dawson helped me find an excellent doctor, a friend of his."

I smiled. Apparently, leaving a jagged scar on her face to punish her ex was no longer necessary. Maybe I'd done something right after all.

"Good luck, Liz! I'll call you when we hear more about the book project. Is Caitlin there? I'd like to speak to her."

Silence greeted me. "I think she's outside..." I heard confusion in her voice. "She's flying in tomorrow. Maybe you can talk to her then."

Unease crept through me. I hung up the phone. This wasn't the first time I'd wanted to speak to Caitlin and had been told she was unavailable. But I wouldn't let it go. It was important for both of us to confront the issue of Anthony's death, standing between us like a double-edged sword.

My mother came into the family room and sat on the edge of the couch. "Can we talk, dear?"

"What's on your mind?"

My mother lifted my hand and gripped it tightly. "Your father and I have been discussing your situation. Is there some way you can turn your business over to someone else? As unusual as you might think the incident was with Anthony Carbone, we disagree. What you are doing, interceding for people who come from all walks of life, has proved dangerous. We'll help you in any way we can to end Straight Talk and become involved with something else."

Feeling as if I'd been punched in the gut, I fell back against the plush cushions of the couch. Straight Talk was a business I'd established with a sense of gratitude for the people who'd helped me when I needed it most. It kept me on the straight and narrow. If I gave that up, what would it do to me? My work gave meaning to my life. Without it, I'd feel lost.

I tugged my hand out of my mother's grasp. "I ... I don't know what to say."

"Just think about it, dear. I'll give you time to become used to the idea and we'll talk about it later." She leaned down and gave me a peck on the cheek. As loving as it was, it seemed like the kiss of Judas.

Sickened by the idea of giving up Straight Talk, worried that other attacks might take place, I dialed Zach's number. His voice mail came on. Disheartened, I flipped on the television and watched competitors trekking through a dangerous jungle on a survivor-type show I'd never seen before. I felt as threatened as they.

Over the next few days, I wrestled with the idea of giving up Straight Talk. Each time I came close to deciding my parents were right, I'd recall the faces of the women who now held respectable jobs or who'd opened businesses of their own with my help. I wavered. I'd fought hard to succeed. Why didn't my parents see the value of my work? I couldn't just step away from people who needed me.

I attempted to reach Caitlin several times. After leaving many messages for her at her mother's house, she finally called me back early one morning. I was pleased to hear her voice. Without my help, who knew what might have happened to her.

"I'm so glad you went out west with Liz and Dawson, where Anthony couldn't hurt you."

"Yeah? I should have stayed right here in Boston. Then Anthony would still be alive." Her voice was cool, defiant, and with a trace of slurring that worried me. "It's all your fault! You *made* me leave, Samantha."

My heart pounded in loud, painful beats. "I ... I'm sorry ... about everything. Fighting him off, the gun ..."

"You *killed* him, Samantha! Anthony didn't deserve to die! You're a *murderer*!" Her voice broke. "I don't care what you say, you killed the man I loved ..."

At her sharp words, shock roiled through me. "I couldn't help it. I couldn't let him kill me! Look what he did to you, for God's sake!"

"Yeah, but then you shipped me off to the west coast. I could've talked to him, convinced him not to hurt you. I know it."

"Oh, no ..."

"I never want to see you again!" she shouted and burst into tears.

The hum of the broken connection burned my ear. Shivering beneath the covers of my bed, my body felt as if I'd never be warm again. She blamed me for Anthony's death!

Guilt flooded me. His words came back to me. Had I played God with their lives? Would he still be alive if I hadn't tried to help Caitlin?

Bile rose in my throat. Sick to my stomach, I hobbled to the bathroom and threw up.

CHAPTER FOURTEEN

Marissa walked into my parents' den and came to a quick stop. "What's wrong? You look awful!"

She took a seat on the floor next to the couch where I lay sprawled, my mind hurting more than my body. I told her about my conversation with Caitlin. "How many lives have I ruined?" I covered my face with my hands.

She tugged my hands away from my cheeks. "Look at me."

I couldn't ignore the command in her voice. Through misty eyes, I stared at her.

She shook me gently. "You've heard of the battered wives syndrome. They keep blaming themselves for everything the abuser does. Caitlin is doing this same sort of thing—blaming herself and you for Anthony's death. Don't you dare buy into it! That would be a huge mistake."

"Anthony told me I was playing God ..." Queasy, I took a moment. "Do ... do you think that's what I was doing?"

She gave my hands a squeeze. "You were helping women who needed it—nothing more, nothing less. Don't let anyone take that away from you."

"My parents want me to close down the office. Maybe they're right. Boston is too painful for me, right now."

Marissa studied me for a moment. "That's a decision only you can make. I know you like to keep busy, and, with all that's going on at Rivers Papers, you can help there."

Even that seemed like something too difficult to face. "Oh ... I don't know ... Allison wants me to go out to California. She says she needs me at Sweet Talk. Their wine and chocolate business is growing by leaps and bounds. I'm happy for her, but I don't know what I want to do."

Marissa gave me a look of sympathy. "Give yourself time to get over the trauma of the shooting before making any decisions. And allow enough time for your leg to heal properly."

I blinked away threatening tears. "Okay ... we'll see," I said shakily.

Depression, deep and real, burrowed inside my mind, my body, my spirit. I spent hours staring out at the woods behind my parents' home, lost in a forest of blankness, unable to perform the simplest daily activities, refusing to do anything but sit and stare. My whole body weakened. It took every bit of effort to use my crutches to move from my makeshift bedroom in the den to the kitchen or the family room. I couldn't concentrate on books or even bear to watch mindless television programs. More than anything, I began to be haunted by the relief alcohol might bring me.

Zach arrived unexpectedly one afternoon.

"What are you doing here?" I pushed lifeless hair away from my face. "I thought you had a busy schedule this week."

"I do." He stared at me grimly. "Your mother called and told me how bad things were with you. Sam, have you seen yourself in a mirror lately? You look like hell."

"Thanks. Some friend you are!"

"Damn right." He knelt in front of me. "You and I have been through too much together to have you end up like this. Are you giving up on everything just because Caitlin blames you for Anthony's death? Is that what this is all about?"

I looked away from him.

"You're going down in a hurry," he continued, "and we both

know where that can lead. I'm not letting you go back there. The choice is yours. I know that, but I'll be damned if I'm going to be quiet about it."

I clutched my hands together. "I'd kill for a drink right now. Help me! I'm a mess, a total wreck."

"Get up!" His voice was as stern as I'd ever heard. He rose to his feet and held out his hand. "You're coming with me. Just because you're on crutches doesn't mean you have to hide in the house like a recluse."

Ashamed, balancing on my crutches, I struggled up onto my good foot.

"That's more like it. Now, let's find your coat."

"Why? Where are we going?" A ray of hope broke through the grayness of my life.

"First off, we're going to a meeting. Then you're coming back here to pack a bag. We're going back to Boston to face your demons. Your mother called your therapist, and he's ready to see you anytime."

Later, sitting in a circle of understanding people, all the emotions I'd held in check came pouring out. I told of the shooting and all the difficulties I'd gone through in trying to make a recovery. My voice rose with anguish. "Caitlin will never forgive me for killing her boyfriend." Tears streamed down my face as I recalled the way she'd looked at me, the anger in her voice. "I didn't want to kill him, but I had to protect myself. Why doesn't she understand that? This was not a nice guy, not even with her. Why doesn't she get that?" The one thing I couldn't confess just yet was the underlying horror that perhaps all the work I had been doing with Straight Talk was more harmful than not.

"Feel better?" Zach asked as we left the meeting.

"Let's grab a cup of coffee. I need to talk to you alone."

We sat in a small coffee shop in downtown Portland, facing

one another across a yellow formica-topped table. I noted his concern and immediately thought of what my mother had said about needing to be friends with any man I thought of marrying. Derek didn't fall in that category, but to be honest, we hadn't had much time together.

"How are plans coming together for the wedding?" I asked Zach, attempting to pull myself out of the doldrums. There was a sparkle in his eyes I hadn't seen before.

He grinned. "I had no idea what I was getting into. Eddie and I have talked about eloping, but both of us know her mother would never forgive us. I told Eddie to just grin and bear it. We're going to Tahiti on our honeymoon. That'll more than make up for the hassle to get there." He gave me a wicked grin. "It should be far enough away from her mother to relax."

I smiled. "I'm happy things have worked out for you. I'm hoping to get to know Eddie better. I've only met her casually, just a quick hello."

"She's anxious to get together with you, too. I've sworn there's nothing more between us than friendship." He winked. "As much as that used to bother me."

I laughed, sincerely pleased for my best friend.

Our talk led to my indecision about Straight Talk. I explained that my parents wanted me to end the business, and my sister wanted me to come to California. "I honestly don't know what to do."

He sat thoughtfully for a minute. "Why don't you just go slowly ? You've got a board meeting coming up at Rivers Papers, don't you?"

I nodded, feeling more optimistic than I had in some time. "You're right. I'll just take things one day at a time and see what happens. I don't have to make any decision today."

As he drove me back to my parents' house, Zach told me about some of the cases he was working on and asked me for my opinion on one of them, a troubling case with an anonymous foster child. Family law was something I hadn't been interested in during school, but listening to him now, I admired what he was doing.

By the time we arrived at my home, I felt as if I could begin to face daily activity again. We pulled into the driveway and I gave Zach a kiss on the cheek.

"Eddie is one lucky girl. If she ever needs to be reminded of it, have her give me a call."

Zach grinned. "I tell her that all the time."

I was still smiling as we entered the front hall . I called for my mother, but there was no answer.

"Hurry, pack your bag. I have to meet Eddie and her mother for dinner tonight, and I can't be late."

I lifted an eyebrow in mock humor. "Sure you don't want me to dawdle?"

He laughed and pointed into the den. "Go."

Feeling much more like myself, I hobbled into the den and hastily packed my suitcase, feeling better as I called to Zach to help me with my luggage. He grabbed the suitcase and followed me while I made my way out of the house, one slow step at a time.

My mother arrived home as we were about to get into Zach's car. She hurried over to me and gave me a big hug, looking deep into my eyes. "Keep in touch, Samantha. Your father and I need to know you're okay."

She turned to Zach and hugged him. "Thank you, dear boy."

He gave her a little salute and helped me into his car.

Approaching Boston, flashbacks of my struggle with Anthony flickered in my head. My body tensed at the images and sounds that refused to leave my mind. I stared out the window and forced myself to breathe deeply.

"You okay?" Zach gave me an uneasy glance.

I took a deep breath. "I'm worried about returning to the scene where Anthony and I fought. I've dreamed about it so many times, but seeing it again is going to be even worse."

"Better to get it over with."

"You're right. I need to be able to put it behind me once and for all. Then maybe I'll be able to let it go. I can't allow someone like Anthony to ruin the rest of my life. He's gone and I don't have to be afraid of him or his memory anymore."

"Straight talk from the straight talker, huh?"

I grimaced. "Your humor isn't getting any better, Zachary Adams."

He laughed, reached over and squeezed my hand. "You're stronger than you think you are, Sam. You'll be fine."

We pulled up in front of my condo building. My stomach knotted as I stared at the spot where I'd fought and killed a man. It seemed so surreal.

"Ready?" Zach stood outside the car, my suitcase in hand.

I opened the car door and pulled myself upright, clinging to my crutches. Slowly, steadily I moved up the walk, keeping my eyes focused on the sidewalk. I couldn't look at the grassy lawn where I once lay wounded, thinking I was about to die.

We'd just reached the front door of the building when Martha Greene emerged with her little dachshund.

"Oh, Samantha!" she gushed, giving me a quick hug. "You're back! Did the police tell you that I gave them a full account of what I saw?" She shook her head. "I saw that man attack you. I couldn't believe it! I called 911, but by the time they arrived, both of you had been shot. What a frightful experience."

I swallowed hard. "Thanks for your help, Martha."

"Winston is the one you should thank." Martha beamed at the small black-and-tan dog at her side, wagging his tail. "He got my attention."

Somewhere in the back of my mind, I recalled hearing a dog bark as I'd fought with Anthony.

"I'm just glad the guy is dead," Martha continued. "We don't need people like that around here."

She left, and my gaze turned to the trampled grass where Anthony and I had fought. Nausea swept through me.

Zach grabbed my elbow. "C'mon. Let's go inside."

We took the elevator up to my condo. As I stepped through the doorway of my apartment, I breathed a sigh of relief at the sight of my familiar things.

Zach carried the suitcase into my bedroom and returned to my side. "Eddie and I restocked your refrigerator. Are you going to be all right? It may be hard at first, but it's important for you to get around on your own. Your mother told me you haven't been doing the exercises you were given."

I waved away his worry with a nonchalance I didn't really feel. "I'll be fine. Thanks for everything."

"I'll call you." Zach checked his watch and waved good-bye.

"Have fun tonight!" I called to him, locking the door behind him.

I surveyed my apartment, enjoying the feeling of privacy. A blinking light on the phone caught my attention. I swung my way over to it on my crutches and punched in the numbers to retrieve voice mail.

At the sound of Derek's voice, I tensed. "Hey, Sam, I haven't heard from you. Because the book is on hold, I'm not coming back to Boston for a while. I'm going to Paris to check out some business. Something I'd promised earlier. Give me a call on my cell. Ciao."

Disappointed by him once again, I unpacked my clothes and started a load of laundry, determined to become the independent woman I used to be. No one, I told myself, was going to take that away from me.

My mother called a little later. "How are you doing on your own, Samantha? Do you want me to come down there and make sure you have everything you need?"

"No thanks, Mom. I'm going to be just fine. You don't need to check up on me." I loved her dearly, but I knew I needed to make it on my own.

I managed to tell myself I was happy, that I'd survived for a reason. But nighttime memories of Anthony and nagging daytime thoughts of the blame Caitlin had placed on me continued to haunt me. After several days of this, I finally admitted to myself that my purpose in establishing Straight Talk had been obliterated by the events that had changed my life forever. It was time to focus on something else, at least until I could finally decide what to do about my charity.

I called Marissa. "Can I ride up to Riverton with you for the next board meeting? I may become more involved, as you'd suggested."

"I'd love it!"

Thoughts of moving to Riverton circled my mind. Big-city living no longer appealed to me. I told myself that moving to Maine had nothing to do with being closer to Derek's temporary quarters, then, chided myself for being dishonest. I couldn't forget him or let go of the memory of the intense feelings that had existed between us.

On the day of the board meeting, I rose early and made my way to the parking lot in the back of the building. I settled in behind the steering wheel of my car, grateful my left leg, not my right, had been injured, leaving me able to drive.

Heading north, I felt as if I were about to embark on a brave new adventure. In a way, I was. I'd spoken to a member of my support group. She was interested in carrying on Straight Talk without me. Details still had to be worked out, but I would be free to do something different with my life.

I pulled into Briar Cliff and parked the car, smiling at Lady's frolicking greeting. Marissa came out of the house and waved gaily at me. We exchanged hugs and I climbed into her car, happy to spend time with her.

Chatting all the way from New Hope to Riverton, we arrived in time to join the other board members for a late lunch. As I got out of the car, I inhaled the fresh pine smell I associated with northern Maine. The October sun shone brightly. I took it as a good omen of things to come.

Inside, the other board members expressed their distress when they saw me hobble into the room on crutches. Though I was grateful for their concern, I steered the conversation away from the painful details. Marissa sat at my side like a watchful guardian, ready to rescue me, if necessary.

Ted Beers seemed especially solicitous, which made me wonder what trouble he was about to cause. It wasn't in his nature to be genuinely worried about me.

Walt Coddington arrived just as we started a discussion of the book project. "Sorry I'm late, but my flight into Portland was delayed."

"Glad you're here," Ted said smoothly. "We're about to make some final decisions on the book project, and I know that you, along with Samantha, had some concerns about my sister writing the text." He made eye contact with each board member before turning to me.

"I've done a little investigation of my own, and, Samantha, you failed to tell us that your friend, Liz Sanders, the writer you have recommended, is the ex-wife of Howard Sanderson, the esteemed advisor to the governor of Maine. After learning that bit of news and with all the political ramifications involved in this project, I spoke to Howard. He was most definitely opposed to throwing support behind us if she is involved. Therefore, I've taken it upon myself to ask the senior editor at Beaver Crossing Press to personally sign onto the project, working with Isabelle, to give us a far better result than we'd receive from anyone else."

His smug gaze pierced me. I flexed my fingers, wishing I could rise to my feet and fly at him with my fists. He was as devious a character as I'd ever known.

"The job rightfully belongs to Isabelle, anyway," he continued. "Are we agreed, everyone?"

Walt glanced at me and shrugged. "I've got no problem with it, just as long as we end up with a superior product."

Fury sliced through the calm demeanor I fought to maintain. Liz hadn't been given a fair chance. Ted had done it again.

Marissa looked as frustrated as I felt, but she remained quiet. Other matters, like establishing a day-care program at the plant, were about to be fought over. We'd save our energy for our pet project.

The meeting dragged on and on. A number of budget items were on the agenda. When the topic of the day-care program came up, Ted wanted to postpone voting on it, but I persisted.

"With all due respect, Samantha, I don't know why you're pushing this. It's another of your liberal ideas, and it's going to cost us."

Ted's condescending tone broke through my effort to remain composed. "It's been proven over and over again that if you take care of your employees, it pays off in the long run, Ted," I snapped. "Riverton is a small town that depends on us for many things. We should show the people here that loyalty is rewarded. Why should we lose our best employees to other mills in the state because they're doing a better job at that than we are?"

Walt quickly came to my aid. "I agree. I've found by

offering my employees a few extra benefits they stayed with me. That costs a lot less in the long run than constantly replacing and retraining people. Why can't we do the right thing?"

Ted bristled at the remark. "We're talking about running a business here, Walt ..."

"As a major stockholder, I agree with Walt," Marissa piped up, causing the color in Ted's face to become an unhealthy red.

"Excuse me, but you're not even a member of the board. This idea of you and Samantha sharing the family seat is totally preposterous."

Sim waved a cautionary finger at Ted. "We've gone over this before, Ted. The board has accepted that proposal."

I wanted to blow a kiss Sim's way, but I remained as impassive as possible, hoping my enthusiasm wouldn't bring forth another underhanded maneuver on Ted's part. A vote was taken and the day-care center was approved.

When the meeting finally ended, Ted came over to me. "Guess it was pretty much a draw today. I got Isabelle to do the book and you got the day-care center. Do you think we can ever agree on things for one whole meeting?"

I was flabbergasted by his approach. Was this some sort of conciliatory action? Speechless, I balanced on one foot while I grabbed my crutches and thought of a proper response.

He turned to go and stopped. "By the way, Alexandra told me that when they get back from Paris, Derek is ready to tackle the book project."

I blinked in surprise. *Alexandra was in Paris with Derek?* My good knee buckled and I sank down in my chair, too stunned to utter a word as Ted left the room. At that moment I didn't know who I disliked more—Ted or Derek.

CHAPTER FIFTEEN

As I headed back to Boston, my mind spun. I felt so betrayed by Derek. I'd given my heart to him. But truth forced me to be fair. He'd only promised me another weekend. Nothing more.

I gripped the steering wheel so hard my fingers lost their color. I'd been such a fool to manufacture real love out of a hot hookup. Now, more than ever, I had to be stronger, to go on with my life, to reshape my future. The thought was depressing but I clung to the idea that it was a new beginning, like so many people had told me.

The moment I entered my apartment, I picked up my phone and punched in familiar numbers. "Allison? I've changed my mind. I'd like to come to California, after all. Monday, I'm due to get rid of my crutches and have my walking cast put on. I'll try for a flight out there on Tuesday or Wednesday."

"Are you all right, Samantha?" she said. "You sound upset."

"You don't want me to come?"

"Of course, we do," Allie said in a soothing voice, and I was sorry I'd sounded so snappish. "I just want to make sure you're okay. Blake and I can hardly wait to see you, and I really need you to help me with Sweet Talk."

My breath caught at the reality of the situation. I was giving up my own business to help my younger sister's fledgling enterprise, a wine and chocolate bar. How strange, I thought. I'd worked hard to become sober and was now about to live in a vineyard, surrounded by grapes and wine.

At my silence, Allie said, "Are you going to be okay living here? Working for us?"

"Y-yes, I think it's going to be fine. I can't stay in Boston anymore and I don't want to move to Maine."

"Lucky for me," Allison gushed. "I've missed you so much, Sam! It's going to be wonderful to have you here! Do you have someone to help you to the airport and on the plane?"

"Zach will help, I'm sure. He and his fiancée are coming for dinner Monday night—a celebration for all of us—me for getting the walking cast, Zach and Eddie for their engagement."

"Great. I can hardly wait!" trilled Allison.

I hung up the phone, confident I'd made the right choice. My sister had been begging me to come to California for months and I'd be able to start a whole new phase of my life out there. My existence here had turned into a horror show.

I spent the weekend sorting through my closet, packing the clothes more suitable for California wine country, leaving my stuffier 'city' clothes behind. I'd decided to hold onto my condo as an investment. Someday, I'd put it up for sale, but not until I was certain what I was going to do for the rest of my life.

I was in high spirits leaving the orthopedic clinic,. It felt so good to be free of the crutches. My shoulders and arms still ached from weeks of hobbling. The walking cast would take some time to get used to, but it felt good to be upright on two feet. On the way home, I stopped at the grocery store to shop for my dinner with Zach and Edwina. I searched for the freshest lettuce, the best chicken, the yummiest dessert. I wanted everything to be nice, a special thank you to them both for their support.

Back at the condo, I managed to carry a bag of groceries and a handful of fresh flowers down the hallway, feeling as if I were flying, compared to the slow shuffles of past days.

I hummed as I worked in the kitchen, putting together my favorite lemon chicken dish. Then I cleaned and hand patted fresh romaine to dry and set the table with my best china and crystal. Eddie, as Zach called her, was accustomed to the best. I smiled as I toweled off my crystal water goblets and buffed my good silverware, amused at myself for fussing so. I was a product of my mother's proper upbringing, after all.

Tired from the effort, I went to my bedroom and lay down. In minutes, I found myself in the midst of a strange dream ...

Caitlin and Anthony dragged me toward an open pit from which flames of fire lit the eerie sky.

"I'm sorry! I'm sorry!" I cried, but they just stared at me as we got closer and closer to the pit.

"You must pay for your sins," sneered Anthony. "You're an evil woman. Look what you did to me."

He opened his shirt. Where his chest should have been was a gaping hole through which I could see blue sky and white puffy clouds, like a Salvador Dali painting I remembered from art class.

I began to weep as Caitlin pulled out a gun and aimed it at my head. Her smile exposed teeth that quickly became fangs.

"Bang!" she cried and then laughed.

I jerked awake, my heart pounding. I lifted my hand to my face and felt wet cheeks. Drawing a calming breath, I rolled over on my side and stared at the blank wall, willing those awful images to go away.

"A dream. Nothing but a dream," I said to the empty room.

Shaken, I got up and washed my face, relieved I wouldn't be alone in the apartment that evening. I brushed my long, dark hair and let it hang straight, then slid into a black-leather skirt and topped it off with a pale-pink cashmere sweater my mother had given me for my birthday. I hooked dangling, silver earrings through my ears and stood back to appraise myself in the mirror. No doubt about it, the accident had taken a toll on me. I looked gaunt and tired. The California sun, I hoped, would help transform not only my spirit but my body.

At the sound of the doorbell, I made my way to the door, praying the evening would go well. Zach was the best friend I had, and I wanted his fiancée to like me.

I opened the door, and couldn't help the smile that spread across my face. Zach had replaced his usual worn corduroys and scruffy deck shoes with gray slacks, shiny loafers and a black turtleneck sweater that accentuated his fit figure.

Edwina looked stunning in camel slacks and a hunter green sweater with a large Hermes scarf casually draped over her shoulders. Her lanky figure was almost as tall as Zach. Not beautiful by any means, she was lovely in her own way. Her brown hair was streaked with blond and her blue eyes sparkled with intelligence. I'd seen pictures of her in the newspaper but they didn't do her justice.

Under her watchful gaze, Zach leaned over and gave me a chaste kiss on the cheek.

I smiled at Edwina and held out my hand. "Zach and I are good friends. I'm so glad to meet you at last."

The stiffness in her shoulders seemed to melt as Zach drew her to his side. Leaning into him, she returned my smile. "I've wanted to meet you too. I'm glad you're just friends. Seeing how beautiful you are, it's hard to believe Zach didn't fall for you."

Zach and I exchanged a silent glance.

"Come in, come in." I waved them inside.

I'd expected the conversation to be stilted and full of comments about various social affairs in which Edwina was involved. But I was pleasantly surprised when most of the conversation centered around her volunteer work in the Guardian Ad Litem program.

"That's how we connected." Zach gave Edwina's hand an affectionate squeeze. "We met in court one day."

Edwina and Zach smiled at one another. I'd imagined Derek would look at me like that when we met again.

"So, when's the wedding?" I asked, tearing myself away from thoughts of Derek.

Edwina grimaced. "It's the last Saturday in June. My mother is insisting we have the ceremony here at their estate in Boston even though Zach and I wanted it at our summer place on the Cape. The wedding is really for my mother. Zach and I would just as soon have the money instead and use it for a down payment on a house."

"That's out of the question, as far as her mother is concerned," said Zach, commiserating with Edwina. "Like it or not, it's going to be one of the great social events of the summer. You're sure you don't mind being part of it, Sam?"

I glanced at Edwina. "Do you agree with him on this? Me as his best man?"

"Zach explained you're a big reason behind his sobriety. I want you to be right there by our sides."

The sincerity in her voice warmed me. We gave one another appraising looks, and I realized we liked one another.

By evening's end, I was convinced Zach hadn't made the only good decision. I'd made one, too. Had I chosen to stay in Boston instead of going to California, the existence I'd known in the past would not be the same. It was a good time to leave.

###

I awoke with a new sense of purpose. The day would end with me in California, where I would create a new beginning to my life—something stimulating and exciting, something that would erase Derek from my mind.

My mother and Marissa arrived as I finished sliding the last items into my suitcases.

"Marissa, I hope you don't mind, but I couldn't bear it if I couldn't kiss my daughter good-bye." Tears sprang to my mother's eyes. "We could have lost you, Samantha. You understand?"

Grateful for her love, I put my arms around her and hugged her tightly.

Marissa smiled. "I'm going to miss you, Sam." She embraced me. "You will come back for board meetings after you get settled, won't you?"

"I'll try." I didn't want to go back to Maine unless I was certain I wouldn't see Derek. The sight of him would be even more painful than the occasional twinges in my leg.

The two of them peppered me with questions as to what I'd packed, making me feel like a young girl going off to overnight camp for the first time. Leaving me alone in the apartment, they carried my two suitcases down to Marissa's car. I stood quietly, saying good-bye in my mind to a part of my life that was over forever. Out of all the bad things that had happened, I hoped some good had come as well.

My mother and Marissa dropped me off at the airport and saw that I had help with my bags. I went through security and slowly made my way down to the gate..

A stronger sense of hope filled me. My sister and I were very close, and I'd missed her. She'd help me find projects to keep me busy while I focused on my new life out west.

I settled in my seat on the plane. I was so tired I didn't even bother with what the airline euphemistically called "food," but succumbed to my weariness and fell sound asleep. When I awoke a few hours later, I stared out the window and reviewed my future plans. Suddenly, I could hardly wait to arrive in San Francisco.

Allison was the first person I saw when I walked into baggage claim. She smiled and waved frantically as she ran toward me. I grinned. Two years younger than I, Allison's blond hair and blue/green eyes were in stark contrast to my dark hair and gray eyes, but there was no question we were sisters. Our features were alike.

"Sam! It's so good to have you here!" Allison rushed into my arms and rocked me back and forth, careful of my leg. "I've been counting the hours! Look at that cast. Are you all right now? Oh, we've got so much to talk about!"

Blake Whiting, handsome as ever with his California golden boy looks, came and stood by Allison. They'd been married less than a year. Observing the happiness radiating from their faces, I thought it was as good a match as any I'd known. Blake gave me a quick hug and stepped back. "You two go ahead and talk away. I'll get the bags. Why don't you head for the limo?" He winked at me. "Allie wanted to greet you in style, so we're using one of the limos we rent to brides."

I threw an arm across Allison's shoulder and gave it a squeeze. "Thanks, Sis."

The smile evaporated from Allison's face. "I've been so worried about you. I know you're still going through a hard time."

I nodded, caught off guard by the emotions ranging through me. "It's like my whole life has been turned upside down."

"Well, your stay here is going to change all that." A familiar look of determination crossed Allison's face, and I felt better already.

"How's Daisy doing, living with Jessie and Rob?" I asked as we made our way to the limo. Daisy was Allison's godchild. Not so long ago, Allison had gone through a very difficult time herself, trying to raise her.

Allison turned to me, a smile on her lips. "Daisy's fine. She loves them and they love her. I see her from time to time, but, Sam, I can't wait to start a family of my own. I never knew I'd like being a mother so much. Talk about someone's life changing! Mine's still doing it. It sounds glamorous to own a vineyard, but I'm discovering it's a ton of hard work. Blake has done a marvelous job of turning it into a hugely successful business. That's why we need your help. Between the winery and my businesses, I sometimes feel like I'm sinking in quicksand."

"But Allie, it's all worth it. I can see how great you and Blake are together. I'm so happy for you."

She gave me a quick hug. "One day, you'll be happy too. I just know it."

I shook my head. "I've been so stupid..."

Allison tugged me forward. "We're not going to look back. We're moving ahead. Got it?"

I allowed her to lead me to the car. She was right. No more looking back.

Allison and Blake lived at the Silver Goose Winery in a ranch house nestled among a grove of trees in a private corner of the property. I knew from previous visits that the simple lines of the tan, clapboard exterior belied the elegance inside.

The limo pulled into the driveway.

"We're here." Allison shot me a grin. "We won't discuss work until you're rested and ready. I've got lots of plans for you."

I laughed. Allison wasn't one to sit around doing nothing for too long. Neither one of us was made that way. I was glad. I'd have to keep busy to keep my mind off the disappointments of the past. After unpacking and settling in the guest room, I wandered out to the deck off the living room and breathed in the cool air. It held a particular earthy smell I attributed to the cultivated areas around us.

My sister joined me. "Beautiful, isn't it?"

I turned to her and smiled. Even though it was late October, the damp cold I'd known in Maine was absent. Trees around the house grew far enough apart that the rolling hills were visible, lined with row after row of vines. There was a sense of order to it I found pleasing.

"Are you sure I won't be in the way?" I asked Allison. "You and Blake are still on your honeymoon, more or less."

"I thought it would be easier for you to stay here rather than in the guest house nearby," she responded. A frown creased her wide brow. "But, of course, it's up to you."

"Let's see how it goes. So tell me about Sweet Talk."

Allison launched into a description of the latest activities of the wine and chocolate bar she owned with Blake and Jessie Hendrickson. "But Treasures is what I need to talk to you about. Some of the artists want to put together an online catalog. I want to be sure to cover all the legal aspects of any attempt to do that."

I perked up. This was the kind of work I liked. "I'd love to be able to help."

"Great." As he joined us, Allison turned to Blake with a wide smile.

He bent down to kiss her, and an image of Derek flashed

before me. I was so startled by the reality of it that I caught the rail of the deck and hung on.

"What's the matter?" Allison asked.

I shook my head, unable to speak for a moment. "Later."

She cocked her eyebrow. "Okay, we'll talk after dinner."

Following our meal, Blake left to check on the customers using the Manor House, the conference and entertainment center on the property. It resembled a French *chateau* and had become a popular place to hold meetings, weddings, and other social events. Allison's own wedding had taken place there.

Allison led me into the living room and tugged me down beside her on the couch. "Okay." She faced me with a resolute look. "Spill. Tell me everything that's going on. I know you well enough to realize when you're hiding something—or trying to. What was the deal out on the deck? You looked like a ghost had walked between us."

I took a deep breath. "I told you about the photographer who's working on the book for Rivers Papers, right? What I didn't tell you was that after we went to dinner following the meeting at the paper mill, he spent the weekend with me at Briar Cliff."

Allison caught the corner of her lip with her teeth and stared at me. Worry clouded her eyes.

In an attempt to calm myself, I took another deep breath. "Our time together was unlike anything I've ever known. It was more than sex. We talked about a lot of things. He's so interesting, I actually felt sorry he was so alone in the world. I thought he was someone I could live with and love for the rest of my life. I know it seems crazy after knowing him such a short time, but that's how I felt about him then."

"Then?"

"I can't believe how stupid I am. He doesn't want to be tied down, least of all, by me." My laugh was harsh, bitter. "What a fool I am."

Allison frowned. "That's not like you at all. You're no fool. What happened?"

"We were going to get together the following weekend, but when I returned to Boston that Sunday night, I was attacked by Anthony. I waited for Derek to call me. Zach even went out of his way to pick up my mail and double-check phone messages at home. I finally heard from him. He'd left a message on the phone in the condo telling me he was off to the Mideast—some business deal for him. He obviously hadn't heard about the shooting and had made no attempt to be in touch with me before then. There was no mention of the weekend, no real apologies from him, nothing. He wanted me to call him, but like everyone says, there's no real future with him. I'm not going to be one of those women who throw themselves at him just to keep him...entertained."

"But, Sam ..." A look of concern crossed Allison's face.

I held up my hand. "Wait! That's not the worst of it. When he called again, it was to tell me he was going to Paris. Some sort of business deal."

Pressing my lips together, I became upset all over again. "I found out later that he met up with his old girlfriend there. He'd told me they'd broken up, but obviously, they hadn't." Unable to face her pity, I looked away.

Allison squeezed my hands. "I could kill him for doing that to you."

I chuckled. We'd always stuck up for one another. This time, though, there was nothing Allison or anyone else could do. My time with Derek was a foolish, short-lived affair, over forever.

And my heart was broken.

CHAPTER SIXTEEN

I awoke to the quiet murmur of voices in the kitchen, next to the guest room where I was staying. A sudden silence dragged on, erupting into soft groans. I pulled my pillow over my head, hugging tight, trying to drown out the sounds of Allison and Blake's kisses. Even though the noises became muffled, nothing could erase the sensual images of me and Derek from my mind.

I sat up in bed and sighed. This kind of stuff had been going on for a few days. The guest house would be a far-better place for me. Allison and Blake needed their privacy, and I needed peace of mind.

Allison agreed to help me move into the white-shingled cottage that sat back from a narrow road not far from Allison's house.

"You're sure you want to do this?" she asked me, hoisting one of my suitcases inside the guest house doorway.

"It'll be best for everyone," I said. I'd had enough of their mushiness.

"Juan, our foreman, his wife, Maria and their family used to live here," Allison said. "They left here a couple months ago. Their kids wanted to be closer to the town where they could participate in more school activities. Blake helped them buy a house and we took this over as a guest house for family and friends. But we were sorry to see them go. They were like family to us."

She took my arm. "C'mon, I'll show you around. I think you'll like it."

We walked from the front hallway through the living area to the large kitchen. It had been newly renovated. Cherry cupboards lined the walls and gray granite countertops glistened above and around stainless-steel appliances. I stood a moment, admiring it. A sliding door by the eating area opened onto a concrete patio edged with a variety of greenery, including herbs and flowers. Someone obviously had a green thumb. A much-used swing set stood in the corner of the large yard, and I imagined Juan's children playing there.

"How many kids do they have?" I asked, curious about the family that meant so much to my sister and her husband.

"Two-plus kids—ages nine and six with another on the way." A pretty flush colored Allison's cheeks. She clasped my hands. "I wasn't going to say anything just yet but I can't wait any longer to tell you. Blake and I are trying for a family."

"Oh, Allie, that's wonderful." I gave her a hug. "With you losing Daisy, I know how much this means to you."

Her eyes glistened. "That's a big part of it. I want to fill that void. Blake feels the same way."

"I hope it happens soon." I threw my arm over her shoulder, and we moved through the dining room and headed up the stairs.

Three bedrooms and two baths filled the second story. I chose to settle my things in the large corner bedroom where I had a nice view of the vineyard.

Allison stood beside me, looking out the window. "Funny, isn't it? I never thought I'd end up here at a winery in California. Lucky for you, it's a quiet time. The crush is over, and we're waiting until we can prune the vines, which Blake tells me will most likely be in early December. If you cut them too early they won't have had enough opportunity to store the carbohydrates necessary to ensure a food supply for the spring."

Impressed, I said, "You sure have learned a lot about this, haven't you?"

Allison laughed. "Just wait. When pruning time comes, we'll have a lot of workers in the fields carefully doing their jobs. One of our tasks will be to make sure the workers are well-fed. And you'll learn a lot more about growing grapes than you ever imagined."

I grinned. "I guess I can be a farmer, even if I can never drink the wine."

Allison handed me the keys to the house. "You sure this is what you want to do? Stay here alone?"

"You need your privacy and I need mine. I haven't been able to sleep well and, this way, I won't disturb you."

Her brow wrinkled with concern. "Are you still having nightmares?"

"Yes." I'd become resigned to working through the terror of them slowly. Time, my therapist had told me, would take care of many things, but it seemed an endless process when, night after night, Anthony stalked me in my dreams.

"Let me help you get settled." Allison helped carry my suitcases upstairs and lifted one of them atop the king-sized bed. Together, we unpacked my suitcases, hanging things in the closet and tucking others into bureau drawers.

She gave me a look of satisfaction. "Okay. Now are you ready to go to Treasures? I want you to see some of our newer items in the gallery so you'll have a good idea of what a sales catalog would look like."

"Sure, let's go." I was more than ready to put my arms around a new project.

Treasures was so much more than an art gallery. I stood inside the cute building and absorbed the colors and shapes of the various arts and high-end crafts that were offered. They were a testament to the idea that things of beauty could be as simple as carved wood or a round pottery bowl. I lingered at one of Dawson Smith's pieces, letting my fingers trail over the brightly colored, uneven glaze on the large vase. Enjoying its beauty, I reminded myself I hadn't called him as I'd promised.

Jessie, Allison's business partner, entered the gallery through the side door. She was a tall, high-energy person with dark hair and brown eyes that snapped with intelligence and warmth. I'd met her on an earlier trip to California and liked her. She came over to me and gave me a hug.

"Hi, Sam! We're so glad you're here." She stepped back, eying the cast on my leg. "I'm so sorry about what happened. Thank God, you weren't killed."

I was tormented by the knowledge I'd been spared. I thought it must be for a reason, the same way I'd been spared in an auto accident of my youth. Now, as then, I wondered why. Had I been given a new mission in life?

Allison interrupted my musing. "Jessie, I've told Sam all about the idea some of our artists have about doing an online catalog. I think with Sam's help, it may work."

Jessie grinned. "Great. I'll take her around and show her what items we want to include in it."

"Okay, see you later." Allison disappeared into her office.

Jessie took me on a little tour, telling me what several items cost, how they were made, and their uniqueness—details I'd need to know for marketing.

"What about supply?" The pain in my leg eased a bit as I was drawn into the project.

"Supply and consistency are problems for some of the items," Jessie admitted. "We'll simply label them 'Limited Supply' or "Each Piece Unique."

"I see. Each contributor will donate its items, no charge to you? Is that right?"

"Yes, they'd be consigned, like we do for some items in the store. However, if an item can be bought elsewhere, it will have a lower rate of return for the artist. They understand how important exclusivity is."

"It's essential to have a clear understanding with each contributor so there are no problems in the future. Have you run numbers yet on the cost of doing this?"

Jessie shook her head. "I'm afraid we simply haven't had the time. Will you do it?"

"Yes," I answered quickly. Aside from the legalities of such a project, I liked to figure out just what profitability was likely for a start-up business. It was something I was good at.

The days passed quickly. Every morning Allison drove me to Treasures, and each afternoon I worked at home on the computer Blake had set up in one of the spare bedrooms in the guest house.

One evening, as I settled down with a cup of coffee after dinner, Dawson called. "'Got your message. Can I take you to dinner tomorrow? There's something I want to talk to you about."

Hearing his voice brought back many happy memories of the time we'd first met, right here at the Silver Goose Winery. Though I wasn't interested in him beyond friendship, I was delighted he'd called. He, like Zach, was a good friend—and a man I could trust.

"I'd love to have dinner with you," I heard myself saying. "Is Liz still staying on the ranch?"

"No, she isn't back from LA, but apparently her surgery went well. That's what she tells me. She'll be back here in a couple of days. I've really missed her." Dawson's voice held a ring of happiness, and I was pleased they were still together.

A moment later, my cell rang again.

"Samantha? It's Zach. Derek called me, angry as hell that he can't get in touch with you. Apparently, he's been trying your number at the condo. He was furious nobody had told him about the shooting. He asked for your cell phone number, but I didn't give it to him. Not after you told me you didn't want to see him again. He left his new cell number with me and wants you to give him a call."

I drew a shaky breath. "Thanks, Zach, but don't bother to give it to me. I'm not calling him."

"Okay, okay. I understand. I'm just doing what Derek asked. The rest is up to you and him."

I hung up the phone, telling myself not to listen to my heart. With Derek back in the country, I already felt as if I were dangling out of control at the end of a string like a worn-out marionette.

I waited anxiously for Dawson to arrive for our dinner date. With a small sense of satisfaction, I checked myself once more in the mirror. I'd lost the hollow look in my cheeks, and healthy color flooded my face. I smoothed my leather skirt, anxious for the day when the cast would be off my leg and I could once more wear slacks. Dawson drove up in his Jaguar. I went out on the small front porch to greet him.

"Hi, there!" He bounded up the porch steps, threw his arms around me and gave me a friendly kiss on the cheek.

I noted the glow in his eyes, the way his mouth curved into a smile so easily- the effect of being with Liz, no doubt. "You look wonderful!"

He grinned. "I think I've found the woman I want to spend the rest of my life with. She just doesn't know it yet."

"She might," I teased. "Liz sounded very happy when I last talked to her."

"Yeah? Well, it might become more difficult. She'll probably have to spend quite a bit of time in Maine if she gets that job you were talking to her about."

I shook my head. "It's not going to happen. Over my protest, the board is selecting someone else. They're supposed to be sending her a letter informing her of their decision. In fact, she may have already received it."

"Oh, that's too bad." He smiled. "Not really, I mean ..."

I laughed and placed a hand on his arm. "I know exactly what you mean. I don't think Liz will be disappointed at all."

He chuckled and held out his arm. "Ready to go?"

We got into his car and headed down the road toward the front entrance of the winery.

Dawson glanced around. "This is quite an operation."

"Blake has done a wonderful job. In addition to the vineyards, he's established the Tasting Barn and the Manor House. When I complete a project at Treasures, I'm going to work at the Tasting Barn, coordinating a promotional program with Sweet Talk."

He turned to me. "So you like California?"

I gave an enthusiastic nod. Away from the pressures of life in Boston, I was happier than I'd been in a long while.

"Do you see much of Allison?"

"Oh, yes." I laughed softly. "In the morning, she walks over to the guest house in her pajamas. We sit under the covers of my bed and sip coffee and reminisce about our childhood. It's nice to have that closeness without being in one another's way."

He turned to me. "I don't have any family to speak of. I'm thinking of reorganizing my charitable trust, establishing a real foundation. Do you have any interest in helping me? I need to be able to have faith in whoever I choose, and there's no one who's more honest than you. Straight Talk was more than just a name for your business. It's the way you are."

I was touched by his compliment and excited by the idea. This would be a way of helping people without becoming too involved in their lives. "I'm definitely interested. Let's talk about it. I could work on it after I'm through helping Allison and Blake with the project I'm doing now."

"Deal. Now let's discuss where you would like to go for dinner. I tried to get into The French Laundry but, as usual, they were booked solid."

"You know what? I'd like something really simple—a salad and a good steak."

Dawson's face lit up. "I've got just the place. Winston's Chop House is a local steakhouse known for its dry-aged, Chicago beef."

"Perfect."

We arrived at a simple, brick building that resembled an old-fashioned storefront. Inside, the ceilings were high. I could hear the strains of a trio playing light jazz from a small balcony overlooking the dining room.

Dawson took my elbow. "This is one of those places all the locals know about and hope not too many visitors find."

We were seated in a red-velvet-covered booth that fit with the 1890s theme of the place. Small electric 'gas lights' gleamed at our table, casting a soft glow. The aroma of grilled meat wafted through the restaurant, enticing my appetite.

After the maitred' left us, Dawson studied the menu and looked over at me. "What would you like?"

"Something simple. A Caesar salad and the petite filet mignon would be perfect for me," I answered without hesitation. My mouth was already watering.

He chuckled. "Sure you don't want anything else?"

I smiled, enjoying myself. It felt so good to spend an evening with this nice man.

Dinner was filled with talk of the business. I took advantage of being with Dawson to test my ideas for the online catalog. Before he'd sold his dot-com business and retired early, he'd been a very successful businessman.

"I think the concept of exclusivity is a valid one. Reward those artists who remain loyal to you." Dawson laid down his fork and studied me a moment. "Speaking of loyalty, I was disturbed by Caitlin's attitude toward you after Anthony's death. I spoke to her about it but got nowhere. Tell me what happened."

The piece of lettuce I'd swallowed stuck in my throat. I felt the blood rush to my face. The memory of Caitlin's accusations still hurt. I fought the emotional surge of disappointment and drew a deep breath.

"Caitlin called me. I'd hoped for a nice talk but she was furious with me. She not only blamed me for Anthony's death, she'd convinced herself that if she'd stayed in Boston, she could have prevented his dying." Reliving the conversation sent waves of regret through me.

"She blamed you?" Dawson let out a grunt of disgust. "That's ludicrous."

"I'm pretty sure she was drunk when she finally called me. I sent her a letter, asking her to give me a call on my cell if she ever wanted to talk again. I haven't heard a word ..." My voice drifted off.

Dawson reached over and patted my hand. "You tried ... we both did ... some people just won't make it. You know that."

I was familiar with stories of people who couldn't or wouldn't kick their habits. But I'd thought I'd been able to reach deep inside Caitlin, to the inner spirit that cried out for change.

"Do ... do you think I interfered too much in her life?" I asked, needing to hear the truth, dreading it.

Dawson shook his head firmly. "Not at all. You gave her an opportunity of a lifetime and almost got killed doing it. End of story. You're a remarkable woman, Samantha. Don't forget it."

I let out the breath I'd been holding. The pain in my leg was nothing compared to the pain that still lingered in my heart.

Later, after Dawson dropped me off at the cottage, I stood on the porch watching, until his car disappeared around a curve. Why, I wondered, did I always seem to end up being just friends with the men who were good for me? Zach and Dawson were both dear to me, but neither one had ever caused the rush of desire that a mere smile from Derek Roberts did.

Staring at my cell phone, I was tempted to get his number and call him. But I knew it would be a mistake. Hearing his voice would send me spiraling downward.

I stood in the kitchen in my robe waiting for Allison to arrive for her usual early day chat over coffee. Checking the clock on the microwave, I frowned. She was late.

A few minutes later, I heard a knock on the door and strolled to answer it, a teasing remark on my tongue. I flung open the door and gaped at the man standing before me, holding a cup of coffee in his broad hands.

"Derek?" I staggered back, so surprised to see him my mind went blank.

"Allison told me to give this to you. She said you were like a cross bear in the morning without it." His smile was entrancing. Even in my befuddled state, I recognized its danger.

"Allison? She knows you're here? She did this?" I vainly attempted to make some sense of the situation. Why would she let him see me when she knew I'd be hurt by it? Or was there more to the story?

Derek walked into the living room, set down the cup of coffee on an end table, and reached for me. "You didn't think I'd forgotten all about you, did you? Let me look at you. They told me you were shot in the leg."

Fighting against the impulse to throw myself into his arms, I stepped away from him and pulled my robe tighter.

"What are you doing here? You're supposed to be in Maine working on the book project—with Alexandra, no doubt." My words were coated with venom as all the anger and frustration I'd felt over the last couple of months snaked through me.

He frowned. "Alexandra? It's her mother on the project, not her. Look, I've been trying to reach you. When I couldn't reach you at the condo, I called Zach. He wouldn't give me your cell number. What's up with that?"

I crossed my arms, still struggling to understand.

"Samantha, please. I'm on my way to Hong Kong, but I had to make sure you're all right. Zach wouldn't tell me anything about it. He said you didn't want to talk to me. I had to work on Marissa to find out where in hell you were. What's going on? Why didn't you want to see me?"

I looked away, full of hurt and curiosity at the same time. Was this the same man who met up with his girlfriend in Paris? That idea didn't ring true. Had Ted been setting me up again?

Turning back to Derek, I forced determination in my voice. "Derek, I'm not the type of woman who has one-night stands and moves on with her life. I would never have spent the night with you unless I felt we'd connected in a way that made me believe we might have some kind of future together. Even as friends we could trust." I drew a shaky breath. "Obviously, I was wrong." I heard the bitterness in my voice, but could do nothing about it. "You keep saying you want to see me, then change your mind and go off on your own. I obviously don't matter to you."

"But that's not true," he protested.

I held up a hand to stop him. "Please. I realize the mistake was mine, not yours. You're a free spirit who roams the world at will. You don't want to be tied down by anything like...like romantic love, not for long, anyway."

His face reddened. He narrowed his eyes. "You've got it all figured out, don't you? Do I even get a chance to say anything?"

I took a deep breath and let it out. "Go ahead. Say whatever you want, but I know this is not going to work."

Derek moved so quickly I bumped up against the living room wall when I stepped away from him. He clasped my face in his hands and kissed me with a barely controlled fury that sent frissons of lust soaring through me.

His lips softened at my response. He groaned as his hard body pushed against the softness of mine. His tongue entered my mouth, caressing me in an exciting pattern all too familiar to me.

With a will of their own, my arms wrapped around his neck, and I drew him closer. It felt like a lifetime ago that we'd spent the weekend together in Maine. I'd hungered for this for so long, it seemed natural to let go and enjoy it.

Derek pulled back, studying me. "I've missed you, Samantha. You can't deny you've missed me, too."

I closed my eyes against tears that threatened to overflow. I couldn't lie to him. I'd missed him more than I thought possible.

"Samantha?"

I looked directly into his golden gaze. My body trembled at the raw desire I saw there.

"Sam, I can't promise I can give you all you want. The thought of being tied down, staying in one place, not knowing what I'd do, scares the shit out of me." With a finger, Derek gently wiped a tear from my cheek. "But I can promise I won't be with another woman."

I straightened, tense all over. "What about Paris? You told me you were going there on business. I found out from Ted Beers you met up with Alexandra there."

He let out a sigh. "Alex insisted on coming to Paris when I told Ted I was going there to meet somebody else on business. She followed, thinking we'd be together again. I told her I'd found someone else, that it was over between us."

"Was it?" I held my breath.

His gaze was steady. "Nothing happened between us. I came home early to surprise you. You know the rest ..."

His lips on mine ended conversation between us. Our bodies spoke the words we couldn't say. All thoughts of propriety left me as he lifted me and carried me up the stairs, cast and all.

Fully clothed, he lay on the bed beside me. Facing me, he gently stroked wayward tendrils of hair away from my face. "I couldn't believe it when I heard you'd been shot. For a minute, I thought you were dead. Thank God, it was just your leg and you're alive. Do you want to talk about it?" His voice, soft with emotion, broke through my normal reticence.

I hesitated, then, told him everything, including all my worries about Straight Talk and Caitlin.

When I was through, the look he gave me was full of admiration. "You're a unique woman, Samantha. Don't let anyone take that away from you. You're strong and full of purpose, always thinking of others. I don't know of any other woman quite like you."

I was silent.

His eyes widened. "You don't believe me, do you? The expression on your face tells me you have no idea how much everyone else admires you."

Hearing his supportive words, I had a fierce need to feel life at its fullest. I rolled over and faced him, then leaned forward and kissed him on the lips, pouring my gratitude into the sweetness of it. "You make me feel so alive," I murmured.

He grinned. "Yeah? You can tell how alive you make me feel."

I smiled. His arousal was obvious.

His face flushed with passion, he drew me closer. "I'll be careful with your leg," he whispered, and opened my robe.

Heat coursed through me as his hands caressed my breasts and moved to the center of me. It wasn't just sex, I thought, as I opened myself up to him. He might not want to admit it, but there was something spiritual about the way he made me feel, as if we'd been searching for one another a long, long time.

He took a moment to remove his clothes and protect himself. Then, with his hands and his lips he made me want him more than anything else in the world.

We rode crest after crest of passion, grasping for every bit of pleasure we could give to one another. I'd never experienced lovemaking like this—even with him—balancing intense, physical passion with such tenderness. I seized that moment in life, knowing it would never happen quite that way again. When we finally lay still, my cheeks were wet with tears.

"I didn't hurt you, did I?" Derek gazed into my eyes with alarm.

I shook my head. "It's just that I feel so grateful to be alive."

"Me, too!" He smiled and traced my lips with a finger.

We lay spooned side by side. Contentment filled me. We'd

shared something almost mystical, and no matter what happened in the future, I would never forget this time together.

CHAPTER SEVENTEEN

The sound of the phone woke me from sleep. I roused and glanced at the clock beside my bed. Noon.

Giving me a sexy look, Derek rose. My lips curved as he turned and walked into the bathroom, every angle of his bare body enticing.

"Sam? It's me," said Allison. "Are you ever going to share the company of that gorgeous hunk who came after you? Will you bring him for dinner tonight? I didn't have nearly enough time alone with him this morning to find out all about him. And I'm sure there's much more I could tell him about you."

I groaned at her teasing tone. "Don't tell me you've already started."

"You don't think I'd pass up a chance like this! No wonder you've been moping around. I would be, too, if I were missing the likes of him. Oh, Sam! He was so serious about wanting to see you when Blake quizzed him this morning. Hearing the two of them, seeing how protective Blake was, I was really touched."

"Blake quizzed him? Why?"

"Marissa warned us Derek was on his way to see you. She gave him *our* phone number, not yours. Blake wasn't going to let him know where you were if it appeared that Derek was out to hurt you."

I watched Derek stroll back into the room like a Greek god and hurried to end the conversation. "Dinner? Yes, we can do that. How about six o'clock?" That would, I realized, give Derek and me the whole afternoon alone.

I hung up the phone and turned to him.

He leaned over and tugged on a lock of my hair. "I love it when you smile at me like that." He chuckled happily. "What's for lunch?"

I laughed and held out my arms to him.

By the time I finally showered, it was late afternoon. In the privacy of my bedroom, I caught sight of my image. There was a glow of happiness about me I couldn't deny. My eyes sparkled and the hint of fun that had always been part of my persona shone through once more. It wasn't as if I'd thrown all my principles to the wind; I'd decided to embrace life with a daring I hadn't shown before. Maybe almost dying gave me this new perspective on life, I thought, feeling a deep contentment within me.

Or maybe it was the intangible feeling I had of knowing that with Derek I realized a sense of self I hadn't known. In the past, I'd strived for acceptance from my father, desperately wanting his approval. I was growing to understand that I had to accept myself first—good and bad. Derek made me see the good and for the first time ever I was truly glad I was a woman.

When I went downstairs, Derek greeted me with a smile. "I took some pictures of the swing set outside. The sun is at the right angle and there is something about it, sitting unused, that caught my eye."

I walked to the kitchen and gazed out. A breeze had picked up, moving the empty swings back and forth as if a ghost or two were pumping away at them, accentuating the sense of their abandonment.

"Sometime, I'd like to see more of your photographs. You have such a good eye for detail."

"I've been asked to do some promo shots for Cathay Pacific. That's why I'm making this trip."

"How long will you be gone?" I asked, trying not to sound as needy as I felt.

Derek shrugged. "It depends on what assignments come up afterward. I promised Ted I'd wrap up the book for Rivers Papers. In my line of work you never know what your schedule will be. In some cases it depends on the weather."

I bobbed my head agreeably, though a sharp pain of disappointment ran through me. If I put too much pressure on Derek, he would feel trapped. But I was already caught in a snare of my own making—loving him, needing him. I'd always vowed to be an independent woman. What had happened to me?

Dinner with Allison and Blake was pleasant. With a mischievous grin, Allison interjected stories of my childhood into Derek's descriptions of his work. Derek's eyes gleamed whenever I protested to her. He now had enough information to tease me for years to come. That is, if he and I were together. I tried not to think about the 'what ifs' and told myself to simply enjoy the moment.

By the time dessert was served, I didn't know whether to hug Allison or hit her. She'd left off no sordid detail of the trouble we'd been in as young girls.

After dinner, Blake rose and turned to Derek. "I've got to check on a party in progress at the Manor Houses. Care to join me?"

Derek smiled. "Sure."

As the two of them headed out together, it felt so good my heart clenched.

After they left, Allison gave me a hug. "Oh, Sam! I can tell Derek really cares for you, but please be careful. He made it very clear his work takes him all over the world, and he loves it that way. He admitted that, after being pushed out of that awful family of his, he's not great about communicating."

"I know. I've fallen for a travelin' man. What can I do? His photographs are famous. It's his life work. Though I can't stand the thought of his leaving, I can't interfere."

"Poor Sam! I just don't want to see you hurt!" Allison gave me a squeeze of encouragement. It did nothing to erase the sadness I felt.

When the men returned, we sat in front of the fire in the living room, sipping coffee, and listening to Blake's explanation of the various seasons in the vineyard.

"We're about to enter another busy season. Pruning the vines is the most labor-intensive period of the vineyard year. As soon as the leaves have dropped off the vines, usually after the first really cold nighttime temperature, we begin." He took a sip of coffee. "Pruning is just as important for wine quality as a careful harvest because it allows us to control the amount of fruit a vine will bear, which affects the intensity of the flavor. The fruit's location on the vine affects its exposure to sun, light, and air, which in turn determines how well it will ripen."

"It's amazing." I was in awe of the whole process.

"And it's a ton of hard work." Allison gave Blake a loving look. "Those vines can be mean to handle. Thank Heaven they don't have thorns."

"I'd like to photograph the workers in the fields sometime," Derek said and gave me a smile.

My heartbeat sped up. Did it mean I was in his future, after all?

Later, when we returned to the cottage, Derek took me in his arms. "I've wanted to do that all evening," he murmured. His lips came down on mine with a gentleness that soothed me. I stored the spicy smell of him, the sweet taste of him, in my memory for the long days ahead when he'd be gone.

The next morning came all too soon. As I watched Derek load his suitcase into his rental car, I felt as if our time together had been little more than a dream.

A sad smile on his face, he approached me on the front porch. "You're sure you understand that I won't see you for a while?"

"I'm sure, but ..." I said softly.

"I've got your cell number on my phone, and I'll call or text as often as I can. I'm scheduled to fly into Boston to finish up in Maine before Christmas. Ted has invited me to his farm in Connecticut for the holidays."

I cringed inside. In my mind, I could see Ted trying to promote a relationship between Alexandra and Derek. No never meant 'no' to Ted.

Derek tilted my chin so I couldn't avoid his eyes. "This has been the best birthday of my life. Thanks."

My jaw dropped. "It was your birthday? Why didn't you say something? We would have celebrated it with cake, and ice cream, and the works!"

Derek shrugged. "I'm not used to that stuff. Guess I've forgotten how that works."

At the injustice of such cruel parents, anger boiled inside me. "Do you mean to tell me your family never celebrates your birthday?"

His eyes turned cloudy. "Not usually. But hey, let's drop it." He cupped my face in his hands, gazing at me with tenderness. "Our time together has been very special, Samantha. You know that, don't you?"

I was afraid to speak for fear I'd burst into tears. He had to be free to go.

His lips lingered on mine, telling me what he couldn't seem to say.

"Good-bye." His voice was husky. "I'll see you sometime. Soon, I hope."

I shut the front and collapsed on the hallway steps, listening to him back the car out of the driveway and drive away. The tears I'd held back, flowed freely now. I wiped at my eyes, knowing that while I had given my whole heart to him, I wasn't sure he'd ever be able to do the same for me.

I heard a knock at the door and Allison popped her head inside. "I saw Derek leave. Are you all right?"

I sniffed and blew my nose, not sure I'd ever be all right again.

Allison handed me a cup of coffee. "C'mon, let's go into the kitchen."

We sat across from one another at the table, sipping our coffee silently. Allison stirred restlessly. I knew how hard it was for her to remain quiet for so long.

"Go ahead, say it. I'm a fool."

"Not necessarily. It's just that some men don't do well being roped in, so to speak. And he's come from a family that hasn't shown him how it can be. Derek is a very strong, independent person who likes his life the way it is. He made that very clear."

I clamped down on the corner of my lip with my teeth. It was too late for me. I'd already fallen for him. Completely.

Allison reached over and patted my hand. "Marissa is worried she did the wrong thing by giving Derek the ability to find you. Did she?"

I shook my head firmly. "No. All in all, I wouldn't have missed our time together for anything. I've changed. After thinking I was going to die during the fight with Anthony, I realize, more than I ever have, how lucky I am to be alive."

Allison gave me a nod of satisfaction. "Good. Let's call Marissa and tell her."

Marissa answered the phone right away as if she'd been waiting for our call.

Soon the three of us were chatting about Derek, the upcoming pruning of the vines and the online catalog. I told myself to relax and enjoy my new life in California, though the little cottage seemed empty without Derek.

I was as busy as I'd ever been as the weeks flew by. Thanksgiving came and went and the pruning started. During this time Derek called to say the project in Hong Kong was taking longer than he'd thought. The Chinese government was now asking to use some of his photographs for a promotional campaign of their own, and he'd be out of cell phone reach. Nothing was mentioned about when we'd see one another again, and I reminded myself that his independence was as important to him as mine was to me.

Allison and I were kept busy overseeing preparation of meals for the workers who dotted the hillsides tediously deciding how many fruit-bearing buds to leave on each vine, balancing the crop load to the vine's age, size, and vigor as had been explained to me.

With the cast on my leg, I wasn't able to move around as easily as I wanted, but I could help in the kitchen. I couldn't begin to guess how many sandwiches or steaming pots of coffee I made.

Most nights, I went home and collapsed into bed too tired to even shower.

Allison kept to her routine of meeting me for a cup of coffee in the morning, though the sky was still dark when she appeared at my door. One morning, she handed me a cup of coffee. "How would you like to be an auntie?"

"You're pregnant?" I threw my arms around her.

Her eyes sparkled. "I'm two weeks late. Blake doesn't even know it yet. I see the doctor next week. When I'm sure everything is all right, I'll tell him."

"Oh, I'm so excited for you! That's wonderful!" I stopped my awkward little dance of excitement, suddenly worried. "Should you be working so hard?"

She waved away my concern. "I've been careful not to do anything out of the ordinary. Don't worry. I want this baby more than anything."

After she left, I headed upstairs. Another long day lay ahead for me.

The phone was ringing when I emerged from the shower. I wrapped a towel around me and rushed to answer it, praying it was Derek.

"Samantha?" My mother's voice greeted me solemnly. "It's your father. He had a stroke last night. Can you come home?"

Unsteady on my feet, I plopped down on the edge of the bed. "Is...is he all right? Will he recover?"

"It's pretty bad. We simply don't know yet..."

My breath left me with a whoosh. My father was such a dominating person, so rigid, so sure of himself. The thought of him being helpless was hard for me to comprehend. "How are you handling it, Mom?"

Silent weeping gave me the answer. I realized how much my strong mother needed me. "I'll pack and be there as soon as I can. Have you told Allison?"

"No, I phoned you first. I'll call Allison, then Hunter."

"I'll let you know when I'm arriving. Maybe Hunter can pick me up in Boston. I'll give him a call when I know my flight schedule."

Funny how fast things can change, I thought, hastily drying myself off. Life was so unpredictable.

###

Allison drove me to the airport. "You understand why I can't go with you? Promise you'll call if I need to be there. Mom told me Father is going to live. She said not to come because it's such a busy time for us. But, Sam, I trust you to let me know if I really should."

"I can't imagine Father letting anything get in his way, including a stroke." My throat grew thick at my first real experience with the frailty of aging parents.

On the flight home, I reminisced about growing up with my Father. I'd worked so hard to please him, to make him see that I was every bit as good as a son might be. But, since the shooting, I felt differently. Having spent time with Derek, delighting in our lovemaking, I'd become much more comfortable with myself . He'd proved I was a woman worthy of love.

Pushing memories aside, I bowed to the wishes of my tired body and settled back against the seat. Eyes closed, I soon fell asleep to the steady hum of the plane's engines.

The sun had already set as the plane descended into Boston. My brother had agreed to meet me in the baggage claim area, and as I entered the noisy, bustling space, I spied his tall figure. A small Japanese woman stood next to him. Kyoko. I studied her. She was lovely, with straight dark hair and lively dark eyes searching the crowd for me.

"Hey, Sam!" Hunter waved me over and gave me a quick hug. "You're looking a lot better than when I last saw you. You remember Kyoko, don't you?"

I smiled. "Yes, though I must admit it's all a bit foggy. I was pretty medicated at the time."

"I'm glad you're much better." She took hold of Hunter's

hand. "I couldn't let Hunter drive by himself. He's been working late shifts at a restaurant in town and I was afraid he'd fall asleep at the wheel."

Hunter gave her a grateful smile. "She drove most of the way so I could rest."

A good team, I thought. Father should be proud of them. Whether he ever would admit it or not was something I couldn't gauge. He'd chosen Bettina and a different life for Hunter.

On the drive north to Maine, I quizzed Hunter on his studies at Statler Hall at Cornell and his life in Ithaca. I'd never seen him happier nor more enthusiastic about life. There'd been a time when I'd thought him shallow and selfish, especially during the months he and my father had battled against Marissa for the family seat on the board of directors of Rivers Papers. That seemed so long ago.

Looking as if she hadn't slept in days, my mother met us at the Maine Medical Center. I put my arms around her and realized how thin she'd become. Or perhaps knowing she might become a widow made her seem so fragile.

"How is he, Mom?"

She let out a long sigh. "They say he's going to live, but he's not the same. He tries to talk clearly and becomes very angry, abusive even, when we can't understand what he's trying to say. The fact that he's even come this far is a good sign. The doctors are pleased."

She turned to Hunter. "Thanks for coming, darling. And...Kyoto is it? It was so nice of you to help my son drive here."

Hunter's eyebrows rose as he struggled to control his temper. "It's Kyoko, Mom. Her name is Kyoko."

She looked at Hunter and then at Kyoko. "I'm so sorry. I'm just not good at remembering names, especially now, with all that's going on."

Kyoko silently placed a hand on Hunter's arm and the angry angles in Hunter's features softened.

"When can we see Father?" I asked.

"The doctors and nurses know you children will want to see him. Until he's stronger, we're only allowed one person at a time in his room and then for just a few minutes every hour. We have to give his body time to heal with plenty of rest."

I turned to my brother. "Hunter, do you mind if I go first? Then if you and Kyoko will stay for a few hours, I can take Mother home for some rest herself. What do you say?"

Hunter looked at Kyoko and said, "We can do that."

My mother's eyes filled. "That would be wonderful! If I could just lie down for a while, it would make all the difference to me. I didn't want to leave your father here alone without any family to watch over him."

"I'll go upstairs to see him. Why don't you get something to eat or drink?"

The expression on my mother's face brightened. "Hot tea would be lovely."

Hunter took her arm and turned back to me. "Meet us in the cafeteria."

In the elevator, I braced myself to see my father as a real person, not the autocratic parent who'd always made me feel inadequate.

I checked into the nursing station. A round-faced nurse smiled cheerfully when I told her who I was. She tilted her head pointedly at the clock on the wall.

"You may go in for just a few minutes. I'm sure he'll be pleased to learn you're here. It's helpful for patients to have their family nearby. His room is right down the hallway, third door on the right."

I made my way down the corridor, trying to be as quiet as

I could, though my walking cast made a distinctive thumping noise on the highly polished, gray-linoleum floor. His door was slightly open. I took a deep breath and pushed it wide.

The man who lay in the bed looked small, not at all like the tall, domineering man who seemed to take control of any space around him. Monitors beeped and lights flashed, reminding me of the toy robot Santa had brought Hunter one year.

I walked over to the bed and stood a moment, studying my father. He was asleep. The right side of his face drooped noticeably, making it appear as if his entire face was made of wax and had mistakenly melted on one side. Saliva dribbled out the corner of his down-curved lip. My father, who was fastidious about so many things, would be unhappy to know that.

I edged around to the other side of the bed and grasped my father's good hand. It, too, seemed much smaller than I remembered.

"Father?" I spoke softly. "It's Samantha. I'm here."

His eyes fluttered, and his left eye focused on me. "Ssss ... sss ... mmmm ..."

Unexpected tears stung my eyes. My father was known as an orator in legal circles, able to soothe and cajole with a silken voice and a smooth tongue. This man struggling to say my name was a pitiful reminder of what could happen to all of us.

"Hunter and I are here to help Mom. Allison will come a little later. Don't worry about a thing. We're here and you're going to be fine." I managed a smile. "Not that any of us believed you wouldn't."

He squeezed my hand.

"I...I love you, Father," I blurted out, unaccustomed to the rarely spoken words. He didn't invite them.

He squeezed my hand once more, a sign of affection that made me want to cuddle up next to him.

A nurse appeared at the door and signaled that my time was up. I bent down and kissed my father's cheeks, stirred by the messages of love that had passed between us.

Downstairs, I walked into the cafeteria, sorting through my emotions.

My mother gave me a quizzical look. "How is he?"

I sat down, feeling drained. "He knew me. He tried to say my name but couldn't. I told him we were here to help you and that he'd be fine." I let out a trembling sigh. "He looked as if he were about to die. Will he, Mom?"

She caught the edge of her lip with her teeth, struggling not to cry. "The doctors are confident he will survive. I just don't know if he'll want to if he's not able to speak well and move about freely. He's always been in such control of himself."

Hunter and I exchanged glances. We knew all about his control over us, but seeing him in this light made me realize how much he'd kept us and others from seeing the person inside. In a way, I suppose, I'd done that, too, until the point in my life when I'd been forced to bare my soul in recovery.

"You ready to go?" my mother asked, and I returned to the present moment.

"Sure. Let's have you get some rest."

We left Hunter and Kyoko sitting in the cafeteria and headed to the parking area to retrieve my mother's car. Walking side by side, I was reminded that, though she seemed fragile, my mother was only in her early sixties.

"What will happen to Father when he's ready to leave the hospital?"

"He'll need to spend some time in rehabilitation, then, he'll come home. We may have to change things around the house to accommodate him, but I'm certain we can do it."

I put my arm around my mother's shoulders. "You really, really love him, don't you?"

She nodded and gave me a sad smile. "It hasn't always been easy, but he's the center of my existence. With you children scattered, we've come to a better understanding of one another."

"Sometime, I hope we can talk."

Her eyes glinted with insight. "It's Derek, isn't it?"

"It is," I replied quietly , wishing the turmoil of emotions concerning Derek would quiet. But then, ours was not a quiet relationship in any aspect.

CHAPTER EIGHTEEN

I drove my mother's Mercedes into the garage of their large Colonial and realized how big and empty it must seem to my mother with us children grown and gone.

As if she'd read my thoughts, she turned to me, a troubled expression on her face. "What am I going to do if your father dies, Samantha? Where would I go? I've lived all my adult life here in this enormous house."

I laid a gentle hand on her shoulder. "Let's take it one day at a time, Mom. That's all we can do for now." The role reversal made me uncomfortable.

She gave me a tremulous smile. "I'm so glad you're here—at least for a while. I know the Christmas holidays might not be the same, but it's important for us to try to go ahead with them. It'll be good for your father."

"And you." I couldn't help smiling. My mother had always loved the holiday time. Each year she worked tirelessly to dress the house for Christmas. I'd do whatever I could to help her.

We hung up our coats, and I hauled my suitcase up to my old room. My mother followed, fussing at me over climbing the stairs in my cast. I turned to her. "I'm going to check for phone messages and then I'll call Allison. Why don't you take a nap?"

"Thanks. I think I will." She went into her room and closed the door.

Disheartened by the changes in both my parents, I called Allison. She cried softly when I relayed the details of my meeting with my father.

"I can't believe it's taken a stroke to mellow him," she said sadly. "You'll keep me informed, won't you? I've scheduled a flight into Maine the day after Christmas unless you tell me to come earlier. Blake and I are having a big celebration for all the vineyard workers and their families on Christmas Eve."

"That sounds good. There's nothing you can do here at this stage. We'll make arrangements to have him speak to you on the phone as soon as he's able—even if you have to do all the talking and he just listens."

"I can't believe he's so bad..." She sniffled into the phone and I understood. We'd never known my father to be so helpless.

After hanging up, I wandered out to the patio in back of the house. A thin layer of snow iced the spidery branches of the pine trees and coated the outlines of the hardwoods among the clusters of trees at the edge of the frost-coated lawn. A red cardinal flitted about—a colorful, cheery symbol of the holidays. My thoughts turned to Derek. Would I see him this Christmas or had our magical trysts in California been just that to him? I hadn't heard from him for a long time but figured he'd be in Maine by now.

I hugged my body against the chilly air and went back inside, determined not to call him. I loved Derek, but I had to be careful. The moment he felt trapped, he'd take off.

Hunter and Kyoko arrived at the house as the afternoon sun was fading. My mother stirred from her chair in the living room and went to greet them.

She hugged my brother and held out a hand to Kyoko. "Let's get you settled upstairs. The guest room is ready."

My brother rolled his eyes at me, but I remained quiet.

Things were still tense in the family over Hunter's decision to abandon the study of law to go into the restaurant arena. Fair or not, my parents tended to blame Kyoko and her family for encouraging him to do it.

Kyoko followed my mother up the stairs, and Hunter trailed me over to the refrigerator. He pinched my cheek playfully. "Packing on a few pounds, Sis?"

I stopped short and gave him a punch on the arm. "I've finally been able to put on the weight I lost after the injury. Believe me, I don't want to lug around any extra pounds. In fact, I can't wait to get rid of this darn cast."

Hunter wrapped his arm around my shoulder. "Just teasing. You look different, somehow. How's Derek? Are you two still seeing one another?"

I shrugged, but could feel my cheeks grow warm at the memory of Derek and me making love. "He calls or texts me once in a while. This fall he visited me in California. That's about it."

"Yeah? I guess he's too busy flying all around the world to settle down."

Hunter's words stung, but I couldn't deny the truth of them. I didn't even know where Derek was.

Dinner was a quiet affair. Each of us kept glancing at the empty chair at the head of the table as if my father would magically appear and dominate the room as usual.

After barely touching the chicken dinner I'd prepared, my mother pushed away from the table. "Hunter? Will you drive me to the hospital? I believe they'll let me in to say goodnight to your father. I can't rest until I'm sure he's settled comfortably for the night."

"No problem." My brother glanced at me. We both knew she wanted time alone with him. I was just as happy to stay at home with Kyoko. After observing Hunter with her, I had the distinct feeling she was going to become my sister-in-law.

My mother and Hunter left, and Kyoko helped me clear the dishes from the table. After setting dishes in the sink, she turned to me.

"So, Samantha, are you also afraid of the relationship between me and Hunter?" Her dark eyes pinned me down, and I realized how threatened she felt in my parents' home.

I drew in a breath of surprise at her boldness and laughed out loud. "No, I see how you are together, how happy Hunter is. I'm glad for you both. My father can appear very forbidding, but sometimes his manner hides a softer side."

"Hunter told me about the difficulties between you and your father, that he won't allow you in the firm." Kyoko's soft voice was full of sympathy.

"He just can't seem to get beyond the idea that I'm not a male and, therefore, not worthy."

Kyoko placed a hand on my shoulder and gave me a hopeful look. "Maybe now that Hunter does not want law, your father will change his mind."

I shook my head. "No. That'll never happen. I'm resigned to it." Eager to change the uncomfortable subject, I said, "Tell me a little about yourself."

She smiled. "I'm the only girl in the family. I have two older brothers. Satoshi is the oldest, and he's in business with my father. Tomi plays the violin and is studying at Julliard. In a way, his love of music helped my father see that I would be needed in the business. Satoshi helped convince him. That's why I'm at Cornell."

"And your mother?"

Sadness swept across Kyoko's face. "She's very old-fashioned and stays to herself. She wasn't happy with the idea of coming to the States as a young bride. It can be difficult."

Understanding, I nodded. Families were never simple.

"My mother was the one who insisted on traditional Japanese names for us children," Kyoko continued. "I don't mind now, but as a young child in school, it bothered me to be so different from some of my classmates. So I made up my own name for myself —Karen."

We looked at one another and smiled. "My father used to call me Sam when I was younger. I liked that name a lot better than Samantha. It made me feel more like a boy. I still prefer it."

We finished doing the dishes in companionable comfort, chatting about the restaurant business and other harmless subjects. A shift had taken place in our acquaintance—we'd taken the first steps toward real friendship.

The next morning I drove my mother to the hospital, eager to see my father. The loving exchange of words and touches between my father and me the day before remained a precious memory. I couldn't help but wonder if he would revert to his old crusty self.

"Your father's career is ended." My mother caught the corner of her lip and stared out the window before turning back to me. "After this, he can never go back to work. Not at his age. That'll be one of the most difficult adjustments for him to make."

"Agreed," I commiserated. "But he's been fortunate. How many men can continue to work into their eighties?"

"True, but I wonder how we'll handle all the changes."

I pulled into the hospital parking lot, stopped the car, and clasped my mother's hand. "We'll take it one day at a time. That's how."

She smiled at me. "You're such a comfort to me. I wish you could stay here forever."

Returning her smile, I refrained from commenting. You can't really go home again. And I didn't want to try.

Father's eyes brightened when I walked into his room. His reaction filled me with joy. I took hold of his good hand and gave it a squeeze. "The nurse told me you had a good night. Mother is going to stay with you this morning. I'll see you again later today."

I bent over and gave him a kiss on the cheek. As I pulled back, I noticed the tears in his eyes and blinked rapidly to hide my own. After years of fighting one another, we were finally softening our stances. Funny how a crisis can do that, I thought, and gazed down at him, lying in bed, helpless as a baby.

I left my parents and drove my mother's car into Boston to meet Zach for lunch. I'd barely talked to him since I'd moved to California and I missed his friendship.

When I hobbled into his office, he greeted me with a bear hug. "Sam! Good to see you!" He held me at arm's length. "I've missed you. Everyone has."

I smiled. "How are things going with you and Eddie?"

He gave me a thumbs-up sign. "We're great! If we could be rid of her mother, we'd be even better. You can't believe all the bullshit I've had to go through over the wedding. Eddie laughs and says it's all part of the game but, jeez..."

I chuckled. "You look too happy for me to feel sorry for you."

He grinned. "Just can't wait for all the brouhaha to be over. C'mon! It's time for lunch. A second Rueben's has opened over on Boylston. Let's hit it."

We entered Rueben's Deli, pushed our way through the noisy crowd lined up at the counter and found seats in a booth.

"Stay here." Zach waved me into a seat. "I'll get our stuff. What do you want?"

"I'll have rare roast beef on rye, with Russian dressing and coleslaw." Rueben's was one of my favorite places. "And don't forget the pickle!"

Zach grinned. "Got it."

I watched him move away, content to be caught up in the excitement of the holiday season in Boston. The air outside was crisp. People bustled about, wearing secret smiles and carrying gaily wrapped packages.

I removed my heavy coat, glanced around the room, and froze. Heart pounding, I inched my way out of the booth toward the red-haired woman sitting at a table in a corner of the room.

"Caitlin! How nice to see you!"

Her face collapsed. She cowered in her seat. "What do you want?"

I swallowed hard. "I came over to say hello and to see how you are." I prayed she would open up to me. I needed her forgiveness. "Are you taking any art classes? You're so good at it ..."

She shoved away from the table so quickly her wooden chair squeaked loudly against the cement floor. Glaring at me, she stood. "Stop it, Samantha! I'll never be able to pick up a paint brush again. How can I, after all that's happened? You, of all people, should know that. It's all *your* fault!"

Giving me a last hate-filled glare, she elbowed her way through the lunch crowd and stomped out of the restaurant.

Mortified by her outburst and the curious stares cast my way, I gripped the edge of her table.

Zach rushed over to me. "Are you all right, Sam?"

Fighting waves of nausea, I shook my head and stumbled back to my seat. It was so unfair of Caitlin to keep blaming me for Anthony's death. He'd wanted to *kill* me! I sunk my face in my hands and drew deep breaths in and out, but the sick feeling inside me wouldn't go away.

In a few minutes, Zach brought our sandwiches to the table. "I'm sorry, Sam. I didn't see Caitlin earlier or I would've intervened." He stared steadily at me. "Don't let her bring you down. You know she's totally irrational about this."

I wanted to dismiss the whole incident, but I couldn't. Never, not even in my wildest dreams, would I have imagined I'd be responsible for someone's death. No matter how murderous his intentions, Anthony Carbone was dead because of me. It was such a heavy burden for me to bear.

Zach patted my hand. "C'mon. Eat up."

Unable to think of food, I merely glanced at my sandwich.

Zach filled me in on some of the work he was doing. And, in an effort to be pleasant, I told him about the online catalog Allison and Jessie wanted to start for their art gallery.

"How's your father?" Zach asked. "You mentioned he's expected to live..."

"Big changes are ahead for my parents. It's unlikely my father will work again. My mother is worried about staying in their home. It's too big for the two of them and won't accommodate Father's disabilities easily."

"Are you going to move back?"

I shook my head. "Today has proved to me all over again that I need more time to heal, far away from here. My sister is flying in after Christmas. We'll make sure they're all right before we return to California."

"How're things with Derek? Still seeing him?"

Gathering my thoughts, I looked away. I couldn't fudge the truth with Zach. He knew me too well.

"So?"

"After he visited me in California, he called and texted a couple of times from China. But I haven't heard from him in some time now. When we're together, it's totally wonderful, but he's been very open about not wanting to be pinned down. After all, he's at the peak of his career."

Zach gave me a steady look. "And?"

"Oh, hell, I might as well tell you. I've fallen for him. Hard. It's stupid, I know, but there it is."

Zach let out a noisy sigh. "I'm sorry I even introduced you to him. He's sometimes a difficult guy to read. You knew that, after his parents divorced, his mother married a real son-of-a-bitch who hated Derek, right? In a way, Derek lost his whole family and even his home in a very short time. I think that's why he travels so much . It gives him an excuse to stay away from the whole mess. How's that for pop psychology?"

I grimaced. "It sounds pretty reasonable to me."

"Look, Samantha, maybe it's better if you just cool it with him. After the whole deal with Anthony, you're very vulnerable."

"Funny, I never knew a guy like you could be so smart." Inside, my heart was breaking. But Zach was right. My encounter with Caitlin had revealed just how defenseless I was against cold reality. I was still feeling queasy.

After lunch, I dropped by Dr. Swenson's office to see if there was any chance they could squeeze me in for an appointment before Christmas. The soft walking cast had, I hoped, done its job and I could be free from it, at last.

I went to the window to check in. When I mentioned my name, the nurse behind the window smiled at me. "Oh, yes, the gunshot wound." She made some notations on a pad. "How's it going?"

"I'm back east for a short time and due to get my cast off. Is there any way Dr. Swenson can do it?"

"He's going to want to see an X-ray of your leg to make sure things have healed well." An assistant handed her my chart. She looked through it. "Why don't I call down to X-ray to see if they can take you? We'll decide from there."

As I was sitting in the waiting room of X-ray, my cell phone rang. I checked the number. Connecticut.

"Samantha?"

Derek's voice sent shivers down my spine. He continued, "When I couldn't reach you, I called Allison. She told me about your father. Guess things are a bit messed up for the holidays, huh?"

"What do you mean?"

"I was going to see if you wanted to come to Riverton for a couple of days..." His voice trailed off.

"Why don't you come to Portland and spend Christmas with me and my family?" I held my breath.

"I guess I could come Christmas Day," said Derek. "My mother and her new family are leaving for a holiday cruise on the 24th."

His words struck me as terribly sad. Zach was right. Derek had lost a lot over the years.

"That would be wonderful," I gushed into the phone. "I've missed you."

"Yeah? Me, too."

A technician stuck her head out the reception door. "Samantha Hartwell?"

"Derek, I've got to go. Call me later, okay?"

"When I can. I'm at Ted's house for a few days."

My euphoria disappeared. What was Ted Beers cooking up now?

After what seemed an eternity, my leg—smelly and hairy—was exposed. I stared at the pink surgical scars on a leg whose muscles had atrophied from lack of use and felt as if it belonged to someone else. The whole leg tingled. But it wasn't

as unsettling as the sensations that crept through my body
when images of that night flashed before me.

"We'll want you to keep your full weight off the leg for a
while until you adjust to it," said Dr. Swenson. "The nurse will
give you some information on exercises you can do at home to
build up strength in that leg. We'll write a prescription for
physical therapy. There must be a place in California you can
use, or you can begin while you're in Maine."

I was disappointed I wouldn't be able to run to Derek like
I'd once fantasized.

CHAPTER NINETEEN

Now that I knew I would see Derek, the holiday season seemed brighter, much more exciting. Between visits to the hospital, I helped my mother dress the house with fresh greens for the mantel, and opened the boxes of Christmas decorations she'd carefully stored over the years. Cradling a ceramic Santa Claus from my childhood, my thoughts turned to Allison. Maybe next year at this time my mother's wishes for a grandchild would finally be realized. I hoped so. Allison had seemed so excited about starting a family.

I was like a child myself, counting the few remaining days until Christmas. Derek planned to arrive mid-morning on Christmas Day. My mother and I planned a brunch in his honor. We pored through recipes, chatting like old times. Hunter and Kyoko would stay for brunch and then travel down to New York to be with her family. With Allison flying in the day after Christmas, my mother was as content as she could be under the circumstances, though the strain of worry about my father continued to take a toll on all of us.

Father continued to make progress each day, but we were fully aware his rehabilitation would be a long process. Final results were still unknown. Each time I saw him, he seemed more alert, more in tune with his surroundings. The usual hard edge to his expression was softened by the slackness of one side of his face. I could almost see the boy he must have been. Rather than my being repulsed by his appearance, his weakness endeared him to me.

Christmas Eve, Hunter and Kyoko offered to cook dinner.

My mother gratefully accepted, saying she was too tired to think of doing it herself. That afternoon, I borrowed her car and went into Portland to try to find the perfect gift for Derek. After searching for some time, I finally decided on a small, digital travel clock that showed various hours in different time zones. Encased in rich burgundy leather, it was made to hold one small photograph. I brought it home and wrapped it, more excited about this gift than all the others I'd bought.

Hunter burst into my room. "C'mon, Sis! Get up!"

I stirred and groaned. Outside, the sky was still gray, waiting for a morning kiss of sunlight.

"Hurry!" He tugged on my blanket like an impatient little boy.

Smiling, I staggered out of bed. Things in this house hadn't changed all that much. Hunter had always been the one who got us moving on Christmas Day.

We gathered in the kitchen, sleepily sipping coffee and juice.

"Okay, everybody, it's time to open gifts." His eyes shining, Hunter set his coffee mug aside, grabbed Kyoko's hand and led her into the living room.

The tree we'd decorated sparkled and glowed in the corner of the room. The fire in the fireplace flickered. Outside, a fresh coating of snow made the whole scenario seem like a painting on a Christmas card.

Amidst a lot of teasing and laughter, we opened our stocking gifts. In our family, they were limited to twenty five dollars per stocking, which meant the key was creativity.

Kyoko pulled a small box out of the toe of her Christmas stocking and shook it. "Another puzzle?"

Hunter shrugged. "Maybe."

She laughed and ripped the paper off. A velvet box lay in her hands. Wide-eyed, she stared at Hunter.

"Open it," he said, and I could read the tension in his face.

She lifted the lid of the box, and we all stared. A round, solitary diamond lay at the end of a white gold chain.

"It's beautiful!" Tears filled Kyoko's eyes. "Is this why you worked so many overtime hours?"

At his nod, she reached out to Hunter, and he drew her into his arms. My mother and I exchanged looks of satisfaction. Kyoko had come into the house a stranger and had made herself a friend. In time, my father would have to let go of his disappointment.

My mother caught me glancing at my watch and put a hand on my shoulder. "He'll be here soon."

Not soon enough for me, I thought, staring at the stalled minutes.

When at last I heard the sound of a car in the driveway, I rushed to the front door and watched Derek emerge from his Jeep. His smile sent a shiver of pleasure through my body. Mindful of the snow and ice, caring little about the chilly air, I hurried toward him,

He wrapped me in his arms. "You'll catch cold out here! C'mon, let's go inside." I heard the happiness in his voice and grinned up at him. With his crooked smile and tawny-colored eyes shining at me, he looked wonderful. Arm in arm, we walked toward my waiting family.

"Merry Christmas, Derek! It's a pleasure to have you here." My mother's formal greeting was in contrast to her warm smile.

Hunter held out his hand. "Good to see you again, Derek."

At my mother's raised eyebrows, I explained, "They met at Marissa's."

Hunter winked at me and drew Kyoko to his side. "And,

Derek, this is Kyoko Matsu."

Derek smiled and shook hands with her. "Kyoko? Love that name. Japan's countryside is one of my favorite places."

Kyoko dark eyes shone with mirth. "I wouldn't know. I've never been there. My family is too busy running restaurants in New York."

"New York? Matsu? Don't tell me your family owns Matsu's!"

She laughed, obviously delighted. "All three of them." She inclined her head toward Hunter. "And he's going to help us run them one day."

The look of pride on Hunter's face gave me goose pimples. He'd found his niche at last. Both my brother and my sister seemed so settled. I stole a glance at Derek and couldn't help wondering about my future.

During brunch, everyone at the dining room table became caught up in Derek's history of his travels. I tried my best to ignore the creases of worry that formed on my mother's brow and the way she kept glancing at me.

When Hunter and Kyoko left the table to go pack for their trip to New York, Derek rose. He smiled at me. "I have a present for you in the car."

My mother pushed back her chair. "I'll do the dishes. You two just enjoy one another."

Derek grinned. "Be right back."

"I'll meet you in the living room. I've got a gift for you, too."

Derek left to go to the car and I gripped my mother's arm. "Isn't he great?"

She hesitated. "He certainly seems nice, dear, but it's obvious his work is very important to him. He loves traveling from place to place. He's made that clear. Be careful, Samantha. I'm not sure he wants what you want."

Disappointed by her reaction, I made my way to the living

room. Derek appeared, carrying a large, flat package. He handed it to me. "Merry Christmas."

I ripped off the paper and studied the framed photograph of the swing set taken from the guest house at Silver Goose Winery. I gasped at the stark beauty of the black and white print, the way Derek had captured the forlorn feeling of emptiness as if the whole yard missed the cries of children playing.

I clutched the picture to my chest. "It's beautiful, Derek."

He leaned over and gave me a tender kiss. "It's a reminder of a wonderful time together."

I looked into his eyes and saw wistfulness there. "Being together was very special for me, too."

As we stared at one another, questions whirled in my mind. *Did he love me? Did he want to spend more time with me? Could I ever compete with his work?*

"So, where's my gift?" Derek's teasing voice broke the silent spell between us.

I handed him the package I'd wrapped so carefully. He grinned, pulled the paper off and caressed the leather case. He opened it, played with the buttons on the clock and slid a finger into the photograph holder. "I know just what picture I'll put in here. Thanks."

He put his arms around me, and I nestled against his chest.

"Do you know what picture I'm talking about?" His voice was soft, tender.

I shook my head and gazed up at him.

"Remember the picture I took of you in the sun at the restaurant where we had lunch? It turned out very well."

Flattered by his sentimental smile, I felt the corners of my lips curve. He did care.

###

Hunter and Kyoko departed for New York. My mother saw them off, and then announced she was leaving for the hospital, to spend the afternoon with my father.

"I'll handle dinner, Mom. Give Father my best." I handed her the container of food we'd set aside for him and followed her into the garage.

"Be careful, Samantha." Giving me a troubled look, she slid into the car and backed out the garage. The overhead door closed with a thud that sounded another warning.

I turned to go back inside. Everyone in my family was worried about me. Why?

Wearing a broad grin, Derek stood at the back door. "Alone at last, are we?"

My heart lurched at the huskiness in his voice. He was as horny as I.

He swept me into his arms and kissed me deeply. His tongue stroked mine until I moaned softly. There was no denying the chemistry between us. We all but sizzled together.

"You taste so good," he murmured. "I'd forgotten just how much. When I'm with you, it all comes back."

Derek's kisses trailed down my neck. I forgot my previous disappointments. As long as Derek kept returning to me, I thought lustily, it would be enough. Wouldn't it?

Derek lifted me up on the kitchen counter so that our height was equal. He lifted my red sweater over my head. His hands circled my breasts, teasing my nipples through the skimpy fabric covering of my bra. "Hm-m-m-m, so nice and full." He bent his head to taste them.

Tingling with sensations that rolled through me in waves of lust, I arched my back. I'd missed him so much.

The jarring ring of the kitchen phone startled me. I shot upright. Cautiously, worried it was more bad news, I lifted the receiver.

"Samantha? It's me. Allison. Blake and I were able to catch an earlier flight out of California. We're driving up from Boston to surprise Father."

Confused, I asked, "Where are you?"

Allison laughed happily. "We passed Portsmouth a while ago. We'll be there in about fifteen minutes."

Frustrated that my time alone with Derek was about to end, I hung up the phone.

He frowned. "What is it?"

I sighed. "Allison and Blake should be here soon. I've got to get things ready for them. Guess we'll have to put ... this ... on hold."

Derek looked as unhappy about it as I felt.

"Sometimes having a close family is a real pain," I grumbled softly, pulling on my sweater and straightening my hair.

Allison and Blake arrived a short time later. She threw her arms around me and smiled at Derek. "Merry Christmas, you two! We thought we'd surprise everyone!"

"That you did, dear sister," I mumbled, glancing at Derek.

Blake shook hands with Derek. "So, how long are you going to stay? Are you going to be here for New Year's Eve?"

My ears perked up. I'd planned a surprise evening in Boston for the two of us, but I hadn't had time to discuss it with Derek.

Derek shook his head. "I'm afraid not. Last summer I made arrangements to meet up with some friends in Rio. It's more or less business. They're clients of mine and I owe them a favor."

I felt the color leave my cheeks. It was no wonder Derek hadn't brought up the subject of the evening on our recent telephone calls. He already had plans—plans that didn't include me. He'd never even given me a thought. Feeling as if

I'd been slapped, I staggered away from the group.

Allison followed me out to the kitchen. "You all right, Sam?"

I couldn't answer. Once again, I'd been foolish. I'd mistaken Derek's interest in spending time with my family at Christmas for something else. "Allie, I just realized a long-term relationship between Derek and me is not going to work."

"You didn't know about Rio?"

"No, he never mentioned it. I'd hoped we'd be together. I even made plans for us for New Year's Eve. I'll have to cancel them."

"So, what are you going to do?"

I drew myself up. No one was going to be allowed to tear me apart, little by little. "Dawson called this morning to wish me a Merry Christmas. He and Liz are having a New Year's Eve party. I think I'll go back to California. Do you mind?"

Allison gave me a quick hug. "I know how hurt you are. Go. Have fun. I'll make sure to follow through on what you and I discussed about finding help for our parents."

The four of us congregated in front of the fire, waiting for my mother to return. Blake and Derek got caught up in a conversation about a new grape varietal Blake was thinking of trying.

Allison tugged on my arm. "Come with me while I unpack, Sam. I can't wait to tell you something."

I followed her up the stairs.

Glum, I sat on the bed while Allison lifted a sweater out of the suitcase. She turned to me, her eyes sparkling.

"I told Blake about the baby. It's for real. It's due in August. We're not saying anything to anyone else until I pass my first trimester. You already knew, so I'm telling you."

I put my arms around her. "I'm so happy for you, Allie. I

really am."

"Me, too. I just hope everything's all right. The doctor told me they'll run all kinds of tests, but I can't help thinking of Daisy. Anything can happen."

I placed a hand on her shoulder. "You'll be fine."

The sound of the garage door had us rushing to the window. Allison grinned. "There's Mom! Remember, don't say a word to her about you know what."

"Don't worry, I won't. Do me a favor. Don't mention that I'm leaving early, not until after Derek is gone. He mentioned my going to Riverton for a couple of days, but I'm not going to do it. Not now."

We descended the stairs together.

My mother greeted Allison and Blake with hugs and kisses. Scanning the four of us gathered around her, a big smile creased her face.

"I'm so glad you're here, all of you. Allison, your father will be so pleased to see you. We'll go visit him after dinner. He's resting now." She let out a sigh. "It's been a difficult day. He tries so hard to be coherent, but getting the words out is a real chore. For a man who's used to being so verbal, it's terribly frustrating."

"Poor Father!" Allison gave my mother a comforting hug. "Poor you! I know what he can be like."

My mother drew a deep breath and stepped back. "Oh, well, we'll just have to deal with it. Let's enjoy the time we have together while we can. I know how precious life can be."

Cocktails were served in the living room. I went into the kitchen to keep busy, away from the drinking. I worked on creating a scalloped potato casserole to accompany the ham my mother had bought. Fresh green beans almandine, along with a spinach and pear salad would complete the meal. Listening to the convivial conversation from a distance, I worked alone.

Derek came into the kitchen and slipped an arm around me. "Need any help?" He leaned down and kissed me.

I closed my eyes, inhaling the spicy scent he wore, locking it into my memory. He would be upset with my decision to break off the relationship, but I had to protect myself.

"You need any help?" Allison came into the kitchen and stopped when she saw us.

"Thanks." I stepped away from Derek. "Help me with the blue-cheese dressing for the salad. We can chat and catch up on all the latest news."

"Uh, oh. Girl talk. See you later." Derek shuffled out of the room.

"What's going on?" Allison whispered.

I shrugged and swallowed hard. Dumping Derek was going to be one of the hardest things I'd ever done, but I knew I was right to do it.

After dinner, my mother, Allison and Blake left for the hospital, leaving Derek and me alone. My nerves tightened. The time had come to settle things.

I stood at the sink rinsing dishes. Derek came up behind me and nuzzled my neck

"What's the matter? You hardly even looked at me throughout dinner. Did I do something wrong?"

I whipped around, as angry as I'd ever been— at myself, at him. "This whole thing between us is wrong, Derek. Did you stop to think that I might want to spend New Year's Eve with you after all we shared in California? I thought you'd want to be with me. But, no, you'd already made plans to go to some far-off place. It's all about you. I'm sorry but I don't fit into that scene. I realize I never will."

Derek's golden eyes flashed. Looking as if I'd kicked him in the groin, he stepped back. "You think you can tell me what to do, where to go, just because we went to bed together?"

I clamped my teeth on my quivering lips. "You make it sound like a one-night stand. It was so much more than that for me."

He rubbed a hand through his dark curls. "That's not what I meant. It didn't come out right. Look, Samantha, why don't I come out to California when I get back from Rio. We'll settle things then."

My breath left me in a gasp. He was still going to Rio?

I shook my head. "No, Derek. Don't bother. It's pointless. You and I are on totally different wavelengths. It's never going to work between us. Your life, your work, doesn't include someone like me."

Derek's eyes widened. I read shock in them. Hurt too. But I knew I was right.

"You're serious?" His lips thinned. "Why don't you say what you mean? I get it. You don't want me around. I'm not stupid enough to stay where I'm not wanted. Been there. Done that. I'm getting my things and leaving now, Sam. Tell your family good-bye." He turned to go and stopped. "On the other hand, I don't care what you tell them as long as they know you broke it off, not me."

He left the room, and I clung to the counter. The room spun around in a sickening dance. I fought to catch a breath between the sobs I couldn't control.

I heard the front door slam and collapsed on the living couch, too shattered to watch Derek drive away. I hadn't wanted to break up with him, but what choice did I have? My wail, a cry that came from deep within me, echoed in the empty house.

When my family returned, Allison took one look at me and hurried over to my side. "What's going on?"

"Where's Derek?" My mother studied my red-rimmed eyes

with concern.

"Gone." I fought fresh tears. "All the things you worried about were true. He doesn't have room for me in the kind of life he leads. It's over between us."

"Oh, Sam," my mother murmured. She sat beside me on the couch and held my hand. "I was so afraid of this happening."

"You weren't the only one." I gave her a steady look. "I'm returning to California a little early. I need to get away and get my life back in order. Do you understand?"

"Allison told me she'd stay here to see that I got the help I need. She said you've already discussed it."

I flashed my sister a look of gratitude.

She smiled. "Blake hasn't spent much time on the east coast. We're going to try to combine being here with a quick tour of Boston."

Maybe having a close family was all right, after all, I admitted to myself as I stumbled up to bed, too emotionally drained to stay awake.

CHAPTER TWENTY

I sat in the car on the way to the airport, more wounded now than when I'd been shot. Fighting the pain in my heart, I knew I'd done the right thing. Glum, I stared out the window. The winter sky was a bright blue, distracting me from the slushy snow piled along the curbs of the streets in gray, forlorn clumps.

Allison and Blake dropped me off at Logan Airport, and I made my way inside, grateful for the chance to return to sunny California and the life I found increasingly comfortable.

In an emotional fog, I emerged from the plane in San Francisco, vowing to be well.

Jessie met me at the baggage claim area of the airport and gave me a big hug. She studied me a moment and, seeing my misery, began to chatter. "I'm so glad to see you. I've got Treasures and Sweet Talk staffed, but even so, someone needs to be around to supervise. With you here, I'll have some time to catch up on other things."

We continued to chat as we waited for my suitcase to arrive on the conveyor belt.

"How's your father?" Jessie's expression softened with emotion. "Allison was so upset when she heard the news."

"He's going to live, though the lives of both my mother and my father will be forever changed." I was overwhelmed by sadness. My siblings and I had been very lucky we hadn't had to deal with the trials of aging parents before now. It made me realize the importance of having one's own family.

Jessie placed a hand on my arm and gave me a worried

look. "Are you all right, Samantha?"

"I'll be fine." I filled with determination. There'd be no more moping over all that had happened to me and mine.

Jessie drove me to Treasures, where I picked up Allison's car. From there, I drove to Silver Goose. I couldn't stop thinking of Derek. We wanted such different things. He wanted freedom, and, though I treasured my independence, I wanted a healthy, steady relationship with a man—something he apparently knew nothing about.

When I pulled into the driveway of the guest house, Blake's black lab, Pepper, greeted me with a welcoming bark. I got out of the car and rubbed her head. This was home—or the closest thing I had to one.

I unpacked and headed to the kitchen, thinking a cup of tea would taste good. While the water heated to a boil, I stood at the sliding glass door and gazed out at the swing set. Derek had captured its emptiness perfectly. I turned away from the scene and poured myself a cup of tea. The hot comforting liquid slid down my throat, and I tried in vain to relax. The trauma of the past weeks slammed into me. I stumbled into the living room and lay down on the couch, grateful Jessie didn't need me until the next day.

Bright sun slanted through the windows. I blinked in confusion. Outside, the chirping of birds trilled musically. I sat up and rubbed my eyes, trying to get my bearings, and realized it was morning. I checked my watch. I'd slept a good twelve hours.

My whole body felt stiff as I rose to my feet and stretched my arms. I had to get ready for work. I staggered upstairs and took a hot shower, reveling in the warm water washing over my skin, forcing me awake.

As I dried myself off, I inspected myself in the mirror and sighed. I'd gained a little weight. It must have been all those Christmas cookies my mother had made. She was a fabulous baker.

Checking the time, I hurried to finish dressing. I'd promised Jessie I'd take over Treasures for the day. Downstairs, the thought of breakfast made me wrinkle my nose. I decided to grab something later.

I'd just reached the interchange of routes 116 and 101 when I realized the nausea I still felt from all the travel was going to erupt. I swerved over to the grassy apron beside the road and got out of the car in time to be sick. Airplane food, I thought with disgust. Even the stuff you had to buy aboard some flights was horrid.

I climbed back into Allison's SUV, hoping the gallery wouldn't be too crowded. I needed some time to recover. Too much had happened to me.

The gallery looked wonderful. It had been packed with merchandise before the holidays and, now, with sales creating more space, it had become easier to showcase specific pieces of art and crafts. Jessie had done a terrific job of rearranging things, I thought, taking a moment to look around.

A customer arrived, and my work day took off.

Liz called me mid-morning from Dawson's ranch. "I heard you were in town. Can you meet me for lunch? I'll drive down to Sweet Talk. We can eat there."

"Sure. Anytime. Margaret will send one of her staff from Sweet Talk over here to watch the gallery." I hung up, pleased to hear from Liz. She'd completed plastic surgery in Los Angeles to remove the scar on her face and I was curious to see the result.

The time sped by. I heard the door chimes tinkle and looked up to see Liz walking toward me, a broad smile on her face. Her dark eyes shone with happiness.

"Oh, Liz," I gushed, beaming at her. "You're beautiful! I mean you always were ... but let me see you!"

She did a pirouette in front of me and, delighted, I clapped my hands. The scar was gone and there was a new confidence about her, attributable in some part, I suspected, to her thriving relationship with Dawson.

She elbowed me playfully. "Let's do lunch."

I nodded, willing my stomach to stop playing tag with the soda and crackers I'd nibbled on earlier. A nagging suspicion rose in my mind, but I brushed it away. Impossible.

Claire, one of the staffers, arrived to watch over the gallery while I took a break. Chatting easily, Liz and I walked out back to Sweet Talk.

Margaret seated us at a table for two by the fireplace in the sunroom. The warmth from the fire felt good on this late December day as I settled in my chair. I glanced around the room, pleased to see the tables almost full. I ordered clear chicken soup, declining the special of the day—a rare roast beef and Boursin cheese wrap.

The food arrived and I stirred my soup, trying to drum up enthusiasm for it.

"You're not hungry?" Liz asked, biting into her sandwich with enthusiasm.

I shook my head. "You know what traveling does to your system. I must have caught something on the plane. It never fails."

She gave my hand a pat. "You do look a little peaked. Dawson has been looking that way, too." Her brow creased into lines of worry. "In fact, I'm very concerned about him. He's seemed so tired, not like himself at all. My son Rick is out here for the Christmas holidays. He and Dawson are having a ball with the horses and playing computer games, but it seems to be taking a toll on Dawson, bless his heart. Rick's own father never had the time for him." Her eyes filled. "Dawson has been just wonderful to both Rick and me. I love him so much."

"Do you think you'll get married?" It would be so nice for both of them.

Liz shrugged. "I thought he was going to give me a ring for Christmas, but it didn't happen. Now, I think it will be New Year's Eve, though, at this point, I don't care. I just want to be with him." A bit of her old sparkle shone through. "Funny thing, when I went back to Maine to pack a few more of my things and to make arrangements for Rick to fly out here, I met with my ex." Her face glowed. "Howard made a pass at me. Can you believe it?"

"Oh, yeah," I said, and we laughed together.

Liz left me at Treasures with my promise to attend the New Year's Eve party she and Dawson were throwing. I was grateful for the invitation, anything to keep busy and take my mind off Derek.

I sorted through contracts with the artists for the online catalog. Steven, our webmaster, was doing a magnificent job of setting up our website with all the variables we wanted. We'd classified the items into categories: Glass, Metals, Jewelry, Fabric, and Paintings. So far, each artist we'd invited to join the project had accepted our offer, with the exception of a metal sculptor who felt he wouldn't be able to meet inventory demand.

Before I closed the gallery for the day, I did a quick survey of the items sold and realized we were almost out of Dawson Smith pieces. I gave him a quick call.

He answered the phone, sounding as if I'd awakened him from a nap.

"You sound sleepy," I teased. "It must be exhausting to

have a full family for the holidays."

"It's been great, really great. I'm glad you called. Remember when I asked you to help me with my charity project? I need to meet with you about it. How about my coming to your house right after the holidays? Maybe on the second of January? Can you do that?"

"Yes, but, won't Rick and Liz still be there?"

"Actually, no. Liz is going back to Maine for a couple of weeks. She had an offer to work on a magazine assignment and I encouraged her to take it."

I frowned. There was something in his voice I couldn't identify. Was he trying to get rid of Liz? Somehow, I wouldn't think so. Yet...

"Liz thinks I'm going to propose, but I can't. Don't say a word to her or anyone else about it. Not until we have everything squared away."

"Oh, but ..." I babbled, hurt for my friend.

"Don't worry. I'll take good care of her; she's given me so much happiness."

Numbed by his words, I hung up the phone. Something wasn't right. This wasn't at all like the Dawson I knew.

New Year's Eve arrived on a blustery day. Though Sweet Talk continued in full swing, we closed the gallery early. The wine and chocolate shop had been booked for the evening by a large group in town. I left for Silver Goose, relieved I wouldn't have to help with the New Year's Eve affair. I was still not feeling well and had decided to see a doctor after the first of the year. I'd heard from a number of people they were recovering from a stubborn stomach bug that wouldn't go away. I wondered if my sad state of mind was prolonging it.

It was dark when I pulled into the driveway at home. A cold

rain fell from the skies. I climbed the porch steps, more than a little depressed with the weather and the way my life was going.

Upstairs, I drew a bath and, hoping to relax the tense muscles in my shoulders, lay back in the warm water to soak.

Fighting hopelessness, I climbed out of the tub and towel-dried my body, trying not to notice the weight I'd put on. It served me right. I'd really pigged out in Maine on all my favorite things, lobster, butter, Mom's baking.

My slacks pinched at the waist, and I became even more disgusted with myself. I fussed with my hair and promised myself I'd try a different style in the New Year. Nothing looked right or felt right.

The phone rang. I set down the brush and answered it.

"Samantha? It's Blake."

"Hi. How are you?" I wondered why he, not Allison, would be calling me from Maine.

"I'm okay, but Allison isn't." His voice caught. "She lost the baby this afternoon. She's in the hospital overnight to make sure everything's okay."

I collapsed on the edge of the bed. "Oh, no! She wanted that baby so badly."

"She's already talking about starting all over again, as soon as possible. You know how she is when she gets an idea in her mind."

"Yes." I blinked back tears. "I'm so sorry, Blake. Will you tell her that?"

"Sure. She wanted me to give you a call to let you know. She's pretty shook-up at the moment but, as she says, you Hartwell women are strong."

I smiled, my heart aching for my sister. I knew how much that baby had meant to Allison. "Tell her I'll call tomorrow."

"Let her call you, Sam. That might be better."

I hung up the phone with a melancholy sigh, relieved the year was almost over. This one had been horrible.

Dawson's ranch was one of those understated, sprawling homes that look unassuming from the outside but, inside, was totally upscale. It reminded me of Blake and Allison's home, though Dawson's house contained a collection of art that most people would be willing to pay to see.

Liz looked right at home as she greeted me at the carved, wooden, double doors off the veranda. She was lovely in silk slacks and a matching emerald-green, wrap blouse that hid a high price tag and showed a hint of cleavage.

"Happy New Year!" I said, trying to get in the mood. "You look so nice, Liz!"

She grinned. "Dawson helped me pick out the outfit for tonight. I swear he gets as much fun out of shopping as I do."

Dawson approached, and I bit back an exclamation of surprise. His face lacked his normal color. Dark smudges stained the skin beneath his eyes.

He gave me a kiss on the cheek. "Samantha, my dear, I'm so glad you're here. There's someone I want you to meet."

Leaving Liz at the door to greet a couple walking toward it, he took my arm. "My lawyer, Reggie Whitfield, is a whiz at setting up and handling trusts and estates. I want to introduce you to him before he's surrounded with divorcees throwing themselves at his feet."

I studied the distinguished, gray-haired man Dawson pointed out. He appeared bored by the blond woman talking to him. At Dawson's approach, he turned to us with a smile that reeked of relief. I couldn't help returning his smile.

Dawson let go of my elbow. "Reggie, this is Samantha Hartwell. I thought it was time she met you. She'll be working with you on my charities."

He took hold of my hand and smiled down at me. "It's a pleasure to meet you, Samantha. Dawson speaks very highly of you. He's assured me of your ability to handle a charitable foundation like the one he's developing."

We chatted for a moment and quickly arranged a meeting after the holidays.

I spent the next hour greeting a number of people, trying to be upbeat, though all I wanted to do was to go home and climb into bed. When I could do so gracefully, I made my exit.

Back home, I undressed and slipped into pajamas, wanting nothing more than to curl up in bed and watch the ringing in of the New Year in the privacy of my own house. I walked into the bathroom to find an aspirin for the headache that hovered behind my eyes. As I opened the medicine cabinet, a box of tampons fell out.

Staring at it, feeling dizzy, I clutched the edge of the sink. I'd come up with every excuse I'd been able to think of, but I couldn't deny it any longer. The nausea, fatigue, enlarged breasts, growing waistline, all meant one thing.

I sat on the edge of the tub, feeling sick to my stomach. No doubt about it, I was pregnant. I knew exactly when it had happened. And I knew very well who the father was.

I staggered into my bedroom, slid under the covers and cried myself to sleep.

CHAPTER TWENTY-ONE

The first day of the New Year turned gray and rainy, a match to my mood, a grim reminder of the unsettled times to come. Fighting nausea, I forced myself to nibble on saltines and sip on ginger ale. I was still rocked by the idea of a baby growing inside me. In these days of birth control and repeated warnings about protection, it seemed foolish for a woman my age to be faced with this predicament. It didn't seem fair that while my sister desperately wanted a child, I didn't. Not like this.

Looking back I admitted to myself that the unbelievable chemistry between Derek and me had wiped out all my good judgment. I couldn't deny it. There'd been one time that wonderful afternoon in California when we hadn't taken the few extra minutes to protect ourselves. We had, instead, thrown ourselves into the passion of the moment. He'd always had that effect on me.

Midday, Jessie called to ask me to join her and Rob and Daisy for dinner. I declined. I wasn't ready to face anyone else yet.

I poured myself a cup of hot tea and wandered over to the sliding door. Outside, the cool wind rocked one of the swings back and forth on the swing set Derek had photographed. The forlorn image made me realize how alone I'd be, raising a child as a single parent. Odd, not long ago I'd abhorred the idea of marriage. Now, I was faced with motherhood and no marriage.

I decided to ask Blake and Allison if they would consider

allowing me to stay on at the vineyard, working for them indefinitely. Theirs was a big enterprise and I felt sure I could be a help to them. Besides, staying here would give me a good hiding place.

Dawson called to confirm our meeting the next day. He explained that Liz and her son had returned to the east coast so her son could get ready for school. Now that he was free, he wanted to see me as soon as possible.

I agreed to meet him at noon the next day.

Restless, I picked up a romance novel and caught up in the story, I wept uncontrollably when the hero walked out on the heroine after a fight. The scene was much too close to home. Blowing my nose on a tissue, I vowed to put order into my life—a life that would not include Derek. *One day at a time*, I told myself. But my mind kept skipping ahead to a bleak future.

Tired to the bone, I climbed the stairs and got ready for bed. Stretched out beneath my soft comforter, I told myself I could do this thing called motherhood. Many women had been in the same situation.

My stomach rebelled.

I jumped out of bed and raced into the bathroom, not as strong as I thought.

Dawson showed up just before noon. He looked no better today than he had two days ago. His coloring was sallow, his cheeks drawn, and, when he greeted me, his voice was hoarse.

I hugged him and drew him inside. "I have a light lunch planned. We can talk while we eat."

"Thanks, but I must warn you, I don't have much of an appetite." He followed me into the kitchen.

"Are you going to tell me what's wrong?"

I became frightened when his eyes filled.

His shoulders drooped. "It's lung cancer. I found out just before Christmas. I haven't been feeling well for some time. That's why I asked you to help me a couple months ago. I didn't know then that it was cancer."

My breath left me in a whoosh of horror. "How bad is it?"

He swallowed hard and fought to gain control of himself. "I've got six months maybe, just maybe. It's spread beyond my lungs. I start chemotherapy tomorrow. That's why I wanted Liz away from here. It's going to be difficult."

My heart went still. "Oh, but Dawson, she, most of all, should be here to help you. She loves you! She told me so."

He shook his head. "I don't want her to see me this way; I want her to remember our good times. The last months with her have been the happiest of my life. That's why this makes it so damn hard."

I wrapped my arms around him. Dawson Smith was one of the nicest, most generous men I'd ever known. Why did it always seem that the good guys got hurt the most? It didn't make sense.

My legs began to wobble as the reality of it hit me. I sank into a chair at the table. "Dawson, I'm so sorry, so very sorry."

"Yeah." He took a seat opposite me. "It's a bitch, but I'm going to fight it. I'm smart enough to know I have to put my things in order, though. I need to be sure my charitable trust is set up and in good hands. That's where you come in, Samantha. I want you to run the trust for me. With your business and legal background, you're perfect, and I trust you implicitly. Your work with Straight Talk was very impressive."

My lips turned down. "I saw Caitlin in Boston. She'll never forgive me for what happened to Anthony."

Dawson reached over and patted my hand. "Liz is going to try to talk to her. Her attitude is ridiculous, but I believe she'll come around in time. She's very immature."

I looked down at our hands bound together. How typical of Dawson to be concerned about others when he faced certain death. I gave his fingers a squeeze.

"What can I do for you, Dawson? I'll do anything to help you."

Silent, he stood, walked over to the sliding door, and looked out. When he turned back to me, his expression was the saddest I'd ever seen.

"Until this news came up, I intended to ask Liz to marry me. I'd like to do something really nice for her and her son. One of the things I plan to do for her is to leave them the use of the ranch for as long as she wants, with enough money to live there comfortably. I'm making those arrangements with Reggie. Should she ever decide to leave, the ranch will go to the trust to be used as you see fit—perhaps as an art school or a children's camp or both." He shook his head regretfully. "I never had children of my own."

My hands crept to my stomach and formed a protective layer over it.

"Over the course of the next few days," Dawson continued, "when I feel up to it, I'll make a list of specific charities I'm interested in supporting and then ask you to research them and come back to me with some ideas of your own. I understand things evolve over time and changes will be made, but the businessman in me wants to have a good idea of where you'll begin."

It wasn't fair! Rising to my feet, I went over to Dawson and clung to him, willing him to be strong, to be magically healthy.

Amidst long sad pauses, the two of us managed to choke down some lunch. I had the strangest feeling destiny had led me to California, to the dear friend who needed my help. I silently vowed to honor his wishes and see that his generosity became a lasting monument to the wonderful man he was.

After Dawson left, I wandered back to the kitchen and sat at the table, still reeling from his news. I caressed my belly, aware of the miracle of life. Having been so heavily acquainted with death in the past year, I was now adamant about having this baby. I'd bring a new being into the world just as Dawson was dying. It was life at its best—and its worst.

I drew a painful breath. The baby and I would survive without Derek. It wouldn't be easy, but we'd make it, just the two of us. I got up from the table and looked out at the swing set. Aware my hormones were going crazy, making me weepy and unsure of myself, I wondered for a moment if I'd been too quick to end it with Derek. Then, in my mind's eye, I envisioned his horrified reaction to the news I was about to bear his child. He'd no doubt offer to help financially. He might even offer to marry me. I shuddered at the thought of entrapping him that way. No, I decided, I didn't even want him to know about the pregnancy. It would be best for everyone that way, including my baby.

Life would go on. I'd be busy the next few months, working for Allison and Blake. The website for Treasures would be launched soon. When I wasn't working on that, my work for Dawson would fill the rest of my time.

Allison called that evening. We cried together as she told me about her miscarriage, and I told her about Dawson.

I took a deep breath, hoping I wasn't being too bold. "Can I stay in this house for the foreseeable future? I have a lot to keep me busy here for some time." I made no mention of the fact that my busy life would include caring for a baby. It was much too soon to tell Allie.

"Oh, Sam, I'd love it! As far as I'm concerned, you can stay there forever. I'll speak to Blake about it and get back to you." She sounded closer to normal. "It's something I've always dreamed of—you and me living near one another, sharing good times."

"And bad times?"

"Yes." Her voice choked. "That, too."

"When are you coming back to California? Are things better with Mom? And Father?"

Allie's voice lifted. "Mother and I interviewed some nurse's aides today. We've found someone who's willing to come to the house on a daily basis. She'll even stay overnight, if necessary. Blake and I will leave at the end of the week. He's anxious to go back to work, and he wants me to have more rest."

"Can I speak to Mom?" I vowed to give nothing away about my situation.

My mother came on the phone, and we chatted for a while. By the time I hung up, I was satisfied she was all right.

The next day, I awoke with a new sense of purpose. I would face my situation head on, do my work for Treasures and Dawson, and build a life for me and my baby.

As soon as I'd settled my stomach, I called Dr. Thomason, an OB-GYN in town, and asked for an appointment.

"Is this for a regular checkup?" the voice asked at the other end of the phone.

I hesitated. No hiding the truth. "I'm pregnant."

"How far along are you?"

"Two months." I knew the exact date and time of conception. I'd replayed it in my mind over and over again.

"You're all set for Friday at two. Come early to fill out the paperwork. See you then."

The phone buzzed in my hand. I set it down, feeling as if I'd been given a major role in a play—and no script.

I gathered my things and left for the gallery. It was time to get busy.

###

Jessie gave me a sorrowful look as I entered the store. "I just got off the phone with Allison. I'm so sorry about the baby."

"Me, too." Afraid I'd blurt out my own news, I hesitated to say more. I wanted the chance to speak to Allison alone before I told anyone else.

Jessie followed me into the office.

"We need to take inventory for the catalog," I said, taking a seat behind my desk. "We also need to make sure the shipping area is ready. I understand Claire is going to be in charge of it."

"She's hired two friends of hers from the community college to help out on a part-time basis. If it becomes really busy, we can hire more people."

As I got to my feet, the room spun in dizzying circles. I gripped the back of my chair, hanging on to it with whitened knuckles.

"Sam? Are you all right?"

I opened my eyes and made a dash for the bathroom. When I emerged a few minutes later, Jessie's gaze narrowed suspiciously.

"I've watched Allie do just that for the past few weeks. You're pregnant, aren't you?"

I staggered to my chair and sat down, drawing deep breaths until I could face her. "Allison doesn't know yet." My mouth turned dry. "She's going to be so upset. She should be having a baby, not me."

Jessie knelt in front of my chair. "Does Derek know?"

I shook my head. "We broke up over Christmas."

Jessie stood and put her arm around me. "It'll all work out, you'll see." But the doubt in her voice told me she wasn't any surer of that than I was.

I gave her a steady look. "I'm going to have this baby and we're going to be fine. After the shooting incident, I'm glad to be adding a life to the world, not taking one away."

Jessie's jaw dropped. "Of course! I never thought of that."

I had thought of it—many times during the last few days. It had become a mantra of sorts each time I wondered how in the world I was going to handle this.

"When is the baby due?" Jessie asked.

"End of July, beginning of August."

Jessie gave me an encouraging smile. "That seems like a nice time to welcome a baby."

I hoped I'd be ready.

After we took inventory of the catalog stock on hand, we sent out emails to the participating artists, asking each of them to give us a time frame on their production. Then we set to work on shipping supplies.

When the work day ended, Jessie and I congratulated one another. Our deadline to debut the website was within reach.

On the drive home, my mind filled with thoughts of raising a baby alone. I'd need to be able to cover the expenses of living at the guest house. I'd receive some kind of stipend from Dawson for handling his estate; he just hadn't told me how much. So far Allison and Blake hadn't made financial arrangements with me. In a sense, I'd been working for room and board, but that couldn't continue for long. I had to become totally independent. Surely, they'd understand.

Liz called as I was pulling into Silver Goose. "Samantha? I'm worried about Dawson. He's not acting like himself. Do you have any idea what might be wrong?"

I hesitated. Dawson hadn't wanted Liz to know about his

cancer, and though I didn't think it was fair of him, I'd promised not to tell her.

Liz broke into my silence. "Do you think I ought to come out there?"

"Yes."

"I knew it. It's something awful. Thank you, Sam. I'll call to let you know when I'm arriving."

"I'll pick you up." I was helpless to do or say any more. I had to reinforce Dawson's trust in me. After all, he was placing millions of dollars in my hands.

My meal consisted of soup broth and a green salad. Too tired even to watch the news, I stumbled into bed. When I thought of what Liz and Dawson were facing, my worries didn't seem so huge.

The phone woke me the next morning.

"Samantha? It's Liz. I'm on an American flight, arriving shortly before noon. Any chance you can pick me up?"

"Sure. I'll be waiting for you in baggage claim." After getting the details, I hung up, wondering what to say to Dawson. He'd have to be warned. That was only fair.

When I called his number, the housekeeper picked up.

"Rosita, I need to speak to Dawson. Is he there?"

"*Si*, just a moment."

"Hello? Samantha?" Dawson's voice was so hoarse, so weak, I gasped.

"Dawson, Liz is on her way here. She suspects something is wrong, but she doesn't know what. I didn't tell her about the cancer, of course, but I promised to pick her up in San Francisco early this afternoon and bring her out to the ranch. She desperately wants to see you."

"Really?" His voice caught and I detected soft sniffling before he spoke again. "I'm so damn sick from the chemotherapy. What will she say when she sees me this way?"

My throat grew thick with unshed tears. "She wants to be with you. She loves you."

"Thanks, Sam. I'll tell Rosita to get Liz's room ready."

I hung up the phone and on an impulse, I called my father's hospital room. He picked up and mumbled something that sounded very much like hello.

"Father? It's Samantha. I just wanted to hear your voice. Are you okay?"

"Betrr. Getting better."

"Good. I won't keep you. Just know that I'm thinking about you."

"Good girr-r-r-l. My girr-r-r-l."

"Bye." I hung up before I started to bawl like a baby. My father had given me compliments before, but not those exact words of acceptance. Life, with its ups and downs, was changing all of us. My body turned cold. What would he say when he found out about the baby?

Looking harried but lovely, Liz walked into the baggage claim area of the airport. I greeted her and she held me in a tight embrace. When she stepped back, her eyes welled with tears. "I realize you can't tell me what the problem is with Dawson, or you would have mentioned it. But I want you to know how much I appreciate your honesty."

I swallowed hard. "Sometimes my straight talk has to be more of a whisper."

She smiled. "I don't know what I would have done without Straight Talk. It provides such a wonderful opportunity for women like me."

I squeezed her hand. "I wish everyone felt that way. Caitlin hasn't forgiven me for becoming involved in her life."

"Oh, I don't know about that." Liz clucked her tongue. "I

had a chance to call her when I was back in Boston. Apparently, she has an aunt in Vermont and she's going to move in with her. Maybe then, away from Boston, she'll be able to reason things out."

Hope spiraled inside me. It would mean so much to me to have closure with her.

Liz placed a hand on my shoulder. "You can't be perfect, Sam. Not when you take so many chances in life, trying to help others. It doesn't work that way."

I squirmed under her steady look.

The drive to Dawson's ranch was mostly quiet. Liz was lost in her own thoughts and I respected her silence. When we finally reached the gate to the ranch, we exchanged long looks. Liz was nervous and so was I. Neither of us had any idea what we'd find when we saw Dawson.

I reached over and gave her hand a squeeze. "He'll be so glad to see you."

Liz's expression remained troubled.

Grassy pastures lined both sides of the long drive to the main house. In one, an Appaloosa and a roan-colored mare lifted their heads from their grazing and stared at us. Puffs of dust billowed behind the car as we drew closer and closer to the main house. Such a beautiful place, I thought and wondered how Liz would feel when she was told it would be her home for as long as she wished. I pulled into the front circle and stopped the car.

Liz turned to me. "You'll come inside, won't you?"

"You're sure?"

"Oh, yes. I don't think I can do this alone." Her lips quivered and then stilled as she gained control of her emotions.

"Okay. Let's go." I opened the trunk of the car and helped carry Liz's luggage up the front steps.

The massive front door swung open. Relief was written on Rosita's brown face at the sight of Liz. She hugged her. "I'm so glad you're here! He needs you. Real bad."

Liz glanced at me and I could read fear in her eyes.

Dreading the scene ahead of us, I gave her an encouraging smile and followed her inside.

Dawson ambled out of the library and stared at us. His eyes blinked rapidly as if he couldn't quite believe we were there.

Liz rushed toward him, and a smile spread across his gaunt face, giving me a momentary image of the skeletal frame beneath it.

Hugging him, Liz burst into sobs that reverberated against the marble floor tiles and echoed from the high ceiling above.

His own eyes filling, Dawson embraced her.

I took Rosita's elbow, and we left the entryway, giving them the privacy they deserved.

In the kitchen, Rosita offered me a cup of hot tea. I gratefully accepted it and the two warm sugar cookies she placed in front of me. My stomach growled. Taking a bite of cookie, I had a strong suspicion this baby was going to be a boy—demanding and big. Aware of the new roundness to my stomach, I smiled at the mental image.

Liz entered the kitchen. Her eyes were red-rimmed, but there was a new look of peace in her expression. "Dawson told me about his cancer." Her voice shook. "We've agreed I'll stay here for the duration. I told him there was no way he was going through this without me."

Satisfaction filled me. "I'm so happy you'll be with him."

Liz gave me a quick hug. "Thanks for everything."

I rose. "Call me if I can do anything. Anything at all."

She nodded solemnly and turned to Rosita. "We're going to

be fine, right?"

Rosita burst into tears.

I left them hugging one another and went to say good-bye to Dawson. He lay on a burgundy leather couch in the family room. I hid a gasp at his frailty. He didn't look anything like the robust man I'd first met over a year ago. He lifted a hand in acknowledgment. "Thanks, Sam. I think you'd better move on doing that research for me. This chemo stuff might kill me before the cancer does."

"I'll get started right away." I gave him a quick kiss on the cheek. "Some days will be better than this, I'm sure."

He took hold of my hand. "Thanks for bringing Liz out here. It means the world to me to have her here."

I gave his fingers a squeeze. "I'm glad."

All the way back to Sarita, the haunted expression on Dawson's face danced before my eyes. More than once, I rubbed my stomach, aware of the miracle that was taking place.

CHAPTER TWENTY-TWO

Sitting in the doctor's office, I felt out of place. Women of varying ages and sizes were reading magazines, leafing through them restlessly, or talking on cell phones. Looking as if she was about to deliver another child any moment, a harried woman was trying to keep an eye on her active toddler. I thought about women's bodies and the changes we all had to go through on a regular basis. No wonder there were so many jokes about PMS and "The Pause". Who could blame us for what we did when hormones went wild?

My own body was feeling very different—heavier, fuller. Or perhaps I was just willing to recognize those differences now that I'd come to a decision to keep the baby and raise it alone.

Marie Rossi, whose husband owned Reggiano's, the Italian restaurant in town that provided Sweet Talk with some of their desserts, entered the waiting room and smiled at me. After checking in at the reception window, she took a seat next to me.

"How are you?" She smiled at me shyly.

I glanced down at her very round stomach. "I'm fine. Is this your first?"

"Sal and I have been trying for some time." She gave me another shy smile. "It's hard with him being in the restaurant business, working so late and all."

"Congratulations."

She waved to someone else and I picked up a worn magazine. Why was it, I wondered, that everyone else seemed to have trouble getting pregnant while one brief episode of being careless had tripped me up? Moments later I entered the doctor's office and sat, waiting nervously for her to appear. A woman close to my mother's age, with short, wavy, gray hair and dark, intelligent eyes bustled through the doorway in a white coat.

"Hello, I'm Dr. Thomason." A bright smile lit her face as she sat in a chair opposite me. "So, Mrs. Hartwell, you're about to embark on a new venture."

_ "It's Miss Hartwell. I'm single. I've never been married." I couldn't stop my cheeks from burning.

She reached over and patted my hand. "I apologize. The receptionist noted it incorrectly. Now, let's talk about you."

We spent twenty minutes going over my family history, my recovery, and my life situation. Blood was drawn and I was shown to the examination room.

Exposed beneath the short, cloth gown that did nothing to hide the changes in my body, I lay atop the hard examination table.

The doctor was matter of fact as she examined me. "Are you sure of your dates?" she asked, removing her rubber gloves.

I sat up and nodded. "Why?"

She shrugged. "I thought you might be off. That's all. Congratulations. Things seem to be going well. See you in four weeks."

I left with a booklet of instructions the office had put together for their newly pregnant patients. As I made my way through the reception area, Maria glanced at the material in my hand and gave me a knowing grin.

I forced a smile, resigned to the fact that my being pregnant was something I couldn't hide. In this small town, everyone would soon know the whole situation.

###

Driving into San Francisco, my feelings were mixed. As much as I was happy to see Allison, I dreaded having to tell her my news. It seemed such a cold slap in the face after what she'd gone through.

I parked the car at the airport and hurried into the baggage claim area just as a fresh stream of noisy passengers emerged.

Allison waved and hurried toward me.

"Welcome home!" I gave her a warm hug.

"How are things?" Blake asked me, clapping a hand on my shoulder. "You checked on the wedding group coming into the Manor House this weekend?"

"It's going to be spectacular." Bright, tropical flowers had been shipped from Hawaii to emphasize the island color scheme of the wedding planner. Set against the elegant formal background of the manor house, it was an unusual contrast of styles that worked.

"And the Tasting Barn?" he asked, all business. "The after-Christmas sale went well?"

I grinned. "I even bought a couple of things myself."

He laughed. "Glad to hear it. I need to talk to you about working at Silver Goose permanently. Allison and I discussed it on the flight out."

"I told him you wanted to stay on at the vineyard." Allison gripped my hand. "He's as pleased as I am. It would really help us out."

I swallowed hard. Would she change her mind when she found out why I wanted to live there?

"You ladies stay here and chat while I get the luggage." Blake left us and I turned to Allison. There was so much I wanted to discuss with her, but I couldn't. The time wasn't right. I searched for something safe to say.

"You look ..."

"You look ..." She glanced at me and we laughed.

"You're looking tired, Allie. We'll have to see that you get lots of rest like Blake wants."

"I was going to say the same about you. Are you all right, Samantha? Is it Dawson?"

"Maybe. It's such a sad situation." I, who was known for straight talk, felt guilty that I wasn't being totally honest with her, but I didn't want to say more. Not yet.

Blake came back to us, wheeling two large suitcases, and, for the moment, I was saved from having to reveal the news.

On the ride home, we discussed my father's health. My parents were going to convert their den into a bedroom for him while he was recovering like they'd done for me.

"Ted Beers called. He wanted to see Father." Allison frowned. "He told Mom it was important. She managed to hold him off, but neither she nor I are convinced he'll honor her wishes."

I pressed my lips together. "I doubt he will. He's a very persistent man."

Allison studied me. "The two of you have always been like oil and water. I don't think he'll ever forgive you for nearly having him kicked off the board of Rivers Papers."

The corners of my lips curved with satisfaction. That showdown was one of my triumphant moments. Still, I knew that Ted was someone to watch. He was always up to no good.

I dropped Allison and Blake off at their place and continued on to the guest house, stopping the car to look at the structure from a different perspective. A new thought made me pause. It might be a good idea to buy the house and upgrade it.

I lay in bed, willing my morning nausea to go away. Half-eaten saltines lay on the nightstand beside a glass of flat ginger ale. They hadn't helped.

At the sound of the doorbell, I reluctantly rose, wrapped a robe around me and went downstairs. I dreaded the conversation with Allison I could no longer put off. I'd practiced it over and over in my mind.

Allison stood on the front porch in her robe, holding a steaming mug of coffee, a broad smile lighting her face.

I opened the door, and she rushed in. "Br-r-r! It's cold out there. I thought you'd be up by now." Her brow wrinkled as she studied me. "What's the matter? Are you sick?"

I sat on the bottom step of the stairway and gazed up at her. All my practiced words fled. "I'm pregnant," I blurted, needing so much to let her know. She was my closest confidante.

"You? Pregnant? How? I mean...Derek?"

A variety of emotions flashed across her features. I waited for anger to settle in.

She lowered herself next to me and shook her head. "You caught me by surprise. It's not April Fool's Day, is it?"

"This is no joke." I burped and covered my mouth.

"Oh, hon. I don't know what to say. What are you going to do about it?"

I gazed steadily at her. "I'm going to have this baby and raise it alone."

She covered her face with her hands. "I wanted my baby so much." Her shaking shoulders tore at my insides.

I put my arm around her. "I'm sorry, Allie. I really am. I wasn't sure I wanted to go through with this pregnancy thing, but after reviewing the past few months, I realize it might help me face what happened in Boston. And maybe it'll help with Dawson's dying. Sort of balance things out."

She turned to me, her cheeks wet.

Sympathy twisted my heart. I patted her on the back.

"The doctor told me I can try again in a couple of months." Allison sniffled softly into the tissue I handed her.

I gave her a teasing poke with my elbow, trying to boost her spirits. "Just think of all the maternity clothes you can borrow from me."

"What are you going to do about Derek? It is Derek, isn't it?"

"Oh, yes, it's him, all right. I don't know how I could have been so stupid. It's just as well it's over between us. He made me crazy."

Allison gave me a sharp look.

"No one better say a word about it to him," I warned her. "It's the worst way to trap a man. It's very clear he's not about to be tied down by anybody. It would ruin everything."

Allison sighed and got to her feet. "Blake is going to Sarita to check out Sweet Talk, and I need to check in with Jessie at Treasures."

My heart fell at the cold resignation in her voice. "Allison? You're not mad at me, are you?"

"Mad? Of course not." She lifted her shoulders in a little shrug. "I just need a little time to myself to become used to the idea."

"Will you come for dinner tonight as we'd agreed? You and Blake?"

Relief wove through me when she nodded.

From a side window, I watched her walk slowly down the road to her house and realized how much I loved her. Her steadfastness as much as anything had helped me cope with Anthony's killing. I couldn't bear it if anything came between us.

The next day, Allison and I had our usual morning coffee together. Things seemed more normal, though we kept the conversation away from my pregnancy, concentrating instead on business.

"Blake and I have discussed it and I'm going to become more involved with The Manor House, here at the winery." Allison beamed at me. "We're busier than we thought we'd be. Blake hopes you'll be willing to oversee the books at both The Manor House and the Tasting Barn."

It would be a good outlet for me. Silver Goose was so much more than a vineyard; it was a fascinating enterprise. "I'd love to take care of it, as long as it doesn't interfere with my work for Dawson. I promised him I'd oversee his charitable funds."

Allison let out a long sigh. "I can't believe that dear, sweet man is dying."

We talked for a while longer and Allison left. I was about to go into the shower when my phone rang. My mother.

"Samantha, your father wants you to help him with something." Her voice held an urgency that caught my attention. "Ted Beers has been trying to get him to sign off on a plan for the condo project they share in Coldstream. You remember him talking about it?"

My lip curled with disdain. "As I recall, Ted wanted to cook up a scheme to enlarge the pond and disturb the marshes without the environmentalists finding out. Honestly, Mom, the man has no principles."

"You may be surprised that your father listened to you. He's leaning toward the idea of making it a very natural setting, a place where nature lovers can retreat either for skiing in the winter or enjoying the woods in the summer."

"Really? Father actually said this?" I couldn't hide my surprise. My father usually regarded my ideas as frivolous or impractical.

"That was the gist of it. Will you talk to Ted for your father?"

My heart raced. This was the first time my father had ever

asked for my professional help. "Of course, I'll do it. But I'm going to need more information. Tell me everything."

Mom filled me in on some of the details.

My mind spun as I hung up. Ted was up to his old games.

I put on my coat and headed up the road into the vineyard. Dr. Thomason had told me how important it was to keep healthy by eating right and exercising.

The vines were still in their dormant stage, row upon row. Blake had told me that activity in the vineyard would remain limited until sometime in March when the bud break would occur and the monitoring of the new buds would begin.

On this gray January day, with a promise of rain scenting the cool breeze, I thought about the forthcoming months. I hadn't talked to Blake about buying the guest house, but at our scheduled meeting tomorrow, I planned to bring it up. Working and living at Silver Goose would be an ideal situation for me.

After I returned from my walk, I sat down and sketched a few ideas for adding a new wing to the house, feeling overwhelmed by all the changes in my life. If, as I believed, one thing led to another with purpose, where was I headed?

I met Blake in his office in the Tasting Barn. He rose when I walked into the room, shook my hand, and offered me a chair, setting the formal tone of the meeting.

"Glad you could make it, Samantha."

I smiled. "Me, too."

He started the meeting off by telling me the structure of his entire operation. His idea of what he was looking for from me was pretty much as Allison had already indicated—someone to oversee the books and financial affairs for both the Manor House and the Tasting Barn and their operations.

Blake cleared his throat. "Essentially, in time, you'd become CFO of the enterprise, with a full-time bookkeeper to assist you, so I'm free to handle the development and distribution of my wine. What do you say, Sam? Is this something you're willing to do?"

"I'd love the job, as long as you allow me flexible hours. There will be times when I'll need to work on Dawson's charities."

"It's a deal." He grinned. "I've put together a financial package for you to look over. Anything else?"

I quickly glanced at the financial figures . "As a matter of fact, there is. What would you say to my buying the guest house and adding on to it? Allison told me you were willing to sell it to Juan, but that he and his wife wanted to move closer to the children's school."

Blake steepled his fingers and gazed at me thoughtfully. "You're willing to pay fair market value?"

"Sure." I'd have to sell my condo in Boston to do it, but it would be worth it.

"Let's have a real estate agent appraise the property and we'll agree on a price. I know how much having you here means to Allison." He smiled. "And to me."

I couldn't hold back my worry. "As I become more and more pregnant, I hope Allie feels the same."

Blake chuckled. "Oh, I don't think that will be a problem. She's determined to try again as soon as possible and you know Allie..."

I burst into laughter. I knew Allie all right. Chances were she'd get pregnant right away.

Excited about my future, I left Blake's office. My life, which had seemed so unanchored, was beginning to take shape. I had an interesting job, two of them, actually, and the chance to have an attractive, safe place to raise my baby.

I returned to the house, intent upon reaching Ted Beers regarding the development in Coldstream. He'd been avoiding my calls. I took a deep breath and lifted the phone, determined to remain implacable against the barrage of justifications for his plans that Ted was sure to hurl at me. Quantity, not quality, was his game.

His secretary answered the phone. "Samantha Hartwell? Hold on, I'll get him. He needs to speak to you."

"Samantha?" His voice was crisp, unfriendly. "Your messages said you were calling about the Coldstream project. I thought one of your father's partners would be calling me. Not you."

I reined in my temper. I'd been as surprised as Ted to be asked to handle this affair for my father, but there was no way I'd ever admit that to him.

Forcing confidence into my voice, I said, "Father asked me to handle this for a very good reason. He's committed to keeping the project environmentally sound. He liked my idea of having it become a natural retreat for nature lovers. It's the right thing to do for many different reasons."

I ignored his grunt of disapproval and continued. "Natural, unspoiled places are becoming impossible to find. Keeping it that way would serve as a good marketing tool. We're talking high-end market, which makes the concept even more attractive."

"Obviously, you know nothing about my detailed plans. Have you gone over the financial projections? I bet you haven't even looked at them."

"They're on their way to me. My mother sent them out yesterday." I wanted to crawl through the line and choke him for talking down to me.

His snort of disgust echoed on the phone line, like a hand to my face. "Well, then," he continued in clipped tones,

"There's no reason to continue this discussion. Furthermore, I won't accept any opinion from you on this matter until you've actually walked the land. When do you plan on returning to Maine?"

"As soon as possible," I snapped, not about to lose this battle with him. "I'll inform your secretary when I'm available for a tour." Hanging up the phone, I sighed. Dealing with Ted was never easy. But I'd do almost anything to prove to my father that I could handle his business for him.

After the call with Ted, I made immediate plans to return to Boston to get my condo ready to sell. An appraisal of the guest house was a technicality I'd deal with later. After doing research of my own, I had a pretty good idea of its value.

As we sipped our morning coffee together, I spoke to Allison about expanding the guest house.

Her eyes lit up. "Great. I've got the perfect contractor to do the addition for you. He's a character, but one of the best in the area, if you don't mind his language and the way he treats us so-called 'little ladies'."

I rolled my eyes. "Can he complete the job in a matter of months? I want everything done before the baby comes."

"Let's call him now. His name is Wayne Jamison. He renovated Sweet Talk."

Allison dialed his number and put him on the speaker phone. "Well, little lady," he said when he heard her name, "what can I do for you?"

"It's my sister Samantha who needs your help." She went on to explain what I was thinking of doing to the house.

"Let me bring our architect over. We'll see what makes sense. The winter months are a good time to carry out a project like this."

After arranging a time for them to come the next day, Allison hung up the phone and gave me a hug. "I'm so excited! You're really going to stay and be part of Silver Goose?"

I nodded and grinned, happy with the whole idea.

Wayne Jamison arrived at my house with a young man named Gary Hanshaw. Gary was a recent grad in architecture who seemed intrigued by the prospect of adding a big addition to a house that was several years old. He walked around with a sketch pad while I told Wayne and him what I had in mind.

Wayne tapped on walls to find studs and went up into the attic to look things over. Gary explained that it was a matter of melding the new with the old so that an unsuspecting person would never guess an addition had been made.

"Will it take a long time?" I asked, fretting over the idea.

"Wayne's the best," Gary smiled. "He brings in the whole crew to do the work so they can get in and out as fast as possible. He makes more money that way."

I waited impatiently for Wayne to return from the attic. He entered the kitchen wearing a grin. "It's a pretty simple matter to tie into the roof line."

"Can we move on this quickly? I'm going to Boston for a week. When I come back, will plans be ready to approve?"

I'd already made up my mind that, if the condo didn't sell right away, I'd take out a construction loan. There could be no delays.

Wayne's eyebrows shot up. He turned to Gary. "Well?"

"We'll make it work, somehow."

Wayne studied me a moment and hitched up his jeans. "Well, little lady, it looks like we can have plans completed and a budget drawn up like you want. Like I told ya, this is a good time for me. Once we're into our summer jobs, there's not a minute to spare."

Later, I met with Allison and gave her the good news. "And when I go back east to work on the condo, I'll meet Ted at Coldstream. He claims I won't get the real picture without a tour of the property."

Allison gave me a worried look. "What if Derek is around?"

My mouth grew dry at the thought.

"Well?"

"There's no reason he should be," I said, shrugging off my concern. "His work for Rivers Papers is over. I imagine he's long gone. Besides, he's not involved with the Coldstream project or Ted would have mentioned it—just to make me miserable, if nothing else."

Nothing could interfere with completing the task for my father.

CHAPTER TWENTY-THREE

I waved good-bye to Allison at the airport. For the first time since coming to the West Coast, I felt like I was leaving home instead of returning to it.

Standing in the security line, I thought of my last conversation with Liz. She'd told me Dawson was failing fast and wasn't sure if he wanted to continue chemotherapy. I ached for them both. I'd promised her that while I was in Boston, I would contact Rosie's Place regarding an endowment for women working in the arts field, much like the arrangement we'd made with Caitlin. She'd also given me Caitlin's phone number, encouraging me to give her a call. Even though I wasn't sure I was ready for that confrontation, I'd tucked it into my purse.

I settled in my seat and picked up a novel. I read only a few pages before my eyes fluttered closed. Morning sickness had eased but I could never seem to get enough sleep. It felt as if my body required all its energy to make this baby, who seemed to be growing awfully fast. Or maybe it was just my surprise every time I looked down at the bulge that rounded under my clothes.

I awoke as we were circling over Boston Harbor before landing at Logan. My seatmate, an older woman, smiled at me when I stretched and yawned.

"When are you due?"

I blinked in surprise. "How ... how did you know?" Was my pregnancy *that* noticeable?

"Five children of my own," she answered with a short

laugh. She gazed at my stomach meaningfully.

I looked down at my midriff with dismay.

"Don't worry, dear." She gave me another smile. "You look healthy. Good luck to you."

In the turmoil of exiting the plane, I lost sight of her, but her words continued to bother me. I'd been so intent on pleasing my father with my business expertise that I hadn't faced the idea of disappointing him or my mother in this way. Now, I knew I couldn't hide my situation any longer.

I took a cab to my condo. Zach had offered to pick me up but I'd declined, wanting to put off a discussion I dreaded. With my being pregnant, there was no way I could be part of his wedding. He might be okay with the idea, but I was sure that Eddie's mother would not. I'd decided to wait for the first trimester to be concluded, then, I'd tell them both.

Climbing out of the cab, I saw my neighbor, Martha Greene, walking Winston, her dachshund. She waved me over. "The manager posted a note in the club room about you selling your unit. I have a friend who plays flute with the Boston Pops. She's looking for a place. Would you consider renting, instead?"

I shook my head. "I'm sorry. I need to sell it." Standing in front of the building where I fought off Anthony Carbone, it all came back. A shudder rolled across my shoulders. The condo would always remind me of that dreadful night.

Martha smiled at me. "Who knows? She may decide to buy, after all. She loves the location."

I told myself not to count on a thing from Martha's friend. It would make things too easy. It would be nice if it happened, but that wasn't the way things usually worked.

Anxious now, I hurried to my condo. Stepping inside, the familiarity of my things comforted me. As I walked through the rooms, I imagined my furniture in the house at Silver

Goose and was pleasantly surprised. Most of it would do very nicely.

A yawn stopped me, and I fought the urge to lie down. I had just a week to get packed up.

I called my mother to let her know I'd arrived safely and confirmed with Ted's office that I'd meet him in Coldstream midweek. Then I called the moving company. They reassured me they'd arrive at the end of the week to pack as we'd agreed earlier.

I worked alone throughout the afternoon, sifting through items I'd saved for years. By nighttime, I was too tired to call any of my friends and crawled into bed. Now that I'd made the decision to leave Boston permanently, I could hardly wait to leave.

Mid-morning the next day, I walked to a Starbucks coffee shop two blocks away for a much-needed break. I'd given up caffeine but still needed a hot decaf brew to jump-start me.

Martha Greene was leaving the shop as I entered.

"I talked to my friend. She's not sure about buying but she'd like to take a look at your condo. Can she come by some evening?"

I hesitated.

"She said to tell you not to worry about being in the middle of packing; she'll understand."

I gave in. "Okay. Just call me first."

As I headed back to the condo, the wind whipped off the water in the harbor, sending blasts of cold air along the narrow street. I huddled inside my winter jacket and realized I wouldn't be able to zip it up for long. I stopped and looked inside a woman's clothing store. A winter sale was going on. Perfect.

Inside the store, I picked through a number of woolen ponchos and sweaters, searching for the right look. A poncho in Hunter green fit me best.

The clerk assessed me. "If you're into that look, we've got a selection of sweaters that are loose fitting. Some of our larger women like them."

My jaw dropped. She thought I was fat—me, who'd always worked hard to remain trim. Not about to tell her the truth, I followed her to an area in the back of the store and flipped through a number of tops that would do a lot to hide my condition.

After purchasing a couple items, I headed back to my condo, feeling blue. My body was changing in a way that made me uncomfortable. Would it ever be the same again? If this was just the beginning, I couldn't imagine what I would look like by the end of my pregnancy. I caressed my stomach.

Marissa called and arranged to meet me for lunch. No stranger to family problems, herself, she'd been a great support to me in the past. I hoped she'd be as supportive of me now.

When the doorbell rang, I hurried to answer it.

Marissa threw her arms around me, then stepped back, a look of surprise crossing her face.

I closed the door as if I could prevent my secret from escaping into the world at large.

"Is ... is everything all right?" said Marissa. "You look ... different. Are you..."

"Yes, I'm pregnant. No one but Allison and Blake knows about it. And that's the way I want to keep it for now."

"Omigod! It's Derek's child?"

I sighed. "I'm afraid so. But I'm not going to tell him; I'm raising this baby alone. Roping Derek into a relationship this way would be the worst mistake I could make."

Marissa caught the corner of her lip between her teeth.

I held up my hand to ward off any discussion. "I've done a

lot of thinking about this. My mind is made up."

She studied me for a moment. "What about your parents? They don't know?"

My heart sank. "It's going to be difficult to tell them. They'll be disappointed, but I can handle it." Caressing my stomach, I gave her a shaky smile. "I want this baby, Marissa."

Marissa hugged me. "I understand. I'll help you and them. They've been good to me and so have you. Are you... are you really okay?"

"I wish things were different, but I'm going to be all right. It's not the worst thing that could happen. Did you know Dawson Smith is dying of cancer?"

Marissa's face froze with shock. "No! Dawson? He seemed like such a nice man when he came to visit, far too young to die."

"It's weird, but in some mystical way, I think this baby is replacing him. I'm sure it's a boy, and I'm going to call him Dawson."

Marissa's eyes watered. "That's so sweet."

"Enough about me. Tell me all about you and Brad. Any more visits to New York?"

Marissa soon had me laughing about life in Barnham, New York, where Brad continued to occasionally practice law with his father.

"Even though it won't be for several months, his Aunt Doris has already picked out her dress to wear to our wedding. She'll act as mother of the bride for me."

I returned her smile, pleased things had worked out so well for her. It was amazing, really, how she'd found our family and was making a good life for herself in New Hope, Maine, dividing time there with visits to Barnham.

After lunch, Marissa came back to the condo and helped me pack up a box of family souvenirs I didn't want the moving company to handle.

"So, what's it like, living so close to Allison?" she asked.

I grinned. "It's wonderful. We've become closer than ever. Blake is happy to have me participate in the business, and it's the perfect solution for me. It's going to be a great place for me to raise my baby."

Marissa sighed. "Sure you don't want to move to New Hope? I miss you and Allie."

"I'll feel safer in California," I said firmly.

Her eyebrows rose. "Safer? You mean away from Derek?"

At the withering look she gave me, I shifted in my chair uncomfortably. Marissa might think it wise to let Derek in on the situation, but I didn't.

She clucked her tongue. "I hope you're not making a mistake. Don't you think he has a right to know?"

"It would make him miserable." After agonizing over it for weeks, I had it all worked out in my mind. He didn't love me. It was that simple, that painful.

I prepared to drive north for my meeting with Ted. Dealing with him in the past had been difficult, and in my present state with hormones going crazy, I felt particularly fragile. To make matters worse, following the meeting I was expected for lunch at my parent's house.

Wishing the cup of decaf coffee I'd gulped down would settle in my stomach, I left Boston as the sun was rising. Snow was still on the ground, making travel conditions less than ideal. A brisk wind gathered puffs of dry snowflakes and blew them across the highway in deceptive sheets of white.

I crossed the state line into New Hampshire and soon entered Maine. Worry about the upcoming meeting with Ted made my head pound. Without my father's approval, his plans to make a killing in real estate would not work. He'd fight dirty if he had to. He knew it. I knew it.

Signs for Riverton appeared alongside the road. I turned off the highway and drove past the apartment complex where Derek had briefly lived. Images of him making love to me hit me like a blow to the body. I sped up.

Coldstream lay to the north of Riverton. Driving into it, I took note of the few businesses and poorly maintained houses. The surrounding woods and fields were beautiful, though, and I knew the tiny forlorn town couldn't avoid development for long. I just hoped it would be done responsibly.

At the crossroads, where the sole gas station and grocery store stood, I turned left, heading west, and traveled down a long, snow-packed, dirt road. Ted's Range Rover was already there. I pulled up beside it.

He was talking on his cell phone inside the car, but he nodded curtly upon seeing me. A good-looking man full of self-confidence, he was not used to defending his actions. He and I had locked horns several times in the past and probably always would.

I got out of the car, grateful I'd worn my warm boots. Wrapping my poncho around me against the cold air, I walked toward the pond, its surface frozen now. A few cattails rose stiffly above the icy coating on the water, reminding me of the marshy quality of this section of land. Tall evergreens edged the rolling fields and seemed to nod greetings as clumps of snow melted in the sun and fell free from their branches.

From the revised drawings my mother had sent me, the scattered buildings envisioned here, with their natural woods and stone accents, would blend in nicely with these native surroundings. Density and preservation of nature were the issues that concerned my father most.

Ted joined me. "You made it in good time. Beautiful here,

isn't it?"

"Though he was disappointed when Rivers Papers didn't buy it, Father has always loved this land."

Ted's lips tightened. "They might have bought it if you and Marissa hadn't interfered." He shrugged his shoulders. "But let's not talk about that. We've got a better, more lucrative plan for the land. Did you like the drawings I sent?"

"My father wants to continue to work with the revised plans he had the architect draw up. He's committed to the idea of keeping the land natural. I understand he's already informed you he doesn't want to enlarge the pond and install a fountain there, that there are too many birds and other species that depend on it being kept the way it is."

Ted glared at me.

Fighting for confidence, I drew a breath. "By limiting the number of units and restricting the buildings to just two floors, he feels the return on investment can be just as good as your idea of packing the place with more and cheaper units."

The muscles in Ted's jaw flexed. "Why is it that every time I come up with a plan, you seem to interfere with it? Your father was perfectly happy with my ideas until you mentioned the nature-preserve crap."

"I'm merely representing him. He's the one who put together the revised plan before he got sick."

"Can't you just stay out of my life?" The venom in Ted's voice shocked me. He clenched his fists, and, aghast, I wondered if he was going to hit me.

My hands held high in front of me, I backed away from him and slipped on the crusty surface of the snow. I landed in a heap on the icy surface. A horrified gasp came out of me. I cradled my stomach, wondering if the baby had been hurt.

"Are you all right?" Looking sheepish, Ted held out a hand to me.

Furious, I ignored his offer of help and scrambled to my feet, still shaken by the fall.

"I came here because you insisted on it, but I'm not staying a minute longer." My voice shook with an outrage I hadn't felt for some time. "What I've seen confirms my support for what my father is trying to do. He's spoken to several people about the type of development he wants. Most agree that to destroy the natural habitats here would be criminal. "

"Your father's a sick, old man who's suddenly got religion. We could have made a ton of money with the project I had in mind," Ted spat out

"My father isn't an easy person to live with, but he's always been straightforward with everyone, including you. He's asked me to represent his interests in this project and I intend to do just that."

I turned and, taking careful steps, made my way back to my car. My body wasn't showing any signs of trouble from the fall, but I wanted to sit for a moment to make sure the baby inside me was all right.

I slid behind the steering wheel of the car and rested my head on it.

Ted tapped on the car window beside me. "Look, I'm sorry. Are you all right?"

I nodded, too upset to say a word.

CHAPTER TWENTY-FOUR

Resolving to be strong, I drove south to Portland. Since he'd become ill, my father and I had made great strides toward a better relationship, and I worried that his criticism would destroy that. I hoped he'd see my viewpoint. For one reason or another, many women today were raising babies alone. I could, too.

I pulled into my parents' driveway and gathered my thoughts before going inside.

My mother greeted me at the door and threw her arms around me. "I'm so glad to see you!"

I hugged her back. Now that I was about to become a mother myself, I had more respect for her than ever.

She pulled away and inspected my face. "You look so much better than when I last saw you—you look rested and, I don't know, well-nourished. From that California sun, no doubt."

"I've been sleeping a lot lately," I admitted, leaving it at that. "You look good, too. Is the new day nurse working out?"

My mother smiled. "Better than we thought. Your father likes her, and it gives me the opportunity to leave the house and continue with my volunteer work." She rolled her eyes. "I'd go crazy without her."

"I know how difficult Father can be."

She laughed. "He's mellowed some, but he's still the same George Hartwell we all know."

"Can we have a private time to talk after lunch, just you and me?"

She frowned. "Is everything all right?"

"Yes and no," I answered truthfully.

She gripped my arm and tugged me to the stairway. "You can't keep me in suspense that long. We'll have our private time right now. I know when something isn't right."

I meekly followed my mother up the stairs, feeling like the recalcitrant teenager I'd once been.

In the master bedroom, I removed my poncho and wordlessly faced my mother.

Her eyes widened as she took in my fullness. "Oh, my word! This is what you wanted to talk to me about?" She sank in the overstuffed chair she normally used for reading and continued to stare at me.

I took her hands in mine. "I found out not long ago. It seems you're about to have a grandchild, after all." My voice quivered with emotion.

"Is it ... is it Derek's?"

"He doesn't know and I'm not telling him. You saw how important his work is to him, how independent he is. Marriage would never work if he felt trapped by me."

She studied me thoughtfully. "When are you due? May? June?"

I shook my head. "At the end of July or beginning of August. The doctor gave me a range of dates, but I know exactly when it happened." Despite my efforts, my eyes filled. "I loved Derek so much."

At my words, she straightened in her chair. "I'll help in any way. Do you want to move back here?"

Gratitude made me smile. "No one can ever really go home again. We all know that. Thanks, but I'm going to stay at Silver Goose. Blake has agreed to let me buy the guest house on the property, and he's asked me to be the CFO for the winery."

My mother clasped her hands. "Oh, my! What did Allison say about your being pregnant?"

"She cried. But you know Allie. I'm betting she's pregnant before I have this baby."

My mother let out a sigh. "It's going to take me a while to get used to all this, Samantha, but I'll support you."

"What will Father say?" My voice sounded hollow to my own ears.

She shook her head. "I'm not sure ..."

Icy tremors ran up my spine. Just when I was gaining his trust, my father would find another reason to be disappointed in me.

"Come." My mother took my hand. "Your father is waiting to see you. He'll want to know all about your meeting with Ted. How did it go?"

"About as well as I expected." Loathing crept into my words at the memory of Ted's anger and my subsequent fall on the ice. For someone as successful in business as Ted, he never seemed satisfied.

Downstairs, I hesitated at the doorway to the den and fluffed my full sweater, wondering what changes I would see in my father's health. He lay propped up in a reclining chair, wearing normal clothes. When he saw me, a crooked smile spread across his face. His right hand lifted in a little wave I found encouraging.

"Hello, Father." I went to his side to give him a kiss. "You're looking better."

"I *am* better," he replied in slurred, but understandable words.

A sturdy, middle-aged nurse stood beside him. "He's doing well, considering his stubbornness."

My mother laughed. "Samantha, this is Eileen McHenry. She and your father are well matched."

I glanced at my father. Though he maintained a stoic expression, a glimmer of a smile lit his eye.

"Too much sympathy never brings results," Eileen said crisply. "Right, George?"

He grunted and waved me closer. "Damn woman doesn't leave me alone. How about getting me a scotch? Make it a double."

I blinked in surprise and glanced at my mother. She shook her head. I'd never heard my father swear like this and he was not a big drinker. But maybe underneath his stuffiness, there lurked a man who might have lived differently.

"Guess we'll have lunch first." I didn't know what else to say.

"Bah! You're all alike," he grumbled. "Where's my son when I need him?"

Hearing his familiar refrain, a flash of hot resentment tore through me. He'd always favored Hunter, his one and only son. I turned to leave with my mother, intent upon helping her prepare lunch.

"Stay here." My father reached for my hand. "Tell 'bout meeting with Ted."

Though his words were a little garbled, the command in his voice brought me to a standstill.

I pulled a chair over to him. "Ted was, of course, unhappy with the revisions you made to the original plans, but I'm hopeful, in time, he'll come around. I'll send him the facts and figures I've drawn up to demonstrate the value in proceeding with your idea. I didn't have the opportunity to tell him about the informal commitments we have from some of your wealthy clients to purchase a number of the units. Don't worry. I'll see that it works out."

"Good job. Should've made you partner."

He reached for my hand again. "Maybe not too late."

My vision blurred. It's what I'd waited to hear all my life. But it *was* too late. My life had taken a turn onto a path I'd never foreseen. I couldn't and wouldn't embarrass him by joining his staid firm in my situation.

The sentimental moment was interrupted when my mother and Eileen returned to the room carrying trays of food, which they set down on the coffee table. I brushed away regret and rose.

In no time, Eileen had my father's soup and sandwich on a rolling tray in front of him. She sat in the chair I'd occupied to help him eat.

My mother patted an empty seat next to her on the couch. "Sit. We can eat right here."

I lowered myself onto the couch, wondering if this was how meals in the house were now shared, so different from their usual lifestyle.

"It appears you have a good routine," I murmured to my mother.

She shrugged. "Progress is slow but steady. At night, we make the effort to dine in the kitchen before Eileen leaves and the night shift comes in."

The sadness in her voice made me realize how difficult my father's illness was for her. Her whole life had changed. Gone were the elegant dinners, the brisk business discussions. I could see how much the talk of my meeting with Ted had taken out of my father. He could barely keep his eyes open.

He was sound asleep by the time we finished our meal. I helped clear the dishes and then sat with my mother in the kitchen, lingering over decaf coffee.

"I wanted to tell Father about the baby, but I couldn't."

My mother patted my hand. "Let me tell him later. He's got a lot on his mind. I'll find the right moment."

My lips quivered. "He wondered if it was too late for me to become a partner in his firm."

My mother's eyes widened, surprised as I'd been by the

suggestion. She gave me an emphatic nod. "No matter what happens in the future, you remember that, in the end, he wanted you there. Okay?"

She didn't have to say it. I'd hold that knowledge close to my heart until my dying day. Too bad I couldn't do anything about it.

Checking my watch, I rose. "I'd better be going." I wrapped my arms around my mother and hugged her tightly. "I love you. Thanks for being so understanding."

"I wish things had turned out differently for you, Samantha, but we'll love this child because I can see that you already do."

I bit back any comment. Of course, I loved this child. It was Derek's and mine.

Back at my condo, I removed a half-full box of packed office items from the top of my desk and sat down to go over the figures for the Coldstream project once more. I'd drawn up a projection of income from sales, taking figures from a feasibility report my father had commissioned, toning them down to what I considered more realistic numbers. I tried not to think of it, but I was forced to face the fact that this would, most likely, be my father's last business deal. It had to be right or my mother would be the one to suffer. The easiest thing to do would be to sell out to Ted, but I knew my father well enough to know he'd never do it, that he considered it a contribution to the future to leave something worthy behind.

After sending off an email to Ted with the new figures, I went to bed, exhausted.

In the morning, I called Margaret. "Time is running out. If your friend wants to see the apartment, I suggest she come sometime today."

Margaret promised to tell her, and I realized that with my departure imminent, I could no longer put off calling Caitlin. I had a number of questions I wanted to ask her regarding the scholarship money Dawson had given her. I hoped her answers would help me prepare an approach to the board of Rosie's Place. I was scheduled to meet with the director the next day. After that, I'd be too involved in my move to do anything else.

My body felt cold as I punched in the numbers to her aunt's residence in Vermont. I drew a deep breath and reminded myself to stay calm.

An unfamiliar voice answered.

"Is Caitlin Rafferty there?"

"Caitlin? Hold on."

"Yeah?" Caitlin's voice sent a flood of memories through my mind—her excitement at the idea of going to the Art Institute, the shy way she'd smiled at Dawson when they first met, her beaten and bruised face when she'd come to me for help.

"Caitlin, it's me. Samantha. I need you to answer some questions, for Dawson, really." My voice broke. "He's dying, Caitlin, and I'm going to be taking over his charitable work."

After a moment of silence, Caitlin whispered, "Dawson? Dying? Omigod!"

I gave her a few moments to pull herself together, and continued. "He has lung cancer. Liz is with him now. She'll stay with him until ... until the end."

"But he's much too young," she protested. "And way too nice. What do you want to know?"

I pulled out the sheet of questions I'd compiled earlier and we went through them one by one, discussing what steps had been most helpful to her.

Perhaps the shock of knowing Dawson was dying, or

remembering how much had been given to her, Caitlin's voice warmed as we talked.

When we completed the questions and answers, I hesitated. "Caitlin, I'm sorry about Anthony. I really am." I waited, needing to hear some words or at least tones of forgiveness in her voice. I'd killed the man she'd loved.

I spoke once again into the silence. "Will you ... can you ... forgive me?"

"Samantha, it wasn't your fault. I know that now." Caitlin's voice, soft and kind, surprised me. "I'm back in the program and I know what a complete ass he was. I blamed you for everything because I didn't want to blame myself."

"You're back in the program?" Relief, warm and sweet, pulsed through me. Caitlin would be all right, and I could let go of this agonizing worry.

"Once I got away from the old friends in Southie who dragged me down, I wanted help. I hated facing myself every morning, knowing what I was doing to myself."

"I'm so glad."

"Please tell Dawson how much he helped to change my life. Because he was willing to give me money to go to school, I started to believe I had talent."

"Your work *is* good, Caitlin. If you want to try to go back to school again, you can apply for another scholarship through the foundation. I'm sure Dawson would be pleased."

"Who knows? Maybe I will." I heard a new note of optimism in her voice. It made me smile. I'd been forgiven by her at last.

CHAPTER TWENTY-FIVE

I was putting the final few things in the last box of give-away items when the doorbell rang. I frowned. Margaret had promised to call before bringing her friend over. I wiped my hands on my jeans and went to open the door, hoping they wouldn't mind the stack of boxes in my office.

I flung open the door and staggered back.

Derek stood there, a smile on his face.

A streak of fire flamed through my body, melting me at the sight of him. I was so shocked I couldn't find any words. I fought to keep my hands from traveling to my belly.

He was as handsome as ever. His black hair curled at the nape of his neck as if he'd just come back from a long trip and hadn't had time to go to a barber. His golden eyes held my gaze, piercing the mental armor I fought to keep in place.

"What? You weren't expecting me? Didn't you get my message?"

"There wasn't any message." My heart beat so fast I felt light-headed.

"I left one on your phone in California, telling you I'd stop by on my way to Alaska and asking you to give me a call. Guess you don't check messages when you're away." He gave me a grin. "When I didn't hear from you, I called Marissa. She told me you were here. Going to invite me in?"

I shook my head. "I don't think it's a good idea."

His eyebrows lifted. "You still mad because I went to Rio for New Year's Eve?"

"It's so much more than that, Derek." I cleared my throat.

"So where are you off to now? You just returned from a trip?"

He smiled. "I stayed in Rio longer than I thought and then went to Chile. I wanted you to go to Rio with me. But you didn't give me a chance to ask you. I think you would have liked it. And yes, I've got another assignment. Sunday, I leave for Anchorage." His eyes searched mine. "Have you missed me?"

I clamped my teeth together to keep from saying yes. I had missed him, body and soul. I'd needed him, too. But his words, his actions, told me he was not ready to settle down, that he would resent both the baby and me if we tied him down. Inside, my heart felt as if it were slowly disintegrating.

Derek reached over and stroked my cheek. "Don't look so sad. I'll be back."

I swallowed the huge lump in my throat. "No, Derek, don't come back to me. It's over between us. It's for the best. For all concerned."

The features of his face fell.

Before I could say the words I really wanted, before I could beg him to change his ways, before I could throw myself in his arms, I closed the door with a click that broke my heart.

My knees felt rubbery as I leaned against the door, listening for any sounds. Silence pulsed in my ears and then I heard his footsteps fade away.

I sank to the floor, hurting so badly I couldn't move. I'd done the right thing. Hadn't I?

Images of Derek taunted me throughout the night. Remembering the way he'd smiled at me, the touch of his broad hand on my cheek, the sound of his voice, I tossed and turned. If only things were different, I told myself over and over again. I wished I'd never met him. No one else would ever be able to make me feel like I did in his arms.

After little sleep, I awoke with a pounding headache. This would be my last full day in Boston, and I was glad. There was a part of me that wanted to find Derek and tell him my decision had been some awful mistake. But I knew I'd done the best thing for me and my baby.

I forced myself out of bed. Seeing Derek had filled me with a desperate need to escape. The packers from the moving company were scheduled to arrive by eight, and I wanted to be ready for them.

The packers worked hard, putting my belongings in boxes, wrapping furniture in plastic, changing my condo from a home to a shell as empty as my heart.

I thought about meeting Zach for dinner and put off calling him, too depressed even to share my woeful tale with him. All I wanted to do was return to my hiding place among grapevines.

Allison greeted me in San Francisco. I drew a deep breath as she hugged me. I'd done it. I'd made the move to the west coast where I could have an isolated life, raising my baby, working and living at Silver Goose.

"Are you all right?" Allison asked, helping me with my luggage. "You looked so unhappy for a moment."

I brushed away the regret that had momentarily washed over me and took her arm. "Let's go. I'm fine. It'll be wonderful to settle in and get started on my work. How's the online catalog doing?"

Allison's lips curved happily. "Better than we thought. It's going to be a problem keeping up with supply, though. I guess it's one of those 'be careful what you wish for' kind of things. Claire is going crazy. In fact, we all have to help her."

My spirits lifted. Something was going right, and I'd helped to make it happen.

Back at the vineyard, I walked throughout the house, envisioning the changes that were about to take place.

Wayne Jamison and Gary Hanshaw met with me later that day to discuss the plans they'd drawn up for the addition. They'd made considerable changes to the simple design I'd sketched, and I was thrilled with each little detail. If I used the new schematics, it would double the size of the house.

Later, after dinner at Allison's, I pulled out the drawings Gary had done.

"Oh, Sam. It'll be lovely," said Allison with enthusiasm.

"Makes all the sense in the world," agreed Blake. "If the time ever comes that you want to sell, we can use the house for a small inn."

Looking over the plans with them, I could hardly believe all the changes happening to me. The new addition would add a master suite, an office, another full bath, a playroom, and an open, two-story, family room between the newly renovated kitchen and the new wing. A catwalk would connect the old and new upper floors at the second story level.

The renovation of the house was a large undertaking, but I could manage it. My condo in Boston was commanding a larger price than I'd thought possible, and Martha's friend was still interested. The old adage of location, location, location, I supposed. With everything going so right, I couldn't help wondering when it would all collapse.

My work on the Silver Goose financials began in earnest. I met with Andrew Stevens, Blake's CPA, to discuss monitoring of income for tax issues. We agreed Silver Goose should consolidate a couple of loans and refinance the mortgage on the Tasting Barn while the rates were low. I offered to do a study of cash flow trends so that a different payment schedule could be implemented. With the seasonal nature of the business, it was difficult to maintain an even stream of income.

My head was still spinning with numbers a few days later as I drove out to Dawson's ranch. Liz had kept me informed of his condition, but I wanted to see him for myself. I knew things were not good.

Smiling shakily, Liz greeted me at the door. I recalled how beautiful she'd looked on New Year's Eve, and it seemed like years, not months since then. So much had happened to us all.

Liz gave me a hug and stepped back. "Wow! You really are pregnant. It looks like it's going to be a big baby. Are you sure of the date?"

I laughed. "I've been counting and I know I'm right. It's the end of July or beginning of August. I hope after it happens, I can lose all the weight." My mood sobered. "Where's Dawson? How is he?"

"He's in the sunroom by the kitchen." Her voice cracked. "He's going downhill in a hurry. I think after fighting the idea before Christmas, he's more or less given up."

I braced myself for the worst, but still couldn't hold back a gasp when I followed Liz into the room. Dawson's head was pink and bald, almost shiny without any of his gray curls. He'd always had a fine, muscular shape to him. Now, in his diminished state, he looked like a small version of his former self. I wanted to cry.

I forced cheer into my voice. "Hey, there!"

He turned and smiled at me. His gaze rested on my stomach. He'd already heard the news. "Well, mother-to-be, you're looking healthy!"

"It's going to be a big baby. A boy, I'm sure." I leaned over and gave him a kiss, then pulled a chair up beside him. Taking his hand in mine, I smiled. "I'm going to name him Dawson. For you."

Dawson's eyes watered. He coughed to hide a sob.

I waited while he gained control.

He shrugged apologetically. "I've become such a damn crybaby. It must be the medicine."

But I knew it was more than that, and by the tearful expression on Liz's face, she did too.

"You got my report on Rosie's Place?"

Liz sat down on the other side of Dawson and held his hand. "We have it, but first, tell us about your conversation with Caitlin. I'm so glad the two of you were able to resolve things."

I told them how Dawson's belief in her had encouraged Caitlin to believe in herself. "That's the kind of thing I envision doing for others," I added, 'whether it's in Boston or here in California."

"Straight Talk did that for me. You know, Samantha, working with Dawson's foundation is like continuing Straight Talk, in a way."

My whole body softened. It had meant so much to me to be able to use my education toward helping women in business. Life had made major twists and turns along the way, but after all the help I'd received in putting my life back together, I'd always try to do the same for others.

We talked about some of the other projects Dawson was interested in pursuing. With Blake and a few others, he'd set up a scholarship for high-school art students in the name of the late Kristin Lewis, Allison's ex-college roommate and former owner of Treasures. She'd be pleased for the scholarship to continue in perpetuity, as Dawson planned.

Dawson's voice grew weaker. Mindful of his fatigue, I

checked my watch. "I'd better be going. I have a doctor's appointment."

I leaned over and gave Dawson a kiss on the cheek. Noting its hollowness, my heart twisted.

Liz walked me to the front door. "Thanks for coming. It means so much to him to see you. Discussing his foundation with you makes him come alive."

"I'm compiling a list of charities with specific ideas for them."

"Wonderful." Liz gazed at my stomach and smiled. "Good luck with the doctor."

My grin was sheepish. "She's going to be angry. I've gained fourteen pounds already."

Liz laughed. "I remember that part of it all too well."

I left Dawson's ranch with a mixture of feelings. He'd looked so frail, yet his spirit was still strong his mind alert. Even so, it gave me relief to escape the atmosphere of impending death and think of new life with my baby.

Dr. Thomason's waiting room was full when I arrived. I looked around for a place to sit. Marie Rossi caught my eye and pointed to the chair next to her. I smiled and went over to her.

"How are you?"

She smiled. "Okay. My due date is almost here."

The nurse called my name, and I followed her into what she light-heartedly called the "doom room", where a large scale dominated one wall.

At her direction, I hesitated and stepped onto the scale. "I've tried to be careful about what I ate," I murmured, though I suspected a lecture from the doctor.

The nurse wrote down my weight in my chart and took a

moment to read through it. "We'll see what Dr. Thomason has to say." She winked at me, and I smiled, though it did nothing to alleviate my uneasiness as I settled in the examination room.

Dr. Thomason walked into the room a few moments later. "Well, well, Samantha Hartwell. Let's see what we've got here."

I lay back on the table while she gently probed my belly and then took out a measuring device. "You say the baby is due at the end of July or beginning of August?"

"I know exactly when I conceived. It's impossible for it to be otherwise."

She lifted her stethoscope. "Let's take a listen."

I lay quietly, watching her face. Was something wrong with the baby? I could hardly swallow.

A smile spread across Dr. Thomason's face. Her dark eyes danced. "I hear heartbeats."

"Good." I let out a sigh of relief.

"Not one, but two."

It took a moment for Dr. Thomason's words to sink in. I rose to my elbows. "Two? What do you mean?"

"Twins." She laughed gently at my shock. "We'll do an ultrasound, but I'm certain. As a matter of fact, I suspected you might be carrying twins at your last appointment, but it was too early to say anything."

My jaw dropped. Twins? How was I going to deal with twins when I could barely wrap my mind around taking care of one baby?

Dr. Thomason patted me on the back. "Don't worry. You're healthy. You'll do just fine."

Throughout the rest of the appointment, I was in a daze. No wonder people had kept asking me if I was sure of my dates. Good Lord! Twins! I hadn't wanted one baby. Now I'd have two to raise. Alone.

I left the doctor's office and went directly to Treasures. Allison looked up when I walked into the gallery office. "What's the matter? Is everything okay?"

My face crumpled. "I can't do it. I can't." Everything seemed to tumble down on top of me at once—helping with the catalog; handling the finances at Silver Goose; overseeing construction on my new house; Dawson's charity; helping with my father's project; and now, having twins.

Her face white, Allison rushed over to me. "Is it... is it the baby?"

I shook my head. "Babies."

She gave me a puzzled look. "Babies? What are you talking about?"

I sniffed loudly. "Twins. I'm having twins."

Her expression went from worried to incredulous. "Twins? Omigod! Really?" She started to laugh. "Twins? But that's wonderful!"

I shook my head. "It's twice the trouble. How am I going to do it?"

She put her arms around me. "I'll help you. We all will."

I didn't know whether to laugh or cry as Allison clapped her hands gleefully. "Wait 'til I tell Blake!" She lifted her phone to call him.

I took a seat in her office, too overcome with conflicting emotions to do anything but cry. My hormones were performing a fast dance I couldn't keep up with, and beneath the hormonal tears lay fear.

And heartache.

CHAPTER TWENTY-SIX

I dreaded making the phone call to my mother. Would she think, as I briefly had, that it was a cruel twist of fate that I would have not one, but two babies out of wedlock?

As usual, my mother's inner strength came through. "My dear," she announced in a no-nonsense tone, "there's something wonderful about love and children. There's always enough love to go around. These babies won't be any different. Your father and I will love them both."

"I still haven't heard from him." I knew my mother had told him about my being pregnant, but we hadn't spoken since then.

"Don't worry. Your father's still getting used to the idea. It just takes him a little longer to adjust. He'll be fine."

During the ensuing weeks, I became more accustomed to the idea of becoming a family of three. My days started with me lying in bed with my hands cupped over my round belly, waiting to feel the movement from inside me that would confirm this miracle of life. The idea still startled me. A few moments of carelessness with Derek had produced this phenomenon that would change my life forever. My circumstances weren't close to ideal, but I couldn't keep from smiling when I caressed my growing belly.

One morning, I lay curled under the covers. Early morning light poked through the blinds and spread in bright stripes across my blanket. Through the open window, I could smell the richness of the earth. Early spring had finally arrived and, with it, a promise of new life.

The sounds of vineyard workers walking down the road in front of the house brought me to my feet. I peeked out the window. Blake had told me several months ago that this time of year prompted the workers back to the fields. I heard their laughter and the jokes they shouted to one another as they headed to the vines. It seemed a good thing for them to begin the day with light-heartedness. I knew by the end of the day how tired they'd be from bending over and selectively pruning the vines.

I slipped on a robe and padded downstairs to the kitchen. Now that my morning sickness had gone, I always seemed hungry. I sat, sipping coffee, thinking of Zach. I'd delayed calling him, but realized it was unfair to him and Edwina to wait any longer. There was no way I could be in their wedding. I already looked enormous. By the end of June, I'd be even rounder.

I smiled at the sound of Zach's chipper hello. "Sam, it's good to hear from you. I've been going crazy dealing with Eddie's mother. You'd think this was the only wedding in the world."

I laughed. Edwina's mother was well known in social circles in Boston and not always in a positive light.

"Well, I'm afraid this is one wedding I'm going to miss." The regret in my voice was real.

"What do you mean?"

I broke the awkward silence. Straight talk was the only answer. "I'm pregnant, Zach. And guess what? I'm having twins. They're due at the end of July, beginning of August. I won't be able to fly at the end of June and Eddie's mother would have a fit if I appeared in the wedding party looking as if I swallowed two watermelons. I'm already big as a house—

or feel that way."

"Does Derek know?" he said softly.

"No," I answered firmly. "And I'm not going to tell him. I saw him a few weeks ago, on his way to Anchorage. Can you imagine what this news would do to him? He'd end up hating both me and the babies."

"I'm not so sure about that. If it were me, I'd want to know."

"The difference is that you'd be thrilled to be a father. I know you, remember? Derek would feel trapped. Did you know he stayed on in Rio after New Year's Eve and then went somewhere else? That's why I never heard from him. There's no room in his carefree life for me or the babies." He'd proved it to me by walking away from me in Boston.

"I heard from him not long ago. He told me you sent him away. Sam, he was all upset about it. He said he was going to wait until you cooled off before calling you. I assumed the two of you had it all worked out by now."

"Well, it's too late. I'm not going to force a guy into marriage. That's just not my style." I knew I sounded defensive, but I couldn't help myself. Derek could have called me, begged me to give him another chance.

"Don't be foolish, Sam. You could at least give Derek the opportunity to give you an honest answer. He might surprise you."

"You and I both know Derek would hate feeling tied down. I'm having twins, for heaven's sake!" I wanted Derek, even dreamed about him, but I wouldn't force him into a situation we'd both regret.

"I'm really sorry about the wedding, Zach. Would you please tell Eddie how disappointed I am? I wanted you to know as soon as possible, so you can have someone else stand up with you." I swallowed hard. "I ... I love you, Zach."

"I know," he replied. "You're the sister I never had. I'd still be hanging around bars if you and I hadn't met. I'll always be grateful to you."

After I hung up the phone, I wondered if Zach could possibly be right. Was I wrong to keep the information from Derek? I shook my head. No, no, as painful as it was, I had to face the truth.

I stared out at the swing set in the yard, trying to imagine two little children playing on it—two children of mine—and Derek's.

My spirits lifted as I threw myself into work. One afternoon, when I was working with Allison on the catalog inventory, a large box was delivered to Treasures with my name on it. Jessie called to me from the front of the store. "Looks like something good for you, Samantha."

Allison and I hurried out to the front room, studied the return label on the box and grinned at one another. Mom.

Allison handed me a pair of scissors. "Be careful opening it."

I slit open the box and lifted the lid. A note lay on top of a stack of clothes. I looked at the words through a thin mist of emotion. "These should help you feel more comfortable, Samantha. Enjoy them, but keep them nice for Allison. She'll need them soon, I'm sure. Love, Mom."

The three of us clustered around the box, holding up one item after the other, the tags still on them. My mother, bless her, had put together a whole new wardrobe of maternity clothes. I watched Allison hold a knit top to her chest and hug it to her. No matter how conflicted I felt about my pregnancy, I knew how fortunate I was to be healthy.

Allison and Jessie helped me lug the box to the car, and I headed back home to work on numbers for Dawson. I had a list of six established charities he wanted to support and a list of eight others that would need one-time financial gifts to help establish themselves. It was these eight that were taking up much of my time as I worked through the weeks following my phone call to Zach.

I was fixing toast one morning when the phone rang. I checked caller ID. My brother. Hunter and I didn't communicate very often, but it was always fun to hear from him.

"Hey, Sis, I'm here at Kyoko's family restaurant in New York and have just a minute to talk. You'll never guess who came here yesterday."

My stomach took a dive. "Derek?"

"Yep. He even asked for me. He remembered Kyoko and me talking about the restaurant at Christmas. He wanted to know how you were. I told him you were fine and so were the twins. Jeez! I forgot he didn't know anything about it. His face went white. I thought I'd better tell you. He was really pissed."

My pulse sprinted in nervous beats. One of the babies kicked and I plunked down in a chair at the kitchen table, shaken by the news.

"Thanks for telling me," I managed to squeak out. "How are things going for you?"

"Great." He sounded so happy. "I really like Kyoko's family. Her father's cool about Kyoko and me. Listen, I gotta go. Take care. Sorry if I spilled the beans, but the guy was going to find out sometime."

Shaking, I hung up the phone. I'd hear from Derek, all right. I just didn't know how or when. I didn't know whether to laugh or cry.

Later that morning, the phone rang. Thinking it might be Derek, I hesitated and then realized it was Ted Beers. I tensed. My last communication to him had not gone well. I'd reemphasized that my father was not about to change his mind about the project in Maine. He'd instructed me to offer to buy Ted out.

"You've done it again, Samantha," Ted growled, "ruined another project of mine."

My eyes watered. Those nasty hormones. I was ready to cry at a moment's notice. Ted's criticism in the past had only spurred me onward. Now, his angry words stabbed my heart. I fought for stability. "I don't understand. The last feasibility study of the newly designed project proves that the end result might be even better than originally conceived."

"We didn't need to go through all that extra expense. I would've gotten the approvals we needed to do what *I* wanted with no questions asked. Howard Sanderson was set to help us."

"Liz's ex-husband?"

"Yeah, that's the one. He's a special friend of the governor. He says he'll help me for a percentage of the profit.

"What do you want with me?" I was sickened by what Ted wanted to do to that property.

"I want you to convince your father to sell to me instead of the other way around."

I pressed my lips together. Didn't he realize how dominating my father was? Or that I would do nothing to destroy the strengthening relationship I now shared with him?

"I'm not going to pressure my father into anything, Ted. But, as a favor to him, not you, I'm willing to discuss the matter with him."

Tension-filled silence followed my remarks.

"Too bad we could never see eye-to-eye." Ted's voice sounded full of regret. "You'd make a good partner."

Surprise cut off any retort I might have been tempted to

make. Ted's comment was as near a compliment as I'd ever received from him.

We hung up and I sat for a few minutes, wondering why Ted always seemed overly greedy and aggressive. Perhaps, it was a matter of control. Yes, I decided, he just couldn't trust anyone else. My thoughts flew to my father. He was someone else who'd always had to be in control. Now he was dependent upon others for help— even me.

I checked the time. One o'clock in Maine. Just before naptime for my father. I dialed the number, uncertain how to approach the topic of Coldstream with him. It had come down to a matter of combating wills between my father and Ted.

My mother answered the phone. Her voice bubbled with enthusiasm as we talked about the twins. "I'm over the shock of it. Just think. There'll be one baby for Allison and one for me when we help you."

Grateful for my family's support, I smiled. There were times in the dead of night when I awoke in a panic, just thinking of what lay ahead. It helped to know they were there.

My father came on the line. I launched into the details of my conversation with Ted. "So, now he'd like to buy you out. I don't know how you feel about it."

"What do you think I should do?"

My jaw dropped. He was asking me? Various thoughts raced in my head. I knew I should approach him in the only way I knew how—my typical straight talk.

"We need to look at the issue from both sides. Regardless of how we felt initially, it might not be a bad idea to sell to Ted, considering your present health. Ted's a difficult person to deal with and, though he's often unprincipled, he's accommodated many of your revisions in the latest proposal. I don't think you can do much better. If he gives you a fair price, you'd have done fairly well financially and still have made it a lot better project than it might have been otherwise. I made sure of that."

"You think that's what I should do? Sell?"

"I think you have two very good choices to make"

"Let me think about it," my father said into the quietness. "I appreciate your honesty." He cleared his throat and I knew something important was coming. I held my breath.

"I've been doing a lot of thinking about you and your ... situation. You're a good woman, Samantha."

"Thanks ..." My voice caught. I knew this simple statement was not an easy thing for my father to say. "Thanks ... Daddy."

My mother came on the phone. "What did you say to your father? He's crying."

My throat thickened. "Tell you later. I've got to go."

I sat in my bedroom as far away from the sounds of construction as I could find and fought to sort things out in my mind. I no longer felt the need to impress my father. Maybe because I'd had the opportunity to treat him like any other client, I realized I didn't have to prove anything to him anymore. I was good at my work and I knew it.

And with his last encouraging words to me, I realized my father had always been there for me when I needed him most. I wanted the same for my children. If and when Derek contacted me, he'd have to understand that.

I waited all afternoon to hear from Derek to no avail. When I climbed into bed that night I told myself my decision was for the best. An absentee father was worse than no father.

But as days and weeks went by with no word from Derek, the depression I'd fought after being shot hovered in view—a black ominous cloud.

CHAPTER TWENTY-SEVEN

The phone rang. Foolishly hoping it was Derek, I lifted the receiver. The sound of Liz's pain-filled voice sent waves of concern through me.

"How's Dawson? Is everything all right?"

"Oh, Sam, it's not a good day. Time is running out for him." Her voice cracked with emotion. "He asked me to call you. He wants you to meet with him this morning. It's important."

Panic threaded through me. I hung up and called Allison to let her know I'd be late for our afternoon meeting and then headed out to Dawson's ranch. I'd presented him with the information he'd wanted regarding the charities and understood that Reggie Whitfield was tackling the legal end of things. Perhaps, with time running out, final decisions were about to be made.

I pulled up in front of Dawson's house, surprised to see Reggie's green Mercedes. In my awkward state, I moved as quickly as I could toward the house, praying nothing bad had happened. I still found it hard to believe Dawson, sweet man, was going to leave us.

Rosita greeted me at the door. "They're in the sunroom."

"Is ... is everything all right?"

She shrugged. "The same." The corners of her mouth turned down with sadness.

Dawson looked up at me and smiled as I entered the room. Reggie rose to his feet and waited while I gave Dawson a kiss on the cheek. Liz came over and hugged me.

"Glad you're here," said Reggie. "We have some paperwork

to go over."

I took a seat and accepted the stack of papers Reggie handed me. "You've been busy."

Reggie glanced at Dawson and turned back to me with a sad smile. "Dawson wants to make sure everything is set up the way he wants it."

"Cracking the whip," Dawson quipped in his hoarse voice.

"Okay. Let's see what you want."

"First of all," Reggie explained. "There's been a change. Liz, here, is going to remain at the ranch with her son, but instead of just living here as Dawson thought she might, she's going to open it up in the summer months as a camp for underprivileged children."

I turned to Liz.

Her eyes shone. "It's going to be wonderful for kids who might never otherwise have the opportunity to ride horses or learn about the arts, or do a lot of crafts. Dawson and I have assembled a staff of artists and ranchers who will help us get started."

She stopped speaking and swallowed hard. This was costing her emotionally. I forced back emotions of my own as she continued. "We hope to have a shortened season this summer as an introduction to what we've called "Carefree Creek Camp".

My gaze swerved to Dawson. A smile of satisfaction lit his drawn face.

Roger's smile was grim. "It's already been set up. We did that last week. The charitable foundation will support this camp as long as it exists, though its contribution will decrease as the camp begins to be self-supporting as a non-profit."

I nodded. A lot of the foundation's money would be used in exactly this way—giving start-up funds to worthy causes.

"Dawson wanted me to draw up papers making you the

head of the foundation effective today. Then he wants the foundation to sign an agreement between it and Carefree Creek Camp, to ensure that this idea goes forward."

Again, I directed my gaze to Dawson.

"Not much time." He spoke with difficulty. His ravaged body told me the same thing.

I held the papers in my lap, perusing the contracts, making sure I was in agreement. When I reached the paragraph regarding my compensation, I gasped. "Ten thousand dollars a month! Isn't that excessive?"

Dawson shook his head and gave me a smile so sweet I wanted to bawl. "Not enough for knowing you'll do what I dreamed of doing myself."

This time, I couldn't hold back the tears. It meant so much to me that he trusted me. It also meant I could raise my children without depending on family help.

"Do you see anything there that we need to discuss?" Reggie asked, his manner formal.

I drew myself up, taking his cue, and assumed a business-like pose. "Everything else seems to be in order."

"Go ahead and sign the contract. Liz and Rosita can witness your signature." Reggie handed me the papers.

After that contract was signed appropriately, we turned to the agreement between Dawson's foundation, now called the D.W. Smith Foundation, and Carefree Creek Camp. In short order, we had the agreement signed, this time with Dawson and Reggie as witnesses.

Reggie rose to his feet. "Congratulations to you all. We've done some good business this morning."

He bid us good-bye, and Liz walked him to the front door.

Dawson waved me over to his side and indicated a chair next to him. "Want to talk to you. Alone." He glanced toward the doorway. "I need you to do a favor for me. Ask Liz if we can talk alone for a minute, will you?"

Puzzled by his secrecy, I did as he asked. Liz seemed as curious as I, but she went off in search of Rosita while I headed back to the sunroom.

I sat next to Dawson and clasped his hand. "What can I do for you?"

A gleam came to his eye. "I'm going to ask Liz to marry me. Oh, I know, it isn't the same as I'd once hoped it would be, but, legally, it will make things a lot easier for me to give her the things I want."

I gave his hand a squeeze. "That's wonderful, Dawson. Now, what do you want me to do?"

"My jeweler in San Francisco has selected three rings for me to consider. Would you go take a look at them for me and choose the one you think Liz would like the best?"

I grinned. "You bet!"

"And one more thing." Dawson eyed my stomach. "I want you to stand up for me at the wedding. Be my best woman. I know you had to give that up for the Boston wedding, but I don't want you to miss out on this one."

"Really? In my condition?"

Dawson's eyes grew misty. "You're absolutely beautiful, my dear. My one real regret is that I never had children of my own. It never worked out, somehow."

I lifted his hand and placed it onto my extended stomach. "The babies are moving around. Can you feel them?"

Dawson eyes filled with wonder when a foot jolted his hand. "It's a miracle, isn't it?"

I was caught off balance by the fact that as one life was ebbing away, I was bringing not one, but two others into the world.

###

Allison and I took the ferry to San Francisco to take a look at the rings set aside for Dawson. She was as tickled as I about the forthcoming wedding. Seeing Liz with Dawson and the way they interacted was inspiring. I knew Dawson well enough to know he'd convince her to accept his riches.

The rings were beautiful. The one that Allison and I loved the most was a large yellow diamond flanked by a cluster of white diamonds on either side, set in platinum. I knew Dawson would like it, too.

The clerk went into the back to wrap it in their distinctive silver and gold paper, and I wandered in front of the display cases, looking at everything.

"Wish you were getting a ring?" Allison asked softly. Her voice held a tenderness that touched me.

I turned and looked her in the eye. "I wish things had worked out between Derek and me, but it wasn't ever going to happen."

She shook her head. "Have you really given him a chance? I saw how he looked at you, Sam. He couldn't keep his eyes off you."

I held up my hand. "Don't. I haven't heard one word from him since Hunter spilled the news."

Allison let out a long sigh. "It's just that you two were so happy together last fall ..."

I turned away. No matter how much I told myself it had all been a mistake, those memories haunted me every night.

We'd just come out of Gump's a short time later when I stopped short. The china and beautiful things for the home we'd seen inside the store made me realize all I was missing. For me, there would be no bridal registry, no wedding.

I stood on the sidewalk of Post Street, unable to hold back the misery I'd felt for so long. People nervously edged around us.

Allison put her arms around me. "I'm sorry, Sam. Sorry how it all turned out. Let's go home. C'mon."

Allison took my hand and I let her lead me down the street like a child. I'd sought safety at Silver Goose Winery in the past. I would again.

I was still in a blue funk two days later. I felt so alone. Everyone else but me seemed to be settled. Liz had joyously accepted the ring from Dawson. Their wedding was next week. Hunter and Kyoko were happy. Allison and Blake were having fun trying for another baby.

The trip to San Francisco had opened up a part of me I'd kept hidden from everyone, including myself. No matter what I said, I still loved Derek. I probably always would.

The phone rang and I sighed. Allison had been calling me incessantly, checking on me. She knew how down I was.

Chuckling, I picked up the phone. "Now what?"

"Samantha?"

My knees weakened at the sound of Derek's voice. I sank down on the bed and gripped the receiver so tightly my knuckles turned white.

"Hello, Derek."

"I just got back from an extended trip to Russia. I suppose you know by now that I talked to your brother. I think you owe me an explanation." His voice was steely cold, yet I imagined those golden eyes of his burning brilliantly with anger.

"If you knew, why didn't you call me then? I waited but your call never came." I heard the sound of disappointment in my voice but could do nothing to hide it. I'd spent too many tormented hours wondering why he hadn't called.

"I was too mad to trust any decent words to come from my mouth. Dammit, woman! Why would you hide something like that from me? Don't you think I deserve to know I'm going to be a father? What did you think? I wouldn't do the right thing by you?"

I could feel the blood drain from my face. Just as I feared, he'd do the so-called right thing. But I wanted more than that.

"Samantha? Answer me."

I pulled myself together. "I never doubted you'd do what you had to, under the circumstances. But both you and I deserve more than that. And it's totally unfair to the babies to have a father who isn't around. No father is better than an angry, absentee father."

"What're you saying?" Derek's voice had lowered to a dangerous pitch.

Mindful of what it might mean to our relationship, unable to stop myself, I forged ahead, even though my body had begun to tremble. "I can't make you want to be with us, Derek. You'd only grow to resent us. I'd rather raise these children alone than to constantly have them disappointed with your resentment and disappearance."

"Are you asking me to quit my work?"

"I'm not saying that..."

"Look, Samantha. I thought we had a lot more going on between us than this ... You told me it was special and I believed you. My time isn't always my own, but each trip back to the States I called you, tried to be with you. You couldn't have meant what you said about us. And this proves it."

"What do you mean?"

"Think about it. You can't really love me."

It surprised me to hear the hurt in his voice. I couldn't lie to him. I wouldn't. "I do ... I do love you."

"Look, I've got to go. I've got a plane to catch."

I heard a click and then the dial tone.

CHAPTER TWENTY-EIGHT

I awoke the next morning with swollen eyes and swollen feet. Gazing into the mirror, I wondered who the sad stranger was who stared back at me so forlornly. I pulled on one of my maternity tees and a pair of Capri pants my mother had sent. The coral cotton tee stretched taut over my round stomach, making me look like an oversized, overripe peach, an image that did nothing to lift my spirits.

"Oh, babies, what are we going to do?" Everything seemed topsy-turvy—weddings, death and birth, all vying for my emotions.

The workmen arrived, and I walked away from the house, finding the burden of carrying two babies more and more difficult. But I knew the more I exercised and kept my body healthy, the sooner I'd recover from their birth. I took pride in knowing I would bring life into the world, not take it away, as I'd once been forced to do.

The dirt road that led into the rows of vines at the top of the hill was dusty in the heat. I pulled my long hair back and twisted it up behind me with a clip, letting the slight breeze cool my neck. I thought back to all the times I'd pushed to attract my father's attention, wanting him to recognize my worth. I realized now how childish that had been. My own children would never question how much I treasured them.

Puffy clouds hung like odd-shaped marshmallows in the sky, white against deep blue. I breathed in the pungent air, puffing a little as I made the climb. Reaching the top of the hill at last, I stood a moment and allowed my heartbeat to slow. I turned, intending to make the return hike down when I noticed a figure walking toward me.

My pulse leaped.

The unmistakable outline of Derek Roberts sent a moment of panic through me. It was useless to think of running away. In my pregnant state, the idea was laughable. I cupped my hands over my eyes, zeroing in on his figure. He was too far away for me to see the features of his face, but I could tell from the way he marched toward me that he was still angry. Telling myself to be strong, I clenched my fists and waited for him to reach me.

As Derek drew near, I studied the set of his mouth with apprehension. And when he came even closer, I was surprised to see the how misty his eyes were. Caught off guard, I uncurled my fingers and waited for him to speak.

"You can't keep running away, Samantha. I'll follow you to the ends of the earth if I have to." He jabbed a finger in my direction. "You have judged me unfairly."

I drew a deep breath. I had to be strong. I was fighting not only for me but for my unborn children.

Derek's voice softened. "I want you and our babies in my life."

"Your life as it's always been?"

"The life I intend to make with you."

I remained silent.

He continued. "I'm not always good at expressing myself with words. My photographs do a better job of speaking for me. Think about the photograph I gave you for Christmas, Samantha. Think about the meaning behind the swing set."

I met his challenge with fresh insight.

"That time with you, here in the guest house at Silver Goose, filled me with a longing I'd never known before." He gazed into my eyes steadily. "It scared the shit out of me—

needing you, wanting you. I know the pain longing like that can bring."

I stepped back, giving myself a moment. "But you left me! You hardly called. I was even afraid to ask you to come to Portland for Christmas for fear you'd bolt and go somewhere else. And when you wouldn't change your plans for New Year's Eve to spend time with me, I knew you didn't care. Not the way I needed."

Derek's jaw flexed. I watched as he gained control over the anger that flashed in his eyes. "You never gave me the chance to invite you to come with me. Then I realized you wouldn't leave your parents during the holidays. Unlike mine, your family is close. When you told me to leave, I knew I could never make it up to you. I've been forced to leave before. My mother and step-father taught me the meaning of those words, ground them into me. I want a life with you and our children, but I won't stay where I'm not wanted, Samantha."

I felt his pain. Even as an adult, he wasn't accepted in the new family his mother had formed. I reached out a hand to him.

"I want you with me—with us."

Derek clasped my hand and, taking a deep breath, closed his eyes.

"You'd better know it's not going to be easy with two babies," I added. "And just look at me!"

His hands caressed my cheeks and moved to my stomach, his fingers gently tracing its shape. "You're beautiful!"

One of the babies kicked his hand. His eyes widened with surprise. Then he laughed softly. He gave me a dazzling smile and drew me into his arms.

Even with the bulk of my stomach between us, I still fit perfectly in his embrace. I leaned my head against his broad chest and could hear the pounding of his heart.

"I don't want to be anywhere, but here," he murmured.

He wouldn't always be able to keep that promise, but I understood the babies and I were the family he'd never truly had.

I tightened my grip around him, filled with a joy I couldn't express otherwise. "I've wanted this for so long," I murmured truthfully. "I love you, Derek. I really do. I always will."

"It's all right, Sam. I'm here." Derek stroked my back, giving me comfort no one else could. "I love you." He cupped my face in his hands and gently wiped the tears on my cheeks with his thumbs. "I want us to be married as soon as possible."

My smile was as shaky as my knees. "For better or worse?"

He returned my smile. "For always." His lips came down on mine with sureness, sealing his promise.

I observed the happiness in his expression, the need in his eyes, and knew he was talking straight.

Eighteen months later, I sat in an Adirondack chair in the backyard of the house at Silver Goose that had become Derek's and mine. Allison sat in a chair contentedly at my side.

We watched little Dawson take tottering steps after his twin brother Darren. Allison's little boy, Brian, cooed in his play seat, watching their every move. I saw the picture in my mind as if I were standing several feet away.

In the center of the activity stood the swing set my husband had hauntingly captured in one of his photographs. It glistened with new color. The image of its dejection slowly faded from my mind's eye at the sound of my children's laughter as they ran toward it.

Happiness filled the air with sugar-coated promises of more such good days to come.

Life was good. Derek and I had formed a wonderful bond,

filled with straight talk, laughter and ... great sex. He still traveled the world, doing his job, but he always came home to me and the boys, and I knew in my heart this little world of ours at Silver Goose was more spectacular to him than any famous location on earth.

My father continued to live a decent existence, though it wasn't what he'd been used to. My mother used visits to California to take a break from life there and to spoil the babies. Hunter was still in hotel school and with Kyoko and loving it, Marissa and Brad were married in a beautiful ceremony on the beach in Maine, and Liz, as Dawson's widow, was carrying on his work at the ranch and was now proud godmother to both of my boys.

Allison smiled at me. "A penny for your thoughts."

"I was just wondering how I would tell Derek that in a few months our little world would become bigger."

My sister's eyes widened. Grinning, she hugged me. "Make it a girl this time. We're getting outnumbered."

I laughed. No matter how outnumbered we might become, the Hartwell women would always remain strong. My mother, Allison, Marissa, and I had each proved it in our own way.

Thank you for reading *Straight Talk*. If you enjoyed this book, please help other readers discover it by leaving a review on Amazon, Goodreads, or your favorite site. It's such a nice thing to do.

Enjoy an excerpt from the fourth book in The Hartwell Women Series, *Baby Talk*.

CHAPTER ONE

On a clear, warm June day, I stood on the front porch of the house I now owned, staring out at the Maine coastline with a sigh of gratitude. I did this as often as I could. For me, taking a moment to appreciate all I'd been given had become a morning ritual I treasured.

In front of me, the blue-gray water met the sandy shore with a moist kiss, reared back like a shy lover then, tempted for more, embraced the shore again. Gulls cried out, swooped down, and lifted up in the air in unending musical acrobatics. A few large rocks, precursors of the rockier coastline down east, protruded from the water's surface like sea creatures wanting a peek at the world.

Almost two years ago, the sandy beach had hosted one of the most important events of my life. Even now, my pulse quickened at the memory of Brad saying "I do" and sweeping me into an embrace that drew applause. The simplicity of the ceremony had touched the hearts of everyone. What a wonderful day that had been! I still felt the thrill of belonging to his family and mine—the family I'd discovered after a lonely childhood. Thinking of the group gathered there, I thought how lucky I was and smiled up at the sun, letting its warmth wash over me.

The screen door opened and closed behind me. Brad stepped out onto the wide porch that swept the front of the seaside estate and wrapped his arms around me. "Good morning, Marissa Cole Crawford!" The sound of my married name on his lips sent a tingle of delight throughout my body.

I smiled and turned to him, inhaling the spicy aroma of his aftershave lotion. Snuggling into his strong embrace, I stared up at him, taking in the caramel-colored hair and toffee eyes that were his alone. I adored this man who'd given me so much love, so much confidence. I treasured our life together, very different from the background that had once been my life.

"You're off to Barnham?" I asked, hiding the emptiness I already felt at his upcoming departure.

He nodded. "Thank God this commuting back and forth will end in another year or so. I'm hoping Dad is fully retired by then and we can finally sell the law practice to someone else." He gave me the lopsided grin I loved. "By then, we'll have started our family, and I can stay settled right here."

I didn't reply but rested my head against his chest. We'd been trying for a baby since the wedding. Brad was anxious to have children but the thought scared me to death. I had so many doubts about myself as a mother. I'd been raised by one of the worst.

"Walk me out?" Brad slung his arm around my shoulder.

We headed through the elegant house I was slowly but surely trying to make into a real home—safe and welcoming to us both. Lady, my golden retriever, followed at our heels. Like me, she hated to see Brad leave for his weekly trek to Barnham, New York.

Outside on the lawn, I gave Brad a lingering kiss, telling him in my own special way how much I'd miss him.

He pulled away and sighed. "See you on Friday. Have a

good week. Love you, woman."

I smiled and played along. "Love you, man."

He laughed and climbed into his Jeep.

Watching him drive away, I wondered if I should confess my reluctance to have a baby. Each time another month went by without my getting pregnant, I was almost pleased about it...until I saw his disappointment. But I was sure he'd be even more disappointed if I turned out to be anything like the cold, heartless mother I'd grown up with.

Moments later, Becky and Henry Cantwell drove their red truck down the driveway toward me, breaking into my disturbing thoughts. I waved and waited for them to park the truck by the garage and cross the lawn. They'd worked for my grandmother for years. I'd inherited them, along with the large house I now miraculously owned. Watching them, I smiled with pleasure. They were so much more than a handyman and a housekeeper; they were the people who'd kept my dysfunctional family spiritually alive with their goodness.

"Brad gone already?" Becky asked.

"Didn't see his car," said Henry.

"He'll be back on Friday."

"It'll be good when he can stay here permanently, don'tcha know," said Becky.

"And how," I quickly agreed. I looped my hand around Becky's arm and we walked together toward the house as Henry headed back toward the garage. She and Brad's Aunt Doris were two of the women I loved most in the world, along with my newfound Hartwell cousins—Allison and Samantha.

We entered the house and I took a seat at the long, cherry table in the kitchen to have a second cup of coffee with Becky. The comfortable kitchen was the heart of the house. It had been upgraded when the sunroom was added on to the house ten years ago. I'd left it pretty much the way it was when the house was given to me. The cherry cupboards, some with etched glass doors, suited the formality of the gray marble countertops. The Sub-Zero refrigerator, its doors covered with cherry wood veneer to match the cupboards, was unobtrusive among the cabinetry. But it was the six-burner Viking range that brought out the cook in me. It was Becky's pride and joy.

We finished our coffee, and when she rose to work in the kitchen, I left her. The kitchen was Becky's domain, which I respected.

I stopped in the front hallway to freshen the flower arrangement. Sniffing the delicate roses, I decided to take a look at the front of the house. Henry and I had talked about planting a variety of flowers and I wanted to see which of the ones he'd suggested would look best.

Lady rushed past me and went to the screen door, barking. Seeing no one, I frowned. It wasn't like her to bark unnecessarily.

I set aside the flower vase and went to take a look. Peering out, I gasped and then forced back a scream. A wicker basket sat on the floor of the porch by the door—a basket that held a baby. And if the light pink blanket meant anything, the baby was a girl.

Heart pounding with alarm, I opened the door, stepped onto the porch, and searched for the person who might have left the little girl there. In the distance, a couple of men were jogging on the sand. In the opposite direction, a young woman was running along the shore, long blond hair flying behind her like angel wings.

I hurried out onto the lawn for a better look at her. Too far away to chase down or catch, I stared helplessly at the retreating figure. I turned in frantic circles to survey the plantings around the house and the lawn beyond. But I saw no sign of anyone lurking.

The baby was now wailing. Pulse skipping in nervous beats, I raced back to the porch. Staring down at the baby's red face and flailing arms, shock continued to roar through me.

Becky appeared in the doorway. "My stars! What's this?"

"A baby." Panic sent my voice to a higher register. "Someone left a baby here on my porch!. We have to find the mother! Why would she do this? I don't know anything about babies."

"Okay, Marissa, let's see what this is all about," Becky said with a calmness I couldn't resurrect. She stepped out onto the porch and lifted the crying baby out of the basket. As she did, a note fell to the floor below.

I snatched it up and read it aloud:

"Dear Mrs. Crawford, I've watched you and your husband for a while now. Seeing as you have no kids of your own, I thought this would be a perfect place for Summer Marie to live. Take care of her because I can't. Please, please don't put her in the foster care system. I know it too well."

I rocked back on my heels. My heart beat so fast, I felt faint. This had to be a joke. Things like this didn't really happen, did they? I stared once more at the note but the words on the page did a dance that blurred my vision. Sick to my stomach, I looked to Becky. "What are we going to do?"

About the Author

Judith Keim enjoyed her childhood and young-adult years in Elmira, New York, and now makes her home in Boise, Idaho, with her husband and their two dachshunds, Winston and Wally, and other members of her family.

While growing up, she was drawn to the idea of writing stories from a young age. Books were always present, being read, ready to go back to the library, or about to be discovered. All in her family shared information from the books in general conversation, giving them a wealth of knowledge and vivid imaginations.

A hybrid author who both has a publisher and self-publishes, Ms. Keim writes heart-warming novels about women who face unexpected challenges, meet them with strength, and find love and happiness along the way. Her best-selling books are based, in part, on many of the places she's lived or visited and on the interesting people she's met, creating believable characters and realistic settings her many loyal readers love. Ms. Keim loves to hear from her readers and appreciates their enthusiasm for her stories.

"I hope you've enjoyed this book. If you have, please help other readers discover it by leaving a review on Amazon, Goodreads, or the site of your choice. And please check out my other books:

The Hartwell Women Series
The Beach House Hotel Series
The Fat Fridays Group
The Salty Key Inn Series
Seashell Cottage Books
Chandler Hill Inn Series
Desert Sage Inn Series

ALL THE BOOKS ARE NOW AVAILABLE IN AUDIO on Audible and iTunes! So fun to have these characters come alive!"

Ms. Keim can be reached at **www.judithkeim.com**

And to like her author page on Facebook and keep up with the news, go to: **https://bit.ly/3acs5Qc**

To receive notices about new books, follow her on Book Bub - **http://bit.ly/2pZBDXq**

And here's a link to where you can sign up for her periodic newsletter! **http://bit.ly/2OQsb7s**

She is also on Twitter @judithkeim, LinkedIn, and Goodreads. Come say hello!

Acknowledgements

Writing involves sitting in a room conversing with imaginary people in a world you've created. Without real people, real friends, in a real world, a writer is without balance. I am so appreciative of my real friends who encourage me to continue writing by giving me their support! You know who you are and you know I love you! Thanks!

Made in the USA
Middletown, DE
07 October 2024

62148008R00184